Lady of the House

Lady of the House

Katie Sanyal

MADVILLE PUBLISHING
Lake Dallas, Texas

To Jean, Sunny, Sammy, and Ella

In the middle of the journey of our life
I came to myself within a dark wood
where the straight way was lost.

—Dante Alighieri

PART 1

The Way of Whisperings

ONE

She hadn't been back to Georgia since, to the old crumbling mansion where terrible, wonderful things had happened. It all felt like a dream now, thin and fragmented, slipping away from her like smoke with each passing year. But Clara Graham, twenty-two and haunted, knew that memories were not so easily erased. A Memory might always find its way back, like some living thing with a will of its own.

As their rental car pulled into the U-shaped driveway, Clara caught sight of her late grandmother's rosebushes, dreadfully untrimmed, a shade of red-magenta that she hadn't remembered existed until she saw it again. Twelve years ago, just as fifth grade was ending, Clara had watched her grandma hand pluck every beetle from the blooms of this bush, throwing them in a bucket of soapy water to drown. Japanese Beetles, they were called, shining emerald and copper; they were an invasive nuisance. "It doesn't matter that they're nice looking," Grandma had said, flicking iridescent body after body into her soapy pail. You could spray them all with poison, an easy solution, but Grandma didn't like to use chemicals on her plants. "They come in, and if I don't do something about it, they'll ruin my pretty roses that were here first. The two can't live together, nature simply won't allow both. They'll just have to find someplace else to burrow," Grandma had said. Now that she was gone, who would deal with the beetles every summer?

Grandma died at the age of ninety-three, a seeming eternity since the Grahams moved across the country to live with her in that giant old house. To help an old woman manage her property and take care of her physical health was the reason Clara and her sister had been told, but Clara now knew that wasn't really the truth. Both Grandma and her house had been in great shape when they moved in twelve years ago. The great magnolia trees showcased in the backyard were neatly trimmed, conical if a bit fluffy, bursting with white blossoms. Everything and anything could grow there, Clara remembered, even dreams and fantasies out of a storybook.

The funeral was tomorrow morning, with a weather forecast for thunderstorms. The whole family would be there, together, and that was a happy thought, even if Cassie was probably going to bring her fiancé along, whom Clara had only met a small number of times before. Five years old than Clara, Cassie fit the model of a real adult. In comparison, Clara felt like she hadn't progressed past high school. She hadn't strayed far from her parents, through college and into her early adulthood. In her senior year of high school, she had applied everywhere with little intent of leaving her home state, and to no one's surprise, that was where she stayed. Never mind that Clara thought LA County was a burning, stinking trash-hole— it was where her parents were, so it was home. The dorms, of course, had been a hard no. She had commuted from her parent's house every single day, almost an hour drive down to UC Irvine in the morning, and then again back up in the evening. She graduated in three and a half years, and then her parents had seriously encouraged her to move into her own place, just twenty minutes from their neighborhood. But Cassie was always far, far away, and currently lived somewhere in upstate New York, a place Clara had never dared to visit.

College... not yet two years finished, but Clara's memory of it was already fading. It held nothing worth remembering, she thought, driving her parents' rental car back into town to pick up groceries from the nearby Publix. The roads were much more crowded than she remembered, looking wider with the addition of bike lanes and occasional chunks of sidewalk, yet it was still nothing compared to LA standstill traffic. It really was like being in a whole other world, barely the same planet as the place she'd lived for the past decade. Coming back as an adult, Clara understood why it had been so easy as a child to pretend she was somewhere else; how seamlessly the rural farms and hills and forests fit alongside her real-life mental map of Middle Earth in Northern Georgia, Cair Paravel of Lake Lanier, and quasi-Hogwarts of Blue Ridge Elementary which was filled with mostly Slytherins and Dudley Dursleys. It had been so easy to pretend her life into something else that it almost became real. Parts of it still seemed like they might have been real.

In the parking lot next to the grocery store was the same old one-room dry cleaner's, barely bigger than a shack but Clara remembered going there once a week with her dad, who let her sit in the front seat even though the physician had ruled her still in need of a car seat. Cassie, of course, had always refused to go anywhere with their dad. Clara had a rare, impulsive urge to go in and see if Miss Tiffany was still there. But she immediately shut the idea down, remembering herself. Who was she to go waltzing in there and expect to be remembered, for her twenty-two year old face and body to be put with the memory of her ten-year-old self. Besides, Miss Tiffany was probably somewhere else now, and Clara felt it was best to leave things as they were, not meddle in the past or its memories.

She parked the car and blinked away all the thoughts that were making her forget where she was and who she was. No one would remember or recognize her, she assured herself. At age ten, she had been a grossly underweight, frightened, unsightly creature. Now, she was considerably less of all those things. Now she followed a daily, sometimes hourly ritual checking to see WWDAS (What Would Dr. Ashley Say).

Part of mentalizing based therapy is being able to stop and recognize that people are preoccupied with their own issues and thoughts, and they are seldom, maybe never thinking about you. Your thoughts are not everyone else's. What's going on in your head is not reflected in theirs.

Inside the grocery store, the shelves were stocked with familiar goods and snacks and candies, yet as she walked down the aisles, she came upon the daunting realization of just how far from home she was. She barely left her hometown in California, with its nearly identical houses—red clay roofing, turf lawns, and endless neighborhood streets lined with parked cars. There was little, if anything, that she liked about her home except that it was where her family chose to be, and that made it home.

Georgia really was a dream compared to that barren, stinking wasteland. It was nearing the end of June, and the heat felt sticky and oppressive, but Clara didn't mind. Here, the summer heat felt different, as if a certain magic filled the air and made everything grow green and wild. Los Angeles in the summer was artificial and bright, the air smoky-brown with pollution. Back down in the south, her baby hairs sprang into little curls that framed her face, and her normally limp hair turned into a wild mess. Every breath she took felt like she was filling up with wet steam; she could have almost believed it was possible for vines and moss to start sprouting up in her lungs like a dark little greenhouse.

She reread the grocery list, ink smudging around her mom's loopy handwriting. It was a small and seemingly insufficient list—but Grandma's church friends and their families would doubtless be bringing enough homecooked food to put together a feast in her name. She had been very active in their local church, and Clara remembered having to go on Sunday mornings while they lived with her for that one year. Twelve years ago, even with the town's smaller population,

Northcrest Church would become so crowded every Sunday that it would take well over a half hour to make it out of the parking lot after service. The preacher... the town had considered him somewhat famous for his lively, intellectual sermons. A couple of years before Clara and her family moved to Georgia, a clip of him speaking had become popular on the internet, and somehow, he had been invited as a guest on the Today show with Al Roker and Savannah Guthrie. The rest was history, according to Grandma and her horde of churchgoing lady friends. Clara wondered if he would be at the funeral tomorrow.

Clara had stopped believing in God at the age of eleven after living in Georgia. But she could not deny that her family owed a lot to the church and her grandmother's involvement. It was, after all, how her dad came to the United States. At almost forty years old, her grandma had been childless, and she adopted a small Indian boy whose family she had been connected with through the church. They had all kinds of programs where families at church would "adopt" or "look over" a family in poverty in some foreign country and write letters and send money. Whatever people thought about it, positive or negative, it was how her dad became a Graham and it was the reason Clara existed. Their church intervened, snatched him right up from India and plopped him into Clara's grandparent's beautiful estate in Georgia. Her dad barely talked about it, his life before Grandma and Grandpa and the church, but Grandma always said he was her pride and joy and reminded her daily of Jesus's divine intervention, and why they owed so much to the church. It made sense, sometimes, the way Grandma spoke about it. How he might have died from being orphaned or some disease or starvation, but because of their church's program he was brought to America to grow up in a wealthy Southern household, graduate from Vanderbilt and then with an MBA from Harvard later. And probably live out a long, healthy, and rich life. Something or the other. Apparently, they owed it all to the generosity of the church.

7

The older Clara got, the more she saw the bullshit in a lot of the things she believed as a child, but she was glad her grandma had the church community after her grandpa passed, and that it had continued to be such a strong presence in her life after Clara's family moved back to California. Clara supposed most grandparents were a little weird in some way or the other, but her grandma was kind and had been a comfort to Clara's loneliness and struggles with school. For months after they moved away, Clara thought about how lonely her grandma must have been, crying to her parents at night when she missed her grandma the most. But eventually, she forgot, and as years turned to months, they passed almost entirely out of each other's lives.

If they owed anything to the church, Clara thought, it was the friendships it had given her grandmother when she was all alone. Maybe there wasn't salvation in Jesus but in simply not being alone.

She picked out the items on the list and quickly worked the self-checkout, leaving the store without a word or nod to anyone. Southerners weren't like Californians though, who looked at others in public with over interest or harangued innocent passersbys. From Clara's limited experience, people in the south acted overtly pleasant, and if they thought anything rude about you it was in silence, or at the very least, behind your back. She had been grumbled at by workers or yelled at by other customers in LA for taking too long choosing an ice-cream flavor, or loudly assaulted by invasive remarks like, "Babe, what are you out here buying cranberry juice for? Better be for cocktails... otherwise, you need the number for my gyno? Cause I bet you're actually hoping that cranberry stuff will help with your issues down there," she winked, and Clara had balked. She never bought cranberry juice again after that. People in LA were always angry or loud or wanted to become unlikely BFF's, and to Clara, at least, these things were always unwarranted and unwanted. In comparison, her shopping experience here had been almost pleasant.

She drove back to her grandma's house in silence, distractedly enjoying the greenness of Georgia. Even the drive out of downtown Atlanta into the suburbs was impressive: Clara hoped it wasn't the Californian in her, but both sides of the six-lane highway were shrouded by forestation that seemed dense enough to make a rainforest.

Just an hour out of Atlanta, her grandmother's house was stunningly beautiful. Rolling hills of emerald grass, with cows and horses and sheep were framed by tall pine, oak, and ash trees that made some streets seem devoid of sunlight, the thick overgrowth nearly impenetrable. Kudzu consumed entire meadows and trees, dripping from the limbs like swathes of fabric. When she was little, Clara had sat next to her grandma and listened to her tell stories of the invasive vine, how it engulfed entire forests in one night, and how someday it might swallow the entire globe, eating Georgia first.

When she pulled into the semi-circular driveway for the second time that day, she saw another car parked to the side. Cassie, finally, she thought, with a small sigh of relief. She had worried that Cassie might not show up at all, that she might pass right through wet, rainy Georgia and go straight down to sunny Florida without even a glance in their direction. Clara shook off the thought. Her mind sometimes wandered into made up realities or theories, sometimes discrediting the truths and intentions of others in the process. WWDAS: You are only yourself. You don't know what other people are thinking or what's going through their mind, even when it feels like you can read their thoughts. Cassie had showed, after all.

But it wasn't her older sister, or the fiancé, sitting at her grandmother's beloved granite-top kitchen bar. She stopped in her tracks, the grocery bags dangling in both hands, suddenly heavy as bowling balls.

It was a middle-aged man, soberly dressed in gray. He was speaking to her mom. Megumi Graham was short and stout, with neat black hair that she redyed every four weeks, and a wide face strewn with sun-spots of all sizes. Clara had wanted freckles when she was little, but her mother had told her that Asians didn't get freckles—they got sunspots, and they weren't small and cute. Indeed, her mom sported those freckle-like spots across her cheeks and temples, some as small as true freckles, others nearly the size of a dime. But her brows were furrowed, deep creases between her eyes that filled Clara with an irrational sense of fear. In under ten seconds, one thousand worst-case-scenarios flashed through Clara's mind, giving her a mental whiplash. But how bad could things be? They were already here preparing for a funeral.

Noticing Clara's return, her mom subsequently wrapped things up with the man, thanking him for taking the time to come over and that they would be in touch. He left the room silently, with a nod to Clara.

Clara helped her mother put the groceries away, and she said, "Mom, who was that?"

For a moment, her mom said nothing, just continued to take the groceries out of the bags.

"What's going on?"

With another dejected sigh, her mom finally spoke. "You should call your sister. We need to put off the service, at least for another week." A sudden, deep dread pooled in her core, and she knew it was something more than the prospect of having to call Cassie.

"Why?"

Her mom didn't look at her as they continued to put the groceries away. "They want to investigate the circumstances of her death. Some detectives will be coming in and out of the house in the next few days."

Clara was stunned. Her grandma had been ninety-three; they had all accepted without question that she died of old age. But what were her mom or the police suggesting?

"Someone sent an anonymous tip." Megumi said. Clara was still confused, and maybe in shock. Her father especially had always had his doubts about his mother living in the giant house alone, but it was more for the sake of her age and capability than of robbery or an attack. Sure, something like that could have been a concern in Clara's neighborhood in California, but never here, not in such a genteel, quaint little town.

"About what?" Clara argued. "Who would have done something? Grandma doesn't have any enemies here. She knew everyone, and everyone knew her."

"They..." Her mom stopped, then started again. "They say they have reason to believe she was practicing occult magic."

Occult magic.

They were both silent, and then Clara laughed. "Occult magic? That's funny." Clara kept laughing, but her mom remained quiet. "What's that even supposed to mean?" Her mom just shook her head, the air around them growing stiff and way too serious. "Oh, come on Mom."

"Clara," she started, rubbing her forehead. "What do you want me to say?"

Time seemed to slow down as Clara slowly began to process her mom's lack of disbelief. How were they not laughing together right now? Occult magic? It was funny. Insensitive? Sure. But what a joke. Debbie Graham had been a picture-perfect grandma with her floral patterned clothes, wispy curls, and strung pearl necklaces. Always a pair of gardening gloves lying about. She had a penchant for lemon bars, and no one made them better than her. Grandma was so good. The word "occult" was unbelievable to the point of hilarity next to her image.

Besides, who in the world would take such a claim seriously? Serious enough to launch a formal investigation? It was absurd. As if coming from somewhere far off, Clara heard herself laugh again.

"I need to go call your father," Megumi Graham said, drawing Clara back into the moment. She felt strange, giddy almost. She couldn't recognize this as her life right now. Her own mother seemed unreal in the way a movie character might, saying the classic lines one would say in a drama, making the somber, devastating facial expressions that an actress might spend her life practicing.

Standing there – frozen – as her mom walked out of the room with her cellphone to her ear, Clara's throat felt tight, her face too warm. She couldn't laugh anymore, and she didn't want to. She wanted to say something now, to scream, to go on a verbal rampage to defend her grandma, but she had never been good at composing her emotions into words, not in the heat of a moment. It was so absurd that screaming, crying, or laughing were not enough to convey Clara's outrage. Debbie Graham had been old and tired when Clara had spent time with her, but she was loving, generous, and so good that Clara forgot her disdain for religion when she was around her grandmother. She liked to knit, care for her trees, and eat coconut creme pies. She had been the brightest light in Clara's loneliness the year they moved to Georgia, a co-conspirator in her childhood creativity. It was okay that she passed away after ninety-three years. It had been fair. But this? And whatever absolute bullshit investigation the town wanted to follow? It was a cruel joke, a disrespect and a disgrace to her name and legacy.

She could vaguely hear her mom on the phone in the other room, but everything that was said passed through her like smoke. She couldn't hear a word amidst the rising anger, the hate; she was so angry, so incredibly angry that these stupid people, her grandma's friends and neighbors, would slander an old woman like that—that they would blacken her name when she was dead and could do nothing about it. They believed in evil? In the devil? Clara hoped with all her heart that they were right.

If Hell was real, this whole town would burn in it.

TWO

12 YEARS AGO

When Clara was ten, she met the devil, and they became friends.

That is, if the devil could be a girl her age, with horns and yellow eyes and sharp little teeth who appeared to her one day in the forest behind her grandma's backyard.

Moving across the country hadn't really been the issue for her. She was a timid girl, and she had no friends that she would be sad to move away from. She hadn't expected she would make friends at her new school in Georgia either, but within the first week of school she learned that having no friends was the least of her problems. There were worse things than not having friends.

It started the first day, when the school bus stopped in front of her grandma's infamous manor.

Clara had always known that her grandparents had been rich. She didn't know why or how it came to be, but she figured that some people just were, and she was lucky that it was her grandparents. They had always sent the most wonderful things in the mail to Clara's house in California for Christmas: elaborately wrapped packages with ribbons and the golden stamps of Von Maur, Grandma's favorite department store. Beautiful children's dresses, hats, jewelry, and toys from her grandparents were some of the true delights of Clara's childhood. Some items were so precious that her mother wouldn't let her touch them, not until she was older, like the string of delicate pink pearls that sat on the highest shelf of Clara's dresser, forever hidden away in a leather pouch beyond her reach.

Clara reasoned that people who sent expensive Christmas gifts probably had other expensive things, like a great big house with three stories and a proper lawn. And Grandma's house was all that, and more.

The day they arrived in Georgia and moved into her grandparent's house was perhaps the most exciting day yet of Clara's ten-year life. She had never seen a place like it before, with its decorative white columns and tall windows and an entire forest full of trees. They had been living in a rented apartment for a few months before moving there, Clara and Cassie and Mom and Dad, and that entire apartment would have fit inside Clara's bedroom here at Grandma's house. She smiled big enough for her horsey teeth to show, without worrying about Cassie making fun of her. And that smile never went away, not until the first day of school, starting with the school bus.

In California, before they lived in the tiny apartment, Clara and Cassie had gone to a K-12 private school together. There were no buses, and their mom dropped them off every day. But here, Clara had to take a bus to Blue Ridge Elementary, and Cassie would take a separate bus to Milton High School.

She had not anticipated that she would have to choose a seat with someone, or that so many kids could fit in one yellow bus. The bus driver was a fat old lady with so much hair gel worked into her hair that it looked wet. She didn't say good morning or acknowledge Clara, just pulled the lever to close the door with a grunt. Clara didn't mind; she preferred it that way. Her dad had instructed her the night before, that it was very important to make eye contact, smile, and address everyone as Miss, Missus, Ma'am, Sir, or Mister. "Even the other kids?" Clara had asked.

Her dad had frowned. "Of course not, Clarybell. Just the adults. No calling them by their first names. Not even the neighbors, and especially not your grandmother's friends."

Luckily, the bus driver hadn't seemed to expect Clara to test that out. She did, however, have to choose a seat—not a single bench was unfilled, and most already had two to three kids occupying one bench. There were no seatbelts either, and that was only one of the many things that terrified her that morning.

She sat right near the front, not daring to venture more than a couple of rows from the bus driver. It felt like too many eyes were looking at her, so she sank down low in the seat. But as soon as the bus started moving, faces popped up over and behind her, around the side of her seat and up from underneath! They looked at her with expectant eyes. She had been coached on the importance of introducing herself, but her parents weren't here to see if she followed through, and Cassie wasn't here to force her.

A girl with curly hair and glasses spoke first. "Is that your house?" she asked.

"Yeah," another girl chimed in. "My momma said no kids live there."

"It's my grandma's house," Clara said. She looked around timidly. The kids around her looked puzzled.

"But…you don't look like her."

"Yeah. That old lady is White." The boy in front of her said, hanging over the back of the seat and absentmindedly picking his nose.

She knew she shouldn't be, but she felt ashamed. "My dad was adopted."

Clara hadn't given too much thought to the way she looked before. She knew that she had tanned skin and black hair and dark, almost black eyes because that's what came from her parents. And kids usually looked like their parents, unless they were adopted like her dad. But he was her real dad, and her mom was her real mom, so that made her and Cassie Japanese and Indian like their parents. Grandma was grandma, but she wasn't their *real* grandma.

The kids in California had ignored her because she was too quiet. Here at her new school, kids didn't jump to befriend her either, probably because she was still too quiet, even though she tried her best to answer their questions about herself. Some things she said seemed to confuse them, like when a boy on the bus asked where she was from and she said California. And they stared. Constantly. Clara knew it was not because she was beautiful, which made her more anxious feeling their eyes on her; their judgment made her fidget and squirm.

The class was enormous—not the room itself, but the amount of kids squeezed into it. When they were asked to take out their pencils and copy sentences from the board, Clara bumped elbows with the kids on both sides of her. Their teacher's name was Mrs. Manning, and Clara was just one of almost forty students in her class. It was never quiet. All morning was filled with the sounds of kids breathing, sniffling, giggling, getting up from their seats, chairs squealing across the waxed floors, electric pencil sharpeners, and eventually a bell that triggered a stampede of her classmates all funneling out the door for recess. Clara was the last to make it out of the classroom.

Recess was a nightmare, as to be expected. Unlike in the classroom, there was no "assigned" place for Clara to be, so she stood frozen before the chaotic playground in front of her. She did not want to go any farther into the sea of her screaming classmates, so she stood by the door they exited from, thinking she'd be safe there. She was not.

Like a wave smacking her backside, Clara was knocked to the ground by a swarm of more screaming kids. It was one of the other fifth-grade classes, and Clara put her arms over her head as kids ran past her like a pack of wild animals let loose on the playground. When she was able to get up, her knees were muddy and her hands were scraped from catching herself on the pavement. She spent the rest of recess huddled against the brick school wall, trying to stay out of everyone's way. The one success from that first recess period was that she was not approached by any kids asking to play.

Her first day of school ended after an eternity, and she came back to her grandma's house looking and feeling like she'd been run over. She was exhausted from all the interaction, even though she'd mostly been an observer.

Cassie had come back fine from her first day, and she had doubtless talked to more people than Clara. Hearing the way Cassie told their mom about all the new kids she'd met, it sounded like she'd actually enjoyed her first day at a new school. Clara ate her after-school snack of apples and peanut butter with her eyes fixed firmly to her plate, unwilling to talk about her own first day experiences.

She wondered if anyone on Cassie's school bus had also been confused by her being Debbie Graham's granddaughter. Surely, they must have. The sisters looked similar enough.

But they weren't really alike at all, Clara thought at dinner that night while studying her sister over the linguine with clam sauce. It was Clara's favorite meal after spaghetti with meatballs and Kraft Mac N Cheese. Cassie ate hardly anything, as usual, and wore her signature scowl, but even scowling, she was pretty in ways that Clara was not. No matter how much calorie dense food her mom fed her (under order of the doctor), Clara barely grew and remained disgustingly underweight. Meanwhile, Cassie ate nothing, but remained strong and healthy. She had breasts, too. Her skin was a shade lighter, her eyes browner, her hair thicker. Also, unlike Clara, Cassie was mean, at least to her family, but maybe not to her friends, and she did have friends. She had them in California, and Clara knew she would make new ones here, too.

After dinner, Clara was too tired to play outside in the big backyard, and too distracted to read. She went to bed early but lay there awake for hours, her mind swirling with anxiety but too exhausted to think actual thoughts. For the first time since they got there, Clara missed California. She told herself it was because her old bedroom had those plastic glow stars on the ceiling, and her bedroom here didn't.

The first week of fifth grade at her new school crept by slowly, and the questions from her classmates dwindled once they decided there was nothing more to know about her. She had no homework most nights, which suited her fine, and by the end of the second week, she had enough energy remaining after school to read or explore her grandma's giant, old house.

Those hours of exploration represented blissful, safe independence to Clara. Even when she was alone, she was still in the same house as her family, and no one else would or could come in. And there was so much to explore—she could wander around contentedly for hours, occasionally hearing the comforting, familiar sounds of her mom cooking or talking on the phone, or Cassie blasting loud music, which she claimed "help her think."

Clara felt mostly free in the house, apart from whenever Grandma's friends were over. She quickly realized that her grandma had quite a few friends, maybe as many as Cassie did. Most of them were like Grandma, powdery old ladies with a distinct smell, and they were all from church. They met once a week on Tuesdays for bible study, toting around fabric bible sleeves and a youthful array of highlighters. Clara kept out of their way when she could, but Grandma sometimes liked to call her to sit on her lap while the other ladies read their favorite passages of the week, highlighted in neon pinks and greens. The pages in their bibles looked almost like those Lilly Pulitzer dresses Grandma would buy for her, adorned with their signature bright, swirling flowers.

About a month into school, Cassie had made new friends she started bringing over to the house after school. Five years older than Clara, she wore makeup, tank tops, and had a cell phone which she decorated with rhinestones to match the other girls at school. Clara thought she was pretty cool, and the friends she brought home seemed to think so too.

But Cassie wasn't the only thing her friends found "cool," there was also old Debbie Grahams mansion. Cassie's friends seemed to find the house as cool as they found Cassie, but Clara couldn't help wondering if they were only there to be nosy, perhaps to explore, same as Clara. They took lots of pictures, and Clara wanted to warn her sister about them, but she couldn't. She couldn't find the words, besides, what did she know about friendship? Nothing, nothing at all.

Besides, Grandma's house was so big that when Clara wanted to get away from all the noise Cassie brought in, she could go to another wing of the house and not hear a thing. No music, no giggling, no talk about boys or words like damn, hell, fuck, or slut. Clara didn't know what slut meant, but judging from the things she sometimes overheard Cassie and her friends say, she figured it was probably just another word for "girl."

The house was so big, she could find a different place to hide every afternoon all the way until dinnertime, but it still wasn't big enough, in Clara's opinion, for all these people who didn't belong there. She liked to be on her own, especially after a loud, long day of school. She liked to be around her mom and grandma and her constantly distracted dad. Mom said work was hard right now, and Dad was stressed out. Clara understood, right? Of course she did, Momma's sweet girl. But Clara thought her dad looked awfully sad in those days, and she didn't understand why.

Clara's favorite rooms in her grandma's house were the sitting room on the main floor, with its long window panels that let weak sunlight through on cloudy days, and the cream couches and the grand piano. She also loved the dining room, with its cabinets full of fine china and sparkling Swarovski crystal figurines of dancing ballerinas, playful little animals, and a great big lotus flower. The walls were painted a cool jade green, the most magnificent walls Clara had ever seen. There was the library too, of course. A real library, all dark wood and a wall entirely made up of books. There was a rolling ladder and twin balconies looking over the sitting room. Those rooms brought a happiness to Clara that she hardly believed could come from a house. People who said money couldn't buy happiness were wrong.

Eventually, it was time to take her explorations elsewhere: outside. This would be a real sort of expedition, one that required a packed bag of snacks, juice, and proper clothing. Her grandma had bought her a pair of green rubber boots for the rain and mud and swamp of Georgia, as her flipflops from California would simply not do.

"Don't go beyond the fence, Clara," her mom said. "You'll get ticks, or poison ivy, or maybe even bitten by a snake."

"But Grandma says there's a creek behind the fence."

Her mom strictly forbade her. "I'll be watching to make sure you don't cross that fence line. I can see, you know. I can see all the way to the back gates right here from this kitchen window."

But Clara knew she couldn't. Still, she would not disobey her mother. If she really did get ticks or poison ivy or a snake bite, there would only be one way to explain that to her mom.

She sunk into her new boots, which fit perfectly, and stepped out through the back porch door. She looked back and saw her mom watching her, arms crossed, but Clara was too excited to feel upset about the look on Mom's face. They didn't have a backyard worth exploring in California, not at their house and especially not at the apartment complex. Most lawns in their old neighborhood had fake grass anyway, good for nothing except a spot for neighborhood dogs to pee on during a walk.

But Grandma's backyard was glorious. It went back so deep and far beyond the house that there really was no possible way her mom could see all the way to the back fence.

Right behind the house was a pool, covered for the coming autumn, but Clara made a mental note to ask her grandma to uncover it for her. She wasn't a very good swimmer, but she longed to see it, if only for the sake of seeing a pool in the backyard of a house.

The grass was deepest emerald and freshly soaked from a light rain. It looked so soft and alive, and Clara wanted to kick her boots and socks off to wiggle her toes in it, just like people always wanted to wiggle their toes in the sand at the beach. She thought the beaches in LA were so dirty, filled with trash and scum, people should keep their shoes on at the beach.

Wiggling her toes in the grass would have to take place another time, though, as there was still the whole backyard to explore, and Clara had barely gone beyond the pool. She was scared for a moment that her mom really wouldn't be able to see her, and she would be completely alone. But it was better to be alone, she told herself. She preferred to be alone, and Grandma's fences were six feet tall by state regulation for a property so large. Grandma said they were so tall that a leaping deer couldn't clear them. Perhaps, she reasoned, the backyard was even safer than the house. No one she didn't know could come in, especially not Grandma's church friends or Cassie's school friends. And that backyard became a real haven—just for her. The trees were so tall and dense that they formed a larger fence, of sorts, all around the back side of the property.

As she explored, Clara unpacked her worries, and wondered why she and her family had so quickly needed to move across the country to Grandma's house. She felt safe—so safe here. Maybe Grandma had been lonely after Grandpa died, all by herself in her beautiful mansion, silent and alone like a ghost. But that didn't feel like the right answer to the question, since as an old lady, Grandma had more friends than Clara had ever had. Maybe the house was simply too big, and Grandma didn't want to sleep alone there at night. *Yes*, Clara thought, *that must be it.*

21

Whatever the reason, Clara was happy to be there, and for the dramatic change in scenery. Since they had arrived, they'd experienced several heavy rainstorms and various light showers at all times of the day. Her mom had forced an umbrella into her arms every day before getting onto the bus, and Clara suspected that only made her appear more pathetic; none of the other kids brought umbrellas, most of them didn't even have raincoats. She felt ridiculous, like the people in southern California who donned puffer jackets the moment it fell below seventy degrees outside.

In the backyard Clara felt a strong, warm connection to this house and land through her grandma. It was the closest thing to magic that she'd ever seen. She decided she would call the backyard and the forest behind it Mirkwood, after Tolkien's evil forest, home to the giant spiders and woodland elves. It felt like a fitting name, though nothing about this place looked or felt evil in the slightest. However woodsy it felt, the area within the fences, at least, was a properly groomed backyard, from the pool to the stone staircase leading down to a little vegetable garden.

The backyard exploration, Clara decided, would require days of careful study. For today, she would start by walking the perimeter along the fences. She was curious about the woods behind the property where everything was untouched and wild, but she would not disobey her mom and go beyond the fence—she would just get close.

But the closer she walked toward the back fence, the further she got from the house. She looked back several times to make sure it was still there. It was, but it was getting smaller and smaller, and she began to feel afraid. This close to the edge of the property, Clara had a sense that she was walking away from the world of her family and schoolmates, and into something else entirely. A foreign land, old and fierce. Lawless.

She reached the edge of the property and stood before the back gate. Painted an oily black, its gaps were filled with thick, mesh wire. It loomed above Clara, and she felt both dread and relief: it was so tall and solid that she couldn't imagine anything that might get through. But what needed to be kept out that her grandparents had constructed such an impenetrable barrier?

Though she had been alone the entire time, she realized that the woods had fallen silent. The absence of small sounds and rustling trees felt dreadful, as if the forest around her held its breath, waiting for something. Clara wondered if trees could be afraid.

Into the silence came one momentous sound. It was only the crack of a fallen branch, but it startled Clara like a gunshot. In that moment, she knew she was no longer alone. Something had arrived.

Clara's heart was pounding like it was trying to break through her sternum, and she took a step away from the fence. She no longer felt like this was her safe haven, or that it was hers at all.

A slight movement just behind the fence caught her eye, and she found herself rooted in place. She couldn't have moved if she wanted to. Something was there, watching her. It brushed up against the other side of the fence and two yellow eyes peered through the mesh wire.

For days and nights after that, Clara tried to convince herself that it had been some animal, some beast she had seen on the other side of the fence. But she knew she had come across something far worse. And it had seen her, too.

She couldn't sleep, could barely close her eyes afterward without seeing it all again. Fear had wormed its way into her heart and chilled her to the bone. The image in her mind's eye of the beast gradually resolved into not a best, but rather a little girl who looked human enough to have been one of Clara's classmates. But human girls her age did not have horns poking out of their heads, or yellow eyes, or pointy little teeth that grinned at her like they shared a secret.

THREE

PRESENT DAY

While they were in town, they were not staying at Grandma's house, which was a relief to Clara. Being in that place, that relic of her past, Clara realized there was a lot she had forgotten about her childhood and her time there. She hadn't forgotten exactly, she had simply forgotten to think about it. Now it felt as if a dam had broken and those memories were flooding back, unstoppable and brutal as the ocean.

They couldn't stay in the house because of the investigation that was going on, but Clara couldn't reconcile the idea of an investigation having anything to do with Grandma. That was something that belonged in books or movies, something that dealt with criminals and not a lonely old woman. Clara's family was told that they would be allowed in during the day when the investigation took place and that they would be under video surveillance, but they weren't allowed in when the police or detectives were away, in case they tried to tamper with any evidence. Clara didn't know what kind of "evidence" they were hoping to find. Her bibles, lovingly highlighted and annotated? Surely not, because nothing with the Lord's name in it could possibly be a tool for evil. Perhaps they considered books like Harry Potter or Clara's beloved Lord of the Rings of the occultist-sort, instruments of witchcraft. It was likely. After all, certain places across the country banned books the way a child eats candy: indiscriminately and by the fistfuls. Her rage deepened.

At least her dad was on the same page when it came to religion. After his own Christian upbringing, her father had never insisted his own kids go to church or think of themselves as religious. Their saving grace, in their grandparent's eyes, had been their mother. When people thought of Christians, they most likely imagined people like Clara's grandparents. Many people, however, did not realize the prevalence of Christianity in many Japanese and Korean communities. Her grandparents had been overjoyed when they learned that real Asian Americans (not like their son, adopted into a white family and indoctrinated into the religion) could be equally as devout, and even had their own community churches.

Raised on the other side of the country, Megumi Graham had attended a Japanese-Christian church every Sunday for as long as she could remember, and she had dragged Cassie and Clara along when they were still young enough to not argue. When they were a little older, though, the sisters became aware that they did not fit into the Japanese Christian community, if any Japanese community at all. Megumi had not needed to explain to her daughters that many East Asian cultures held a high importance on colorism within their own race. Cassie and Clara were not simply tan Japanese girls, they were mixed children, and it was frowned upon. Kids and parents alike gave them sideways looks at church. Their dad never attended, for his own reasons, and eventually their Megumi let them stay at home while she went alone.

She remained dedicated to the religion and the Japanese Christian community. Apart from the one-year break when they lived in Georgia, Megumi still attended the same Japanese church that she had been raised in and tried to raise her own daughters in. Having lived in California most of her life, she didn't buy into the southern superstitions about witchcraft or black magic, but Clara could hear in her mother's voice that she was troubled by the accusations. "What if she got herself mixed up in some cultish sect in her old age? Maybe she was hoodwinked."

Clara's dad was not just troubled by the accusations; he was enraged. Danny Graham was not a devout Christian, but he was a devout son. From her room next-door at the hotel, Clara could hear him shouting through the shared wall. She couldn't hear everything, but she could pick up clear phrases like "ungrateful" and "gossiping liars" or "goddamned religious hicks." Eventually, she fell asleep with those words swirling around in her brain.

Clara woke the next morning to three text messages. One from her mom saying that she and Dad had left early to talk with the detectives over at the house, and that Cassie had arrived last night and would come to pick Clara up.

The other two messages were from Cassie, the first sent thirty-four minutes ago, and the second one nine minutes ago:

> text me when u wake up and ill come get u
> are u up yet???

Clara sent a quick text back and gathered her nerve to get out of bed. One of the many things she hated about traveling was the way it disrupted her everyday routines. Back at her little apartment in California, she filled her days with diligent, comfortable routine, and very little ever happened to throw her off course. This morning, though, she woke up late in a strange room, and no dog. Petra was back in California with the sitter, so Clara would miss her morning walk in. She could walk without Petra, of course, but that would mean taking a foreign path here at the hotel. Back at home, Clara and Petra took the same exact loop around the same two blocks in the neighborhood every single day. They passed by the same apartment complexes, Shell gas station, donut shop, and the same neighbors walking their own dogs around the same time every day. The weather in California was predictable and consistent. After all, it was a place where the idea of four full seasons sounded like a hassle. No, Clara could not bear to go for a walk today, even if Cassie wasn't coming to pick her up in a half hour.

As she brushed her teeth and got dressed, she hoped Cassie would be coming alone. It would be nerve-wracking enough for Clara to see her sister again after almost eight months, and the first time since Cassie had gotten engaged. Clara hadn't seen the ring in person yet, only the pictures Cassie posted to her Instagram. Her fiancé's name was Tristan Becker. He was incredibly handsome with his neat blonde hair and gray-blue eyes. He dressed well, too: crisp button-downs, sweater-vests, and khaki pants. Add beautiful Cassie, and they were quite the pair.

Clara had met Tristan several times before, but she probably hadn't acted very welcoming toward him. Cassie had many boyfriends before—most of them whirlwind romances. They usually ended with some drama and Cassie crying over how the boys she dated always seemed to hurt her.

Every boy Cassie dated made her miserable or furious, so Clara thought her sister would be better off alone. That's why Clara had never tried to befriend Tristan. She hated how boys made Cassie cry, and she had thought Tristan was the next in line to terrorize or be terrorized by her sister. It worked both ways with Cassie.

Her phone buzzed.

—*here.*

Clara stuffed some things into her bag, hoping she wasn't forgetting anything important, and hurried out the door. In the elevator on the way down, she thought about Petra and imagined the little dachshund on her walk. She hoped Petra would be okay with the different walking route with the sitter until she could get back.

The elevator doors parted at the lobby. And there was Cassie. No matter how long they were apart, Clara always spotted her sister instantly. Cassie appeared effortlessly cool in baggy sweatpants, baby tee, and high ponytail—the picture of a causal yet fashionable twenty-something-year-old, with a giant engagement ring sparkling on her left hand. She spotted Clara, rooted in place by the elevator, and impatiently waved her over.

Clara's feet moved, and her mouth smiled—all on its own, and now that Cassie was here, right in front of her, she felt much better. They hugged, and although Clara felt dizzy from her sister's strong perfume, the tension flowed out of her body. They were together again, and would reunite with their parents at Grandma's house, dispel the evil lies about her, and it would all end up okay. She looked around for Tristan, but he wasn't here. Maybe he hadn't wanted to come to their grandma's funeral.

"Aw Clara, it's been a while!" Cassie pulled away, smiling radiantly. She had always been capable of the most genuine cheerfulness as well as the most horrid hatefulness. "Tristan went to park the car, but we can go meet him out there."

Clara's heart sank. He was here.

The sisters chatted on the way to the parking lot, but it was mostly Cassie talking excitedly and only occasionally waiting for a response. Clara had to be alert; she didn't want to come across as uninterested, but her morning went from peaceful quiet to Cassie without much time to orient herself. Cassie showed her the ring up close. It was both huge and delicate, pure white sparkle. It was like the Arkenstone under The Lonely Mountain, and Clara was thoroughly charmed.

"Well?" Cassie said expectantly, pulling her out of her thoughts.

"It's wonderful. Stunning. I would like to have a ring just like it."

Cassie laughed and squeezed Clara's arm. "Well, you'll only have to get engaged for that to happen. Got anyone in mind?" But they both knew the answer to that. Clara was generally terrified of making friends, even as an adult. It was a long time ago, but the kids at school had been so cruel to her, *especially* in Georgia, and contrary to her therapist's beliefs, she worried that the bad experiences would outweigh any of her small, interpersonal victories. Being a commuter student in college had given her the perfect exit to any and all social situations. She could not fathom having to be in a relationship. What would they talk about? What would they *do*? It was a situation she was glad she had never encountered.

A boy was waving at them. No, not a boy—a tall man, Cassie's fiancé, Tristan Becker. He smiled easily at her like he had already won her good graces. "Good to see you again, Clara," and stuck his hand out to shake.

Good looking guys like him probably thought they had nothing to prove. But Clara was a harsh critic when it came to who she believed was good enough for her family.

The three of them got into a rental car. Luckily, Tristan didn't seem interested in catching up with her, or rather, getting to know her, which she was okay with Clara. She was glad. She learned the most about people by observing them and their interactions with others. When most people talked to her, she got too flustered to think. She listened to the two of them conversing easily in the front seats, only one of Tristan's hands on the wheel so that the fingers on his right hand could be laced with Cassie's. Clara realized she was grimacing and made a conscious effort to keep her expression neutral. Positive, if she could manage it. Dr. Ashley would remind her that she didn't know what was going on in other people's heads. It was possible that Tristan didn't have any ulterior motives, and that maybe he and Cassie would be married for many happy years.

But these two seemed far too at ease in the wake of Grandma's death and the loathsome rumors about her involvement with black magic. It felt disrespectful, possibly sacrilegious. The scowl fell right back onto Clara's face, and she allowed it to stay there for the time being.

There were two police cars in front of the house, along with her parent's beige rental car. Clara expected her sister would have already given Tristan the rundown, but apparently, she hadn't. "Witchcraft?" His laugh was incredulous. "You're joking. There's no way they'd actually run an investigation on a claim like that in this day and age."

Clara thought he was right. But she supposed the police in LA county had to look into some weird stuff as well, probably weirder than this. With a sigh, she pushed open the car door and followed Cassie and Tristan up the driveway. She didn't like the way Cassie made Grandma sound, as if she had been just a crazy old lady. But she overlooked her misgivings. She and her sister had been reunited for less than an hour and Clara didn't want to taint their reunion.

To her great relief, there were only two detectives in the house, and they stopped talking with her parents as soon as the three of them came through the main entrance. Twelve years had passed, but Clara still felt breathless taking that first step into the grand foyer, all creamy tile and open space, adorned with its majestic floating staircase that arched up to the second floor. As a child, she had avoided using that staircase. It really did look like it was floating, only attached to the ground and the second floor with nothing visible supporting its middle.

"My daughters, plus one fiancé." Danny Graham said, clearing his throat.

The detective closest to them, a Black woman with long, copper-colored braids looked over at them with sympathy. "We'll get to the bottom of this. It appears your late grandmother had some untraditional… interests."

"That's not true," Clara blurted, surprising herself. Embarrassment washed over her, but now that she'd started, she couldn't hold back. "She loved stories about magic, but she didn't have any interest in that sort of thing in real life. She didn't believe in that stuff. She knew it wasn't real. Everyone knows that." But as that last part came out, Clara had a small, fearful doubt.

The other detective, a tall, thin man scribbled something in his notepad, and Clara hoped she had not made things worse—her mom was making weird faces at her, twitching and blinking designed, apparently, to communicate "just stop talking."

"Well, we're going to go ahead and start looking around," the female officer said.

Clara hated the idea of police and detectives wandering about in her grandma's beloved home in an effort to find some evidence of her interest in the occult. As a child, her grandma had nurtured her love of fantasy encouraging and fueling Clara's imagination, and her creation of fantastical worlds and beasts when other adults told her that fairies and elves and dragons existed only in books for young children. She knew that, but it couldn't stop her from dreaming up such creatures.

There had been a period shortly after they moved to Georgia when Clara's mom and dad decided to set her up with a child psychiatrist. It was only a couple of months into fifth grade when she started to have trouble with the kids in class at her new school. Coincidentally, it was also around the same time that she started catching glimpses of the little girl in the woods and made the mistake of telling her parents out of fear.

Clara hadn't thought of that yellow-eyed girl in years... maybe twelve years. Her memory hadn't been sparked when she learned of her grandmother's passing. It was only when she stepped foot on her grandma's property again that the memories started floating around in the peripheral areas of her mind. Now it felt like those memories had been there all along, and she just hadn't been paying attention. It was like something silent standing behind her, and she was only now turning around to see it.

A part of her now longed to go back behind the house again like when she was a child and lay in the grass, explore the flora and fauna, and wait for the girl to come. Instead, she went to breakfast with her family and Cassie's plus one.

FOUR

THE PAST

Clara started to properly realize she'd be in trouble for more than just her quietness when Grandma took her and Cassie out for dinner for the first time, just the three of them. It was a weird little restaurant set up in an actual house in some half-way point between the rural suburbs and historic downtown, which was not Atlanta. They were far enough into the suburbs that they had their own little downtown made of bricks, devoid of any skyscrapers or tall buildings. The restaurant was quite literally named Midway Meal House. Grandma said they had her favorite fried chicken and waffles, and Clara wondered why her grandma would want to eat chicken and waffles at the same time when one was clearly for breakfast and the other was not.

She didn't exactly notice at first, but a certain hush seemed to fall when the three of them entered the place. It was almost all old people: old married couples, grandparents with grandchildren, old people sitting alone. Everyone stared with unabashed interest. Really, though, Clara hadn't felt anything much out of the usual, and she might not have if it hadn't been for Cassie. She was uncomfortable around most strangers anyway, and old people were worse with their cloudy eyes and pale, wrinkly skin. The rooms of the restaurant-house were filled with them, silent and staring like zombies.

Wordlessly, the hostess led them through the house and into a less crowded room. Grandma liked to eat dinner early, around four in the evening, so it was still bright outside, and the usual weak sunlight came in through the windows from behind the clouds. Almost all windows in Georgia, Clara noticed, had screens so that when you opened the normal window part, the air came through, but you couldn't stick your hand or face out the window. Grandma said it was to keep the mosquitoes and little critters out. *What's critters* Clara had asked. Just something pesky, according to her grandma. Then Clara wondered what sort of thing that might be, or if *she* was a critter.

Two kids menus, which was maybe the first thing Clara noticed that set Cassie off, because she was a real, proper teenager. Or maybe it was having to go out with Clara and Grandma, neither of whose company she seemed to particularly enjoy. As they were reading their menus, Clara caught Cassie shooting glares at the other people in the room at their booths and tables. Clara didn't really think anything of it because Cassie was always angry with everybody, even when Clara didn't see a reason.

"You already know what I'll be getting," Grandma said cheerily, seeming unbothered by everyone's continued staring and Cassie's glaring. Clara started to think Cassie was glaring at the other people for staring at them, and maybe she had a right to. The good thing about being with Cassie was that she fended off everyone and everything for you, sometimes unprovoked like a cat with its claws out. "What about you girls? Clara, honey?"

Clara was still pondering the menu. Kids menus were usually small, they always had good options: mac-n-cheese, chicken tenders, hot dog, or cheeseburgers with fries. She was content, feeling safe with her grandma who had lots of friends and money, and the protection of mean, always-angry Cassie. "I think maybe I—"

Cassie slammed her fists down on the table so hard that

the plastic water cups trembled. "What the hell are they all looking at us for still, huh Grandma?"

"Cassandra!" Grandma exclaimed, something between a whisper and a scream, but Cassie had started now and would be hard to stop.

"Don't call me that, Grandma." She stood up abruptly, facing the restaurant crowd. "You hear that? She's our grandma, you old frumps! You never seen two brown kids with a white lady before? Well, here you goddamn go!" The restaurant that had been silent since they walked in was now alive with cries of disdain and scorn. Clara could see people from the other rooms standing up, some even getting out of their seats to come take a look. Then the waitress was coming over quickly, looking red in the face.

"Is there something wrong?" she asked. The question was clearly directed toward Grandma, but Cassie plowed on like a hot engine.

"Yeah, I'll tell you what's wrong—these racist old freaks won't mind their own fucking business!" At those words, more shrieks erupted.

Grandma looked horribly resigned, and the waitress had a hard look on her face. "Ma'am, we don't use that kind of language in here or talk about other guests that way. I'm going to have to ask your party to leave."

Grandma had already packed up. "Come along girls. Let's get going."

They went through a McDonald's drive through on the way home. Clara hated McDonald's, but Grandma clearly wasn't in the mood for another fight and Clara shoved the flat, slightly cold kid's cheeseburger into her mouth. It was hard to chew and swallow when you were also trying to cry without making a noise. It's not like Cassie was mad at her or Grandma, in fact, she had been trying to protect them in her own way. But sometimes Clara hated Cassie's methods, and she had embarrassed Grandma horribly. Now they had to eat McDonald's, and Grandma ate nothing.

*   *   *

After that day at the restaurant, Clara started noticing whenever people stared. Not just the kids in her class, but adults
too. She had only thought people were curious because she
was new, but Cassie's outburst made her begin to think it was
more than that. In class they had assigned seats, and one time
Izzy, the girl at her table, asked her, "Where are you from?"

Clara knew she had already explained that to the class,
but she said, "California."

Izzy's sparse eyebrows were crinkled, as if she was confused. "But what about before that?"

It was Clara's turn to be confused. "I don't know, I was
born there."

Then, Izzy seemed annoyed. "How about your parents.
Did they come from China or something? Or Mexico?"

But Clara was from here, and so were her parents. Why
did this girl want to know about her parents when she barely
knew Clara? She didn't really know why, but suddenly she
felt very upset.

Another time, she had just bought her lunch and sat down
at their long class table with her tray. It was a nasty piece of
pizza which she only ate the cheese off of, mushy fruit, and
strawberry milk—the only part she liked. Mary Kate looked
at her tray, and then at her. "Why do you never bring lunch
from home?"

Clara was caught off guard. She hadn't given it much
thought before, but Mary Kate's PB and J and juice box did
look nice. She also had a beautiful purple lunchbox. "I don't
know."

Mary Kate wasn't satisfied with that answer. "Do your
parents not know how to cook American food?"

Again, Clara was confused. Of course her parents knew
how to cook American food; they'd lived here their whole
lives. Well, her dad had had been adopted when he was four
years old, but he didn't know how to cook Indian food when

he was four, and he still didn't know how to this day. Her dad didn't even like Indian food. After that, Clara asked her mom to pack her a home lunch. She didn't have a nice lunchbox, but she proudly walked with her brown paper sack to the cafeteria with her class. It was okay because many other kids in her class didn't have real lunchboxes either. In fact, some kids only carried little plastic zip-lock bags to hold their squished sandwiches. Apparently, it didn't matter how bad or meager your home lunch was. The important thing was to be like everyone else.

But there were no questions asked, no suspicions raised about the White kids who bought school lunches every single day.

And it wasn't just kids who pointed out the ways in which Clara was different. P.E. class was twice a week on Mondays and Wednesdays, and it combined two whole classes into one gym. There were thirty-eight kids in Clara's class and thirty-six in the other fifth grade class that they were combined with, so that was almost eighty students for two gym teachers. One day they had to sit and learn about wearing sunscreen and sun protection, which was a treat because it meant Clara didn't have to run laps or try to dribble a deflated basketball.

Mr. Johnston was an older man, old enough to look strange wearing a tank top and gym shorts. Clara thought it was kind of silly that he was teaching them about sunscreen when it looked like he hadn't touched that stuff once in his life: everywhere his skin showed looked charred by the sun (he said he did triathlons). He was kind of like a rotisserie chicken with his unnaturally browned, sunbaked skin. It could have been self-tanner. But Clara could also imagine him paying to lay inside those tanning beds they had around town that looked like coffins.

He said the higher the SPF number, the more protection. "The lightest-skinned folks need high SPF's, around fifty to seventy, or else you'll burn real bad," he said. "Now, if you're naturally more tan, an SPF of thirty-five, or even fifteen, will probably do just fine." The room erupted with chatter, kids comparing what SPF number might be best for them. Mr. Johnston blew his whistle so ferociously that some kids whined or covered their ears. "Hush! Settle down, I'm not finished," he said. "Now, there are some folks who are so dark that the sun won't touch them at all. I'm talking about my friends here like Colston, Abbey, Monica, Clara." Clara knew Colston and Monica; they were in Mrs. Manning's class with her. They were Black, and Clara and them were the only non-white kids in their class. There was one Chinese girl, Chloe, but she was very pale, so Mr. Johnston didn't include her with the four of them. "Brown people don't need to wear sunscreen, so consider yourselves lucky." But nobody whined or complained about Clara, Colston, Monica, and the other girl he called lucky.

Clara thought about it the rest of the day, and she just couldn't make sense of Mr. Johnston's words. Her mom always made her wear sunscreen. She had been slathering it on Clara since she was old enough to go in the pool. Clara didn't think it was true that "brown people" couldn't get burnt by the sun: Cassie disobeyed their mom all the time and came back from the pool or beach with pink shoulders, chest, and even her nose that looked painful and eventually became all nasty and started peeling after a few days. Wasn't that the same thing as a sunburn?

Besides, Mr. Johnston was about the same color as Clara, natural or not. Why hadn't he thought to include himself in that category?

Clara then wondered if putting on sunscreen every day, not just for pool days, would make her become lighter. Light enough, at least, where she couldn't be one of four called out in a room of almost eighty kids.

It turned out that being quiet wasn't enough for her to get by unnoticed.

Grandma's big, lovely house didn't exactly help her situation either.

There was still the issue of the school bus and all the things that came with it. Grandma's house was the very last stop which meant that there wasn't a kid on the bus who didn't watch Clara as she climbed up the steps onto the bus. To make things go quicker, she had gotten into the habit of going a little early and waiting right at the edge of the long driveway so that when the bus arrived, she could quickly clamber in and then they would drive away from the house. However much she loved it privately, she could not think of it as her house, or even her family's house. It was too special, too magical. It did not belong in the world of Clara's family, and she thought it would be best to remember that.

Living in that house made her wonder about other things. Like how much money Grandma and Grandpa had and why they didn't give any to their son. Clara thought a small allowance from his parents could have done their family a lot of good. They wouldn't have had to live in that small apartment in California. Maybe they could have bought a house with a real backyard and grass instead. But she knew that adults and children lived differently, with a set of separate rules. Adults weren't allowed to get allowances from their parents, it seemed, however rich they were.

The kids at school started to ask questions again. Clara and her family were new to the town and didn't have any friends, but Grandma certainly did. Clara didn't want to blame her, but how else would people in her class know the weird scraps of details about her family and situation if it didn't start with Grandma. She was old and didn't have a phone, but gossip among old ladies spread quickly through Sunday church or Tuesday evening bible study.

The town was relatively small, and its inhabitants felt entitled to the details of their neighbors. Izzy, the girl at her classroom table who Clara was starting to really dislike, was the first to bring it up. She was staring at her for a couple of minutes before she spoke, which made Clara so uncomfortable that she squirmed in her seat. "My Momma says your daddy was a hotshot CEO in California." The words sounded wrong in her mouth, and not just because of her southern way of speaking. "A bigtime millionaire! A bajillionaire! Is that true?"

The other kids at her table were all very interested, and Clara had the sudden bad urge to use the bathroom. "Yeah, is it?" Adam, the boy across from her said.

"I don't know," Clara said. She didn't know how much money her parents had. She didn't know if her dad had ever been a millionaire. Maybe he had, at one point, but certainly not now, and certainly not when they lived in that apartment in California right before Grandma's house.

"What do you mean you don't know? How can you not know what your daddy does for a living?" Izzy said, pushing on.

"I—he used to be, I think. A CEO."

"But not a millionaire?"

Clara looked around helplessly, wondering why Mrs. Manning wasn't coming over to scold them for being so loud and not working. She was sitting at her desk, staring down blankly at the papers on her desk. Clara had a nasty, uncomfortable thought that maybe Mrs. Manning wasn't actually grading papers, and that maybe she wanted to know the answers to Izzy's questions as well.

"I don't know."

The kids at her table seemed annoyed with her response. "She's hiding something, I tell you," said Luke. "I just know it."

There were murmurs of agreement. Clara felt a bad feeling, something that she could not name but that made her want to scream and cry. It required a good deal of concentration to keep a normal face. She found that if she kept her eyes still and didn't let them dart around, she could keep the tears in place until the burning in her eyes subsided. She wasn't quite sure where the tears went, if her eyeballs sucked them back up, but at least they didn't come out for the time being.

In that moment, and more moments to come in the next few months, Clara hated Mrs. Manning for not doing anything. It was supposed to be the adult's job to stop bad things from happening. She later learned that was not the case, and sometimes it was the adult's fault that the bad things began in the first place. Maybe adults like Mrs. Manning and her parents got uncomfortable and scared too. Still, Clara couldn't help being angry.

She hated the kids at her table, too, for not leaving her alone and for forming an agreement that she was hiding things. For a brief moment, she wanted to hate Grandma for her stupid gossiping, even if she was just trying to brag about what kind of job her son used to have. Or maybe she wanted to hate her for that wonderful house that made them stick out like a big fat fly in a pot of sugar. Clara was different for enough reasons already, and that house really just made matters worse.

FIVE

June 2022

Cassie and Tristan were alike in that they both talked end-
lessly. About themselves, each other, their jobs, their apartment, the ring, glorious, glorious New York, and the like. It
was draining to listen to, but her parents looked happy, and
at least it saved Clara from having to talk about herself and
what she had been up to. It wasn't like she still lived at home
or wasn't working. It just felt small in the face of Cassie and
her twenty-something blissful success: her "dream job" as a
fashion and style writer for some online beauty magazine.
Before that, the dream had been to be a doctor, then a nurse,
for a short period of time, which later switched to an interest
in becoming a veterinarian, but that turned out to be more
disgusting than nursing. She'd had a crisis a couple of years
ago (but not the kind like Clara, apparently, which required
weekly therapy), and she became a nail tech for a couple of
months. Then she thought she could become an artist, but
eventually, it turned out she had a knack for online writing,
and was quite tech savvy, and well-versed in the languages
of social media. She kept up with the latest beauty and fashion trends, and that knowledge proved incredibly useful for
her. She had been writing for an online publication called
StyleCraze for almost a year now, and it seemed like it would

stick. She *was* good at it, Clara thought, having visited the site to read some of her sister's articles. She actually wanted to take some of Cassie's advice from those articles, but she didn't know where to start.

Tristan had graduated from NYU, and more recently from Boston University with a graduate degree in business. He was still job hunting, but surely those credentials would open some doors for him. He was charismatic and might have seemed charming if he wasn't trying to become a part of their family. But he *was*, and he was here sitting right in front of them and holding Cassie's hand like he owned her. Cassie thought there wasn't room enough for both of them in the family.

Or maybe he wasn't trying to become a part of their family at all; what if Cassie was trying to become a part of his? He might try to take her away from them, and Clara should stop it. She was the only one who seemed to care about preserving their nuclear family and it was up to her to save the Grahams. No, no it was not. Cassie was a full-blown adult with a dependable income and had every right to begin her own family. Clara did as well. She was supposed to *want* to do that.

Luckily, the bagels kept her distracted that morning. When they had lived here before, Clara and Cassie's favorite bagel place had been Bronx Alley Bagels, the strangest, coolest little restaurant they had ever seen. Right off the side of a main road, it was a shiny old trailer, the kind that belonged to trailer parks where people lived. It was relatively big and must have been made up of more than one trailer, and it had been repurposed on a plot of dead grass to become a restaurant.

Cassie had begged like a child in right in front of Tristan, pleading with their parents to make the half hour drive out and see if it was still there. Secretly, Clara was glad, almost grateful that Cassie was making such a scene, because she wanted to go just as badly. Their parents had relented, but no one was certain it would still be there, as it hadn't been very popular twelve years ago and didn't look like it would make it.

But when they got to the place they remembered, it was entirely different. It was still there, but it didn't look like the same little restaurant. The grass was no longer dead and yellow, for starters. Perhaps they had seen the importance of appearance and pleasing landscaping in this particular corner of the south, because there was a real parking lot now, beautiful grass, and an outdoor seating patio framed with potted plants and flowers and plastic windmills that spun whenever the breeze picked up. Cassie squealed and clapped her hands, seemingly unphased by the new look and dragged Tristan up to the steps. Another big difference was the line snaking out the door. There were more people simply waiting in line than could fit in the entire restaurant. It was completely changed, but the Bronx Alley Bagels sign was the same; it could have been pulled right out of her memory. Slanted red font painted on a wide oval, framed with twinkling yellow bulbs and slowly revolving on its axis.

"What's wrong, Clary?" Her dad asked, and she really did feel ten years old again. "Looks like it's still here after all!"

"It's so different." Clara said. Then, "I hope they still have the Kit-Kat cream cheese."

Her mom laughed. "A lot can change in twelve years. Georgia's even a blue state now after the last election."

They waited for over forty minutes in the sticky morning heat. Early June's humidity was oppressive, and it felt like some slant variation of altitude sickness, the way Clara had to fight for her breath. It started to feel silly, waiting so long in line for a bagel in some small little town in Georgia, but then it was their turn and they stepped through the doors.

They did still have the Kit-Kat cream cheese! Despite every other change, the display of cream cheeses right at the front entrance was still the same, and Clara was smiling without even realizing. They still had sixteen flavors, laid out in two rows in a display freezer like at an ice-cream shop. They were the most beautiful cream cheeses Clara had ever seen, whipped and fluffy, a mix of savory or sweet choices with marvelous toppings: real full-length Kit Kat's sticking out of Clara's favorite one, strawberry and fudge drizzles, fruit chunks, nuts, and vegetables. Even Tristan looked impressed, and he was from New York where all the good bagels were supposed to be.

"Isn't it wonderful?" Cassie asked, gleefully tugging his arm.

He smiled down at her. "Well, I supposed they don't name it after the Bronx for nothing!"

They got a table in the corner by the windows, which were cracked open. There wasn't air conditioning in the restaurant, but for once it seemed nobody had anything to complain about. Or maybe they were just older. It was a weird feeling, like being pulled from their present lives and plopped right into the past. It had been one thing to be back at the house but sitting in a restaurant like this made it feel less like a dream.

In her excitement, Clara almost forgot why they were all back here together in the first place, and what waited for them back at the house.

After all her begging and pleading to go there, Cassie didn't even end up ordering anything. She said she would share with Tristan, because they both wanted to watch their weight for the wedding. Clara wondered how you could fly two and a half hours on a plane, drive forty-five minutes out from the city and another thirty to the restaurant, all to wait in line for another forty minutes and order *nothing*.

Her mom and dad both got sesame bagels with salmon lox, Tristan-Cassie got a blueberry raisin, and Clara got two cinnamon sugars with Kit-Kat cream cheese (one was for to-go). There were a few things in life that brought her constant joy, and you never could go wrong with food. Even her other joys like reading and Petra had some drawbacks: too much reading caused eyestrain, and she became very stressed whenever Petra got sick from eating things she shouldn't or something else like sniffing dog poop. But Clara had a big appetite and an endless sweet tooth. It was a good thing she didn't keep baking supplies at her apartment in California or else she might not ever stop.

Without food to eat, Cassie continued to talk, and Clara became busy with her second bagel that she had planned on saving for later. Someone else might have been uncomfortable the way Tristan nearly ignored his sister-in-law-to-be, but Clara was fine to keep to herself. Sure, she thought it was strange, not exactly a great sign how Tristan couldn't even pretend to want to get to know her, but her fear of speaking about herself or saying the wrong thing was greater than her need to get along with him.

But then they had to drive another half hour back to the house, with Tristan and Cassie's voices amplified in the small car. They weren't saying anything particularly rude or obnoxious, as they mostly talked about themselves and gushed over each other, but they were coming up on three hours of non-stop talking and Clara was beginning to feel exhausted and a bit agitated. She closed her eyes in the back seat and forced herself to not cover her ears with her hands. The two of them would doubtlessly leave once they all got back to the house, or at least Clara hoped they would. If not, she would go out into the backyard and hide like a child. She told herself she deserved that much, or else her social battery might explode.

When they got back, however, there was a strangely familiar car parked right in the middle of Grandma's driveway. It was empty, which could only mean they were already in the house. "You've got to be kidding me." Danny Graham said, a calm anger rising in his voice. "That better not be whose car I think it is."

It was. Sitting at the kitchen counter was their old neighbor, Stacie Adamson, and her ugly son Luke. They were deep in conversation with the detectives, looking pleasantly comfortable as if they had been invited in. "What in the name of God is going on here?"

Miss Stacie turned around with a gasp so dramatic, it could have only been fake, a withered hand flying to her bosom. "Do not use the Lord's name in vain, Mr. Graham!"

Megumi Graham had seen and heard enough bullshit since they arrived. "No, you do not tell my husband what to do in his mother's house. What exactly do you think you're doing here, *Miss* Adamson?"

So, it was them who had sent the "anonymous" tip. Of course it was.

Clara remembered Miss Stacie well enough. Grandma had two enemies: Satan, and Stacie Adamson who lived in the house across the street. They went to the same church, but Miss Stacie was *not* welcome at the Graham's for Tuesday bible study. The Adamson's were the type of people who liked to do and say things because "God told them to." Stacie and her husband Paul saw angels in their backyard every so often, and those angels brought them messages such as, "Tell Debbie Graham to stop trying to have kids of her own. If she's not gettin' them, then it's not God's will." This was something Clara had heard a long time ago, a discussion between her dad and Grandma about why the neighbors were so hostile towards each other. Clara had learned many years later how Grandma had tried with fertility treatments for years before letting go of that hope and adopting her dad instead. When it came to pregnancy, apparently, it really all had to be God's will: in-vitro fertilization was immoral in the way that abortion was. There was to be no replacement or substitution of the marital act for procreation.

In some ways, though, Debbie Graham and Stacie Adamson weren't so different. They believed in a lot of the same basic principles, and Clara wondered about how her grandma would have really felt about IVF if she hadn't needed to try it.

It was a nasty thing to think, but Clara thought it worked out better for Grandma in the long run. Danny Graham was her son, and Luke Adamson was Stacie's son. It was shocking to see him in the flesh, twelve years later. A lot of weird looking kids grew into their faces, but Luke had not been one of them. Now, he sat at Grandma's kitchen table with a stupe-fied yet smug look on his waxen face, and his dull yellow hair combed to one side where the dried hair gel left flakes. He had a thin, patchy moustache that was really nothing more than a few long hairs. When he looked over at them, his eyes were small and beady, blank like a puppet. He gave her the heebie-jeebies, as Grandma would have said. As a child, Clara had been secretly glad for the rivalry between her grandma and Miss Stacie, because that meant she hadn't been forced to play with him. In fact, she had been forbidden to.

Miss Stacie clasped her hands together. "We're here for the investigation, of course. And why are you here?"

Clara wished now that Cassie hadn't left. She thrived in these situations of conflict, and it was a gift to be on her side. Cassie could intimidate, out-scream, and verbally abuse the most pig-headed, bigoted fool to the verge of tears if they tried to cross her or her family's path. But she wasn't here this time, and the rest of the Grahams had to stand up for themselves.

Danny went first. "This is my mother's house. That's why we're here."

Miss Stacie sneered, her pale blue eyes foggy with age. "*Her* house. Not yours. Not then, not now, and not ever as long as I live across the street."

Megumi jumped in, addressing the two detectives. Clara hadn't learned their names yet. "This isn't okay. You can't let these people in here. Danny, call up the lawyer and get us a copy of the will. He is her only heir, and this house is right-fully his to ask you to leave."

Miss Stace laughed, but it was ugly and spiteful. "Heir? That woman should have never had an heir of her own. Not after the things she did."

Danny was silent, and everyone was looking at him. What did she mean, *after the things she did*. What did Grandma do? Clara wished her sister were here. Her dad turned away from the nasty woman and cleared his throat. "You're right, Meg, they have no right to be here, and I suggest you'd remember that for next time before we have the lawyers step in," he said, now addressing the detectives. "But you're right, Mrs. Adamson," he continued. "This isn't my house."

Clara felt a wave of defeat. She was tired of people treating her dad like less than his mother's son just because he was adopted from another country. She was tired of people questioning *her* because she didn't look like her own light-skinned mother. She was too busy fighting the surge of emotions to notice that her dad had turned to her.

"My mother left this house and everything in it to her granddaughter," he said. He was smiling now. "So, what do you think, Clara?"

She didn't understand what he meant, but she would deal with that later. "You need to leave," Clara said, quieter than she had meant to. "And don't come back." She couldn't bear the weight of Miss Stacie's hateful look, but her parents looked pleased and that made her feel good. She would deal with it all later: the shock, the fear, the confusion about the house and the contents of her grandma's will. For now, it finally felt good to be able to do something about the bullies.

Last Will and Testament
of
Deborah Jean Graham

I, Deborah Graham, resident in the City of Milton, County of Fulton, State of Georgia, being of sound mind, not acting under duress or undue influence, and fully understanding the nature and extent of all my property and of this disposition thereof, do hereby make, publish, and declare this document to be my Last Will and Testament, and hereby revoke any and all other wills and codicils heretofore made by me.

SIX

Georgia, 2010

Grandma told stories about her house and its forest.

It was not an *old* house, not in the way that some of the houses in Georgia were. Grandma and Grandpa had built the house together and chosen everything, starting from the plot of land and which trees to cut down. In Georgia, you needed the state's permission to cut down big trees, and their house cleared almost four acres worth of building space. Once the house was finished, of course, they would have to plant more trees to make up for some of what they cut down.

So, the house was older than Clara, older than Cassie, and older than their father. It had been Grandma's first "project" before trying to have kids. They had chosen the plot before it was even a proper neighborhood. "How did you know it was the one?" Clara had asked.

Grandma smiled fondly, a distant look closing off her thoughts. "We just knew."

And she almost knew what Grandma meant. It was a beautiful place, the way the trees seemed to reach the sky, so dense and woody that they created a natural wall between the property and the rest of the world.

She asked why they hadn't thought to include the little creek inside their property, extending the fences enough to have that slow moving creek shining with mica and silt as a part of the backyard. Clara could see it there, a little ways out behind the fence, sparkling in the afternoon sunlight when she sat on the roof of the old playhouse in the backyard. She wanted to go there so badly, but it was very much outside of the fence and forbidden by her mother.

Grandma just shook her head. "We had to stop somewhere. There are other things that live here too."

What had she meant by that? It was just forest, stretching as far back as the eye could see. At least, Clara didn't know what existed beyond what she could see from inside the gates. But surely, nobody lived there, save for wild animals. Untouched by development, it looked truly uninhabitable.

One day in late October, a tree right outside the property fence had died and became a danger to the house. Grandma explained that if it fell the wrong way, it could destroy a part of the house and injure Mom and Dad, who slept in the room closest to where the tree might fall. They had to call up some people to come and safely cut the tree down, and Clara watched through the window of her parents' room before it became boring, and she left to go read a book.

That night at dinner, her parents were deep in conversation with Grandma about what had been found high up in the tree: a nest of five young copperhead snakes. Wikipedia said it was a venomous species of pit vipers found in the deciduous forests of North America. Clara didn't know what a deciduous forest was, but it must have been what Grandma's forest was. She hadn't realized snakes could climb so high into the trees, or that they would want to. How did they do it, with no arms or legs?

Because of this new development, Clara was given another lecture by her mother about why it was dangerous to play outside the fence, or close to the fence for that matter. "In California, it's the people you have to worry about," she said. "But here there are wild animals and ticks and poison ivy."

Her mom hadn't mentioned the other scary thing that

lived in the woods: the girl who Clara had seen in the first few weeks of moving in and only caught glimpses of if she went over by the back fence. *That* was what kept her from playing near the fence, not the threat of animals or ticks or poison ivy, or poisonous snakes that could climb trees up into the sky. Maybe she didn't know about the girl, maybe she hadn't seen what Clara had seen.

So, she decided to tell her mom one day, a while after the incident with the snakes, about the girl in the woods. She thought it might be important to tell an adult, in case they were in danger. It might even have been her responsibility to tell them. Her mom had listened quietly, asked very few questions, and a week later, Clara visited Dr. Hartman's office for the first time.

At first, she was confused about why she was seeing a doctor—she wasn't sick, and it wasn't time for her yearly checkup. Besides, their old doctor was still in California. Dr. Hartman's office wasn't like a regular doctor's office because it had a big plastic container of Legos, building blocks, and a stuffed animal so dirty that it had become gray. There was a couch and a rug, and a nice little window lined with potted plants, but there was no examination bed, scale, or other things that belonged in a doctor's office. Dr. Hartman didn't look like a doctor either with her bright dresses and lack of stethoscope or clipboard. She was rather young, perhaps in her early thirties, and she tried to make too much eye contact with Clara.

And Mom didn't get to come in.

Dr. Hartman asked weird questions, like how did Clara like school? Did she get along with the other kids? Had she made any friends? What about her family? Did she get along with them? She encouraged Clara to play with the blocks while they talked, but all the toys in the room were sticky and grimy and she didn't want to touch them because they weren't hers. She wasn't a mean lady, but she wanted Clara to talk, and Clara didn't want to.

She had a feeling that she was in trouble for something.

Eventually, Clara admitted, while gnawing on a stale toot-sie roll, that she didn't like to go to school because the other kids were sort of rude. "Rude how?" Dr. Hartman asked, her pink lips turned down in an inquisitive frown.

"I don't know," Clara admitted. "They just ask me a lot of questions."

Dr. Hartman leaned back in her chair. "Maybe they want to get to know you, Clara," she said. "I'm sure they're not used to getting a new classmate, or even someone new to town."

"Someone like us," Clara said, swallowing the last bit of tootsie roll, still rock hard but slimy with her saliva. It went down slowly and left a dull ache in her throat.

"Who do you mean by *us*, Clara?"

"Me and Cassie. And my mom and dad. They think we're from somewhere really far away." Dr. Hartman laughed as if she had tried to crack a joke. "Well, I would say that California is quite a long way from here. Wouldn't you, Clara?"

She didn't get it.

"I mean from another country."

"Oh, I see." But Clara didn't think she did. And that was that.

The next Thursday evening, Clara's mom finished cooking dinner and told her to get ready to go. "Go where?" Clara asked.

"To see Dr. Hartman again. She's a nice lady, isn't she." It wasn't a question.

"But I went last week."

Her mom put the dish rag down, leaning against the sink. There was a large stain of water across the belly of her shirt where soapy water had splashed up while she was doing the dishes. "She told me she would like to start seeing you every week."

"Why?" Clara argued, her confusion emboldening her. "Nobody goes to the doctor every week. And there's nothing wrong with me!"

Her mom had a strange look on her face. "Of course not, Clary. But I think it would be a good idea to talk with her. She's a very smart woman, and she's good with children your age." Clara asked why she couldn't just hang out with Dad, who was also very smart and good with Clara, but her mom said it wasn't the same thing.

So, Clara went to see Dr. Hartman, again and again. On the second visit, she tried looking around the room for signs of what kind of doctor she might be. Perhaps she had fooled Clara's mom and wasn't actually a doctor because she only asked Clara questions about herself and how she *felt*. About halfway through their second meeting, Clara had a horrible feeling that maybe her mom had paid "Dr. Hartman" to hang out with her since she didn't have friends like Cassie or Grandma. It would explain the toys in the room.

She mustered up the courage to ask a question of her own during their third meeting. "Why am I here?" After all, it was only fair that she got to ask some questions too. "Is there something wrong with me?" Dr. Hartman was wearing pretty tortoise shell glasses that Thursday evening. It was mid-November, and the sun was starting to set earlier each day, and it was getting much colder than it ever got in California. She wondered if it ever snowed in Georgia. It certainly didn't in California. But Dr. Hartman was trying to talk to her.

"Your parents would like me to help you become more comfortable with being at your new school and your new home," she said. "I'm sure it hasn't been easy to start over."

She said it like there was something to feel sorry about, but Clara hadn't left anything important behind in California. "No, I like it here," she said. "Especially my grandma's house."

By the way Dr. Hartman sat forward a little, it seemed Clara had said the right thing. Or perhaps the wrong thing. "Yes, of course! Tell me more. What do you like about it? Do you have any friends in the neighborhood?" She always wanted to know if Clara had any friends, and it exhausted her the way she kept asking the same question in different ways as if she was hoping for a different answer one day.

"No, I don't mind playing by myself."

It wasn't the right answer. "Do you have any imaginary friends? Or pets, I suppose?"

"I'm too old for that," Clara said.

She was twirling a pen in her left hand. "Yes, it would seem so. You seem like a very mature young lady, Clara." The pen stopped. "But tell me, have you seen anything strange since you moved here? Something that maybe you think you shouldn't have seen... when you play alone, perhaps?"

She knew she kept giving the wrong answers, and she didn't want to make Dr. Hartman disappointed. She wanted to say the right thing, so she told her about the girl behind the fence. She didn't spare any details, from the flat yellow eyes and strong horns and the tips of those sharp little teeth. Dr. Hartman seemed very interested then, reaching for a notepad and finally using that pen she liked to twirl.

It seemed that she had finally said the right thing.

There was a little orange bottle for her on the kitchen table the next morning, sitting right next to her morning glass of orange juice. It was the kind of bottle that held pills, little white ones like the ones her dad sometimes took, although these ones looked a bit different. It had her name on it, Clarissa Abigail Graham, and Dr. Hartman's name on it too for that matter. Below that it said ARIPIPRAZOLE 5 MG CAPSULES. She looked up at her mom, who was spreading butter on whole grain toast. She didn't look up, so Clara looked back down at the bottle. TAKE ONE CAPSULE BY MOUTH ONCE DAILY.

It looked like Dr. Hartman was a real doctor after all.

So, Clara started taking the pills, one chalky white tablet every morning with her breakfast, and no one told her a thing about why.

From her visits with Dr. Hartman, she was starting to understand that it was more complicated than "right" or "wrong" answers. There were some things that adults weren't supposed to know about. It would scare them.

The pills that she took in the morning seemed to be doing something to her, like an anti-medicine: whatever it was they were supposed to be doing, it didn't seem to be working unless the goal was to make her feel worse. She was sleepy and groggy at all hours of the day. She felt more angry than usual and always on the verge of tears. Little things agitated her, from hair brushing her face to the way certain clothes felt against her skin. But the matter of the girl behind the fence went uninvestigated. Neither her mom nor Dr. Hartman seemed concerned by it, which meant that no one was going to seek her out and ask her to leave, or who she was. Clara began to worry that it might be up to her to protect her family.

She had been too nervous lately to play any farther out than the pool area, which was quite boring; Grandma didn't like to uncover the pool because then leaves and frogs and pine needles would get in and they would have to hire someone to clean it out with a net. But something had to be done, eventually, and to keep herself awake in school one day, she planned a quest to venture out again, right after school when the sun was still high.

When she got home, there was a plate of sliced green apples and orange cheese waiting for her at the kitchen counter. Her mom always prepared after-school snacks for her, but today Clara felt sick with fear of her upcoming expedition to the back fence, and she hid the food under a few layers of trash already in the trashcan.

Her school backpack was too big to bring if she was going to have to escape or run at some point, so she filled her favorite owl-patterned crossbody with only the necessities: a few sharp rocks, a little bit of water, and one medium sized kitchen knife. She didn't expect to use them, but if she encountered that girl, Clara would be up against horns and sharp teeth, and she had neither.

With a house so big, it often felt empty, and she could go in and out as she pleased. Anywhere inside the fence was safe in her mother's eyes, probably because there would be no kidnapping or assaulting. Clara wasn't exactly sure what the second part meant but it showed up enough on the television and news channel back home in California that she had some idea of how that word should be used. She opened the back door to the patio, choosing her ugly tennis shoes over the wonderful boots Grandma gave her. Today, it would be more important to run fast than to keep her toes and socks dry.

At this point in the year, the sun started to set a little after five-thirty. She didn't wear a watch like some kids at school because it felt uncomfortable on her wrist, but the digital one on the stove had read 4:17. That meant she had a little over an hour to go there and back and complete her mission. As she walked down the pale stone steps and along the edge of the covered pool, Clara had to remind herself that she was only going to the back fence to speak with a girl, and not to The Lonely Mountain to steal from the terrible dragon Smaug. But she had to abandon that thought because truly, she would rather stand before a dragon than talk to that girl with strange, scary eyes. The girl who was so different from what a little girl should be.

The late November air was cold and unwelcoming. It made her face tingle and her eyes water, and she wondered a little distractedly if Grandma would buy her a pair of gloves for the winter. She had never worn gloves before and made a note to tell Grandma later that her favorite color was dark purple. Then she thought it might be best to go back inside and try again another day when she had those dark purple gloves to wear. They would surely make her feel both warmer and braver. But her fear, her need to protect her family, was so large that it surpassed her desire to turn back.

57

The pool area ended, and the grass began. What once seemed marvelous to her now looked foreign and uninviting. She was walking much slower and could not manage to go any faster. She wished she knew what time it was in case it was already getting too late. In the corners of her vision, she thought she could see movement, but when she whipped her head around it was only the last of the dead leaves falling from their branches. It reminded her to be careful of where she walked, because the crunching of those dried up leaves might alert the girl of her presence before she was ready.

She hadn't considered that the girl might already be waiting for her.

She didn't see her at first, blending in with the earthy greens and browns of the forest. Two yellow eyes blinked slowly behind the fence, revealing that she had been there all along, watching. Clara was frozen like a deer on the street, unable to move in the presence of the unknown. She was too afraid to look away—the girl might lunge the moment she was distracted, and maybe she could leap right over the fence. Or fly. Anything was possible for someone who looked like that.

Clara was trapped in a stare down and it needed to be broken. The words came out of her mouth with a will of their own. "Who are you?"

She didn't know what to expect. The girl might not speak English, if she could speak at all. For a moment she only heard the wind in the trees. And then, like a whisper between the trees, "I don't have a name."

Hearing her voice made Clara less afraid. She sounded human enough, like a little girl whose voice she might hear in class or on the school bus. If she closed her eyes, she wouldn't be able to tell the difference. But she wasn't trying to make a friend; she was on a mission to take back her forest. "Why are you here?"

Her voice was light and airy like a fairy even though she

had the face of a devil. "She keeps me here." The girl said *she* like it was someone's name.

Clara's confusion emboldened her. "Where?" She couldn't mean out in the forest. "This is my grandma's land. Where do you belong?"

The girl didn't answer. She barely moved except to blink, but for some reason Clara didn't squirm beneath her stare. Those yellow eyes had an inhuman glow, more like a wild animal than a human girl. Somehow, that made Clara feel less afraid, because she had always preferred animals to the company of kids her age.

The girl spoke again. "I belong to Her." Clara thought of Grandma and how she was letting Clara's whole family live in her house. In that moment, she understood.

If Clara and her family were Grandma's guests, then Clara didn't have the right to send away one of Grandma's other guests. They were both under the care and protection of Grandma, and Clara knew then that the girl would not hurt any of them. Now that she understood the girl, how they were alike, she was no longer afraid.

The light was going now, turning the grays and browns of November to a dull blue twilight. The girl seemed to be retreating into the shadows of the forest, or maybe it was Clara who was falling back toward the warm light of Grandma's house. "I have to go now," she said, and perhaps the girl said it too. "Maybe I'll see you gain."

Clara turned around and ran up the hill to the house, leaving the back fence in darkness and not daring to look back. She reached the pool area and slowed down so that she wouldn't fall. She could tell which rooms people were in because of the soft yellow light that shone out the windows. Cassie was in her room upstairs with the curtains drawn. She could see movement in the kitchen and wondered what Mom was making for dinner. She had returned to her world and the farther she got from the back fence, the less real all of it seemed.

She swung open the back door and the warm air that hit her face and made her instantly aware of how cold her nose and hands were. Her mom was at the stovetop, stirring something in a pot. Hopefully it was Kraft Mac N Cheese.

"Clara."

She nearly jumped out of her clothes, startled by Grandma's voice at her side. She was sitting in her armchair, looking out the window into the cold darkness. "What did you find out there?" But she said it like she already knew.

SEVEN

June 2022, Georgia

The car ride back to the hotel was uncomfortably silent, and Clara could feel an air of unspoken upset radiating from her mom. They had gotten Miss Stacie and her son out of the house, and her dad had reminded the detectives that this was *not* a criminal investigation. Witchcraft, if it somehow *was* that, was a religious freedom, legal to practice even in places like Georgia, with some nuanced rules from town to town. Danny had reminded the detectives about Roberts v Ravenwood, a case from the eighties right here in Fulton County ruled in favor of the Church of Wiccans, recognizing them as a legal and legitimate religious group not in need of paying taxes for their meeting place. Lastly, he had reminded them that the only reason they were hired was to investigate the events of his mother's death, and surely that did not involve the neighbors, especially those with a grudge against the family. If anything, he had said, you should be investigating *them*, as they seemed so vengeful and invested that maybe they had something to do with her death. He didn't really mean it, of course, but it was enough of a confrontation to send them away for the day.

Clara thought her dad had done a fantastic job with the detectives, so why was her mom still upset? Miss Stacie had been properly humiliated when Danny announced that his mother had given the house to Clara. She had mumbled something about Clara being a mute on her way out, and that the family should "go back to where they came from" and Clara knew she hadn't meant California. Clara wasn't too upset over it though—maybe it was her work in therapy that helped Miss Stacie's hate slide right off her. A lot of southern women prided themselves on being outwardly pleasant (and talking absolute shit about people behind their backs), but Miss Stacie was shameless. She didn't care what people thought of her or her actions, or that she spoiled Luke to his detriment. Back when Clara's family had lived with Grandma, Miss Stacie had spent three thousand dollars on a pure-bred golden retriever puppy named Buttercup, which she sent to the pound no more than a month later because Luke didn't like it. Anyone who treated a puppy like that surely treated other humans the same way, at least in Clara's opinion.

Clara's mom sighed, and her dad said, "Out with it, Meg."

She didn't hesitate. "We've always agreed to no secrets. Don't you remember what happened the last time you kept such a big secret?" As an adult now, Clara knew that they were talking about the events that had led them to have to live with Grandma for a year, and how it had little to do with her old age and more to do with Danny Graham needing time to get his feet back on the ground.

"This wasn't a secret," he said calmly. "I had wanted to surprise Clara with it… not like that, of course, but I think we can all agree that it was worth it to see the look on that woman's face." Clara did agree. It had satisfied an urge she didn't know she needed met. Sure, it had put her in a tight spot, but it had also put her in a rare position of power, and she was grateful to her dad for giving her that moment of agency. It had been a good feeling, and she was still relishing it. Later she would think about its implications. But…

Would she have to live in Georgia again?

No, impossible. Not without her parents.

They could all be closer to Cassie, too.

Maybe, they could all live in that house together again.

She felt foolish, like she was thinking like a child. She was twenty-two, graduated from college, and Dr. Ashley said she needed to start building a life for herself. Create a family, if only a circle of friends for now. But that felt so impossible. Dr. Ashely really didn't seem to understand how hard it was to make friends in your twenties once you were out of school. It should have been easy back in middle school, high school, surrounded by the same group of kids every day for years. But if she had had so much trouble then, how was she going to pull it off now?

They pulled into the hotel parking lot, and the thrill of the interaction back at the house had worn off. For a moment she sat frozen in the backseat, a heavy feeling washing over her. Why did Grandma do this to her? What was she supposed to do with a 17,000 square foot house all the way across the country? Nine bedrooms, eleven bathrooms, a pool and a library and a home theater—out of all people Grandma should have known that Clara had no friends to help fill that house. And she would never sell it, could never...

Her dad tapped on the window, his voice muted behind the glass. "Come on, I have to lock up the car." Her parents would help her figure it out. They probably already had a few different ideas for a solution. With that thought to reassure her, she was able to get out of the car and go to her room.

Once upon a time, long before they had to move in with Grandma, Danny Graham's career had blown up in a good way before it blew up in the bad way. He got to bring along the family for many of his extravagant business trips: Pebble Beach, San Francisco, Seattle, even Mexico once. Clara and Cassie spent days with their mom by the poolside and spas, and the hotels always left chocolates on their pillows when they came back in the evening. After everything happened, they had never had those experiences again.

Clara had not been a very curious child. She had never thought to ask where babies come from or what God looked like, and she only started to wonder why they really moved to Georgia after she heard things from her classmates. Years later, once they were back in California again, she just knew. It wasn't something that had ever been explicitly explained to her, but over the years her brain put together the bits and pieces of a thousand conversations she heard between her parents, snide remarks from Cassie, and Grandma's reminiscing about fresh out of college, go-getter Danny Graham. Clara knew that her dad had his struggles with depression, but she wasn't sure if his failing work had caused the depression or if his depression had caused his failing work. As close as she felt with her parents, they rarely talked about anything personal or serious and sometimes she forgot that her parents even had a life outside of the family.

It wasn't like that with Cassie though. It sometimes made a pit form in Clara's stomach when she thought about how she, Mom, and Dad were only a small part of Cassie's big life. She wasn't close with any of them, yet she still told them *everything*. Clara suspected that she told everyone everything though, and their family wasn't unique in what they knew about Cassie's personal life.

However, there seemed to be some things, even for Cassie, that were too personal to talk about face-to-face with another human being: in the last few years of her online writing career, Cassie had written a few personal stories that Clara enviously wished her sister had chosen to share with her instead of the entire internet. They had titles like "I Made Myself White at Sixteen" in which she talked about her phase of wearing blue colored contacts and trying to dye her hair blond at home until their mom finally took her to a salon before she burned off all her thick, black hair.

Clara hadn't realized that someone like Cassie, a girl who seemed to belong in the spotlight, could ever have those kinds of self-doubts. She wished her sister had told her those kinds of things when they were kids and going through the same struggles living in a homogenous community. Cassie had tried to help Clara in her own way—yelling and swearing, telling off strangers, or even that one time fourteen-year-old Cassie had beat their thirteen-year-old cousin Ryan bloody for saying that their mom had made them weird looking for marrying a non-Japanese man. It was at a family reunion, and it was a miracle she hadn't broken his nose given how much blood there had been. Ryan was their first cousin, too, the son of their mother's sister.

After reading some of Cassie's more personal articles, Clara had fantasized about what it would have been like if they had told each other things, if they could have been sisters like this instead of Cassie's displays of violent anger and Clara's silence. Reading those articles, she felt closer with her sister than ever before, but it had been said online to anyone and everyone, and not for Clara only.

Now, being together again in Georgia had thrown Clara into a muddle of memories that she hadn't thought of in years, if at all in the twelve years since they moved back to California and the year spent in Georgia receded into the darker corners of her memory. She got undressed and stood in the hotel shower, so absorbed in her thoughts that she wasn't bothered by the slimy tub or the lukewarm water. She felt as though she was being dragged backward in time, forcefully, like Grandma was pulling her by the scruff of her neck. Only the raisining of her fingers reminded her that she should get out of the shower. She turned off the water but couldn't remember if she had used conditioner on her hair.

The hotel bathroom was poorly lit, and the unnatural yellow light made her skin look sallow and waxy. As a child, her brown skin had been naturally enhanced from time spent playing outside, but now she looked drained of color. It was strange to think that she might have been happier as a child than she was now, because Clara Graham could not have been called a happy child. She had hated going to school, and everything made her so scared and nervous that she still associated her elementary and middle school years with a feeling of ever-present stomach sickness. She had dealt with bullies and unfair teachers, but hadn't every child? After college, she expected she would feel liberated and happy, finally. She had chosen a simple, quiet job back in California at the Cerritos Public Library, which was a place that could make grown-ups feel like kids again. From the outside, it looked like a modern arts museum with its smooth metal structures and the beautiful, simple curvature of its architecture. It had been a wonder of her childhood in California: multiple stories, themed floors, water features, and the grandest children's section that she'd ever seen. The children's entrance was made of giant replicas of classic children's books that leaned into each other so that you felt like a little person walking between books on a shelf.

She wasn't unhappy. Maybe this was the happiest life she was capable of. Her job suited her well enough, and it paid for her to live comfortably (enough) in her teeny-tiny apartment with Petra. It was all *enough*, and who was she to ask for more than that? Truly, she didn't know what she was looking for to make her happier. Her parents suggested a boyfriend, but Clara didn't think that would do the trick.

But now, Grandma's will threatened to upturn the careful life she had laid out for herself. Selling that house... it wasn't an option. Clara couldn't imagine it. But she wasn't financially capable of maintaining the upkeep of the house all the way from California. Neither, she suspected, were her parents. It might have been one thing if it was a more normal house, maybe somewhere between two to five thousand in square feet... but what had Grandma been *thinking*, just handing off that mansion of a house?

What do you want from me, Grandma?

She changed back into her day clothes. It was gross, but they were comfortable, and she hadn't brought enough clothes or pajamas because they had only planned to stay a few days. But now, they'd have to sit around, twiddling their thumbs and waiting for the investigation to conclude. She'd have to call work and ask for time off. She'd need to reschedule her therapy appointment. She'd need to check in with the sitter and ask to extend Petra's stay. And poor thing—how could a dog know if its owner ever planned to come back? Clara felt the tension building up between her furrowed brows, and she massaged them until her forehead turned pink. She had just gotten into bed when there was a knock at her door.

She had no intention of answering it, of course, until her dad's voice came from the other side. "Clara, it's just me." He had probably come to talk over what happened, which she didn't really have energy for, but maybe it would bring her some peace of mind so she could fall asleep. She threw back the stiff bedcovers and went to open the door, quickly finger combing her wet hair. Her dad had never been one to accept sloppiness, and she had learned from a young age to keep her hair tidy or else her dad would take her in to get it cut short. He used to get his hair cut by a man who had cut hair for the military, and whenever Clara was taken in for "tidying up," she came out of the barber shop with a blunt, short cut and tears in her eyes.

But behind the door was not her father, not exactly. Rather, it seemed like her father as he was twelve years ago: a man trying to conceal his pain in front of his daughter in the way that parents tried to protect their children from their own disturbing or shameful realities, wearing that smile that he used when he called her by her childhood nicknames. He used to ask her about her day, but she could always tell that he was actually so distracted that he wasn't hearing a single word out of her mouth, and he was perhaps only using his daughter's voice to soothe his own stress. He was secretive in the way that she supposed all fathers might be, slow to reveal the details and events of his life before wife and children so that Clara felt that she hardly knew who he was outside of the role of her dad, that perhaps Danny Graham *didn't* exist outside of father to Clara and Cassie, husband to Megumi Graham, nee Kitayama, adoptive son of Debbie and Clayton Graham. It was possible that he didn't exist outside of the family, or maybe he didn't want to in the same way that Clara didn't exist outside of the family, just holding onto the past and its baggage in case something worse waited outside, in the future.

"Are you already going to bed?" asked, looking past her to the thrown off bed covers in a bemused way. "It's not even eight."

"I'm pretty tired," Clara said, even though her brain was still spinning at a rate that would make it unlikely for her to fall asleep anytime soon.

He nodded, sympathy almost bleeding from his eyes. "I'm sure. It's been a long day, and I know how much you hate confrontations like that." It was true. Any other day, such a nasty interaction like the one they had with Miss Stacie and Luke would have completely thrown her off, calling for hours of recovery time curled up beneath her bedsheets with Petra, but today had been different, and she was waiting for her dad to mention it.

He didn't, at first. "He got even uglier, didn't he?" And they both laughed about Miss Stacie's horrid son, with his limp hair and piggy nose, even though there were a million more important things to talk about. "I almost wished Cassie had been there to tell them off," he said, and they laughed about that too.

He was still standing in the doorway. "So, how are you feeling?"

She didn't think she could describe it, at least, not now, so she said. "Pretty good." It usually proved to be a sufficient answer when she didn't want to talk about something.

He eyed her carefully, the lines around his eyes and mouth tightening almost imperceptibly. She was terrified by how old he looked these days, his once thick, black hair now sparse and almost entirely silver. He seemed so small too, even though he was still a good five or so inches taller than her. "Can I come in for a moment?"

So "pretty good" hadn't been good enough. She stepped back to let him into the small, dingy room, and he took a seat at the desk chair. "Your grandma loved you best of all," he said, fondly, but also far away sounding. "You kept her better company than the rest of us, took all the strange things she said to heart, and loved her without judgement."

Clara felt a pressure behind her eyes. She hated crying in front of her parents, and the gesture of reaching up to wipe her face felt humiliating. The emotion felt sudden and surprising; she had already grieved her grandmother, whose death at ninety-three had hardly been unexpected. If she was being entirely honest with herself, the only time she had felt really close with her grandma was during that year they lived in this house, when it felt like Grandma had been her only friend in the whole world. She hadn't considered that she might have been an important part of her grandma's life as well. But that had been twelve years ago, and they hadn't been able to spend more than a few days together in the years since.

"You know," he continued. "It had been her plan for many years to give you the house."

"Why me?" Clara broke her silence. "What does she want me to do with it?"

He didn't answer right away. Clara could hear a weak tapping noise above her, and she looked up to see a beetle-like insect fluttering about inside the rectangular ceiling light, trapped behind the surface. She hated the sound. In its efforts to get free, the insect was killing itself, thumping against the glass again and again. She wished she could open the panel to let it free, or at least smash it and end both of their suffering.

Clara's father spoke at last. "I don't know, Clara. But now it's up to you, and I think she chose you to inherit her house because she trusts the decisions you alone would make."

She tried to think of something reasonable to respond with, but all that came out was, "I don't know what to do. I can't sell it."

Danny smiled, for real this time. "No, you wouldn't. Perhaps only you would keep the huge, old house instead of putting it on the market." As he said that, Clara thought of how much that house would be worth if they found a buyer. A couple million, at least. A horrible guilt gripped her, and she wondered if it was selfish to keep the house of her childhood fantasies when it could be sold to help her parents. They were okay, now, since dad regained his footing, but still not like how they *used* to be.

But maybe they would never be like how they used to be, and maybe that was okay.

Still, it seemed like an irresponsible financial situation to keep the house and try to maintain its upkeep from California. She could only afford a small apartment at home, so how could she expect to add four acres of land to her name. Keeping it would be stupidly sentimental.

But she could see Grandma, once young and in love, putting every fiber of her being into building her dream house. Didn't Clara have an obligation to her as well?

She knew what Grandma would have wanted.

EIGHT

September 2010, Georgia

Clara and Cassie used to take piano lessons before things got bad and they had to move to the apartment, and then away from California altogether. When they arrived at their grandma's house for the first time, they were both immediately delighted by the shining grand piano in the foyer, nestled beneath the floating staircase. Even Cassie had joined Clara in banging senselessly on those white keys the first day they stepped into the house, laughing half because of the discordant notes and half from the sheer joy for their absurd new home.

Grandma, who had not been pleased with their lack of musicality, promptly re-enrolled them in music lessons with an old Russian lady who came to the house every Monday evening. It started less than a month after they moved in. Her name was Mischa Voskoboinikova, but Grandma said they could just call her Miss Mischa since her last name was tricky. Clara believed she'd be able to learn it if they were given the chance, because her mom's name before she married her dad had looked tricky, but you only had to read the letters carefully and anyone could say it properly. She figured Miss Mischa's last name was probably the same way, but Grandma had only said it once and declined to write it down, which meant that she probably didn't know how to spell it either.

The first evening that she came, Clara and Cassie both shrank in fear at the sight of her at the door. She was old, not like Grandma, but a good deal older than their mom, and she was very tall and skinny. A year ago, their mom had taken both girls to see the new film *Coraline* in theaters, assuming it to be appropriate and enjoyable for Clara mostly, since it was rated PG. It had not been either of those things for either sister, and Cassie had let Clara sleep on the floor of her room for almost a week afterward without a fight. Miss Mischa reminded Clara of Coraline's Other Mother with her long bony fingers, razor sharp haircut, and red heels with tips so pointed that they could absolutely be used as a weapon.

Grandma looked just the opposite, like Cinderella's sweet, plump fairy godmother. But Clara thought only a monster would call this kind of lady over to their house, and she couldn't piece together how her grandma might have ever had anything to do with this horrible lady. Miss Mischa didn't ask for their names. "I'll start with the younger one," she said, and Clara could feel her knees knocking together. In the months since they'd stopped their lessons, she had completely forgotten how to read notes. Cassie had fled from the room as soon as it had been determined that Clara would go first, but Grandma remained, watching with a smile on her face.

"Play something for me," the lady said, and Clara looked over at Grandma fearfully.

"Play something, Clara, so that Miss Mischa can see what level you are at."

Clara didn't have anything to play. Even if she did, she wouldn't have been able to remember anything under the towering gaze of Miss Mischa. She stuck her pointer finger out, and it trembled as she moved it toward the white keys, which looked menacing like big teeth instead of how inviting they had seemed the other day. She pressed middle C, the only note she could still identify, with the tip of her pointer finger, so lightly that the key only went halfway down and barely made a sound. She was too afraid to raise her head and look over at Grandma again, so she did the only thing she could think of and pressed the next key to the left with her pointer finger again.

"STOP." It was like a bark, and Clara felt tears quickly welling up in her eyes. "What are you doing." It was hardly a question.

Grandma jumped in. "It's been a while since her last lesson, and she is only ten."

"I've seen two-year-olds with more musical ability than this. Leave us, Debbie. And bring the other one in thirty minutes."

So, Grandma left. Clara's vision of the keyboard right in front of her was blurry from her tears. Her stomach was starting to hurt, and she was squirming on the narrow piano bench out of fear and the need to pee. She could barely comprehend what Miss Mischa was saying, not only because of her fear and nervousness but also because of her accent. In a different situation, Clara might have laughed at the strange sound of it, the way that words had a different shape in her mouth, but right now it only filled her with more fear.

She managed to make it through the thirty minutes, and it was a heavenly sight to see Grandma dragging Cassie into the room by the arm. She looked dreadful, like maybe she understood better than Clara how inept their lessons in California had been. If Miss Mischa didn't like how ten year old Clara played, she would absolutely loathe the way fifteen year old Cassie played.

Clara darted from the room with barely a glance at Cassie or Grandma. She ran straight into the kitchen and nearly knocked over her mom, who was standing by the window with the telephone at her ear. She made a noise of angry surprise when Clara ran into her, smashing her face into her soft belly and letting out the wail she had been holding in for the past half hour. Her mom tried to pry her away, holding the phone off to the side to hiss, "Not now, Clara!"

Clara waited for her mom to get off the phone with tears streaming down her face, fingers throbbing even though she'd only played a few meager notes. She begged her mom not to make her do these lessons, too ashamed to go directly to Grandma about it. Her mom had a flat look on her face though, devoid of sympathy. "Clara, honey," she said, impatiently, "You and your sister are both being so melodramatic. Grandma wants you to learn to play properly, and she's paying for your lessons, so you're going to go along with it without any more tears or complaining. She's doing enough for us as it is." Had Cassie been crying about it as well? Even though she was cool and not babyish like Clara, she had her occasional tantrums too. Her dad said it was puberty that made Cassie act up like that, and that they should try to be patient with her. And what did Mom mean about Grandma already doing enough as it is? Mom was the one who cooked and cleaned and made phone calls all day.

But by the look on her mom's face, Clara knew that any more begging on her end would only cause trouble, so she went to sit by Grandma in front of the TV. Her first impulse had been to go and watch Cassie's lesson, but she realized that would mean having to be around that dreadful lady again, and she just could not do it.

Grandma was watching something on Hallmark, and she sat quietly with a bowl of dark cherries in her lap. She had a separate bowl on the coffee table to spit the pits into. Clara's mom usually liked to watch reality shows like Real Housewives of Beverly Hills or Keeping Up with the Kardashians, but Clara hadn't seen her watch those kinds of shows ever since they moved in with Grandma. "How was your lesson, darling?" She asked. Clara was looking straight at the television but not actually watching the show. She felt a little mad at Grandma, but she wasn't comfortable enough to say that yet. "Don't feel discouraged after today. You did a wonderful job participating and it was very brave of you to go first. That Cassie of yours was having World War Three with your mother back here trying to get out of it. You girls don't have to be afraid of Miss Mischa, she's a little strict but a gifted teacher."

"Was she your teacher?" Clara asked, wondering if Miss Mischa was older than she looked.

Grandma laughed, and Clara noticed how her teeth were stained dark red from the cherry juice. It didn't look right. "No, sugar," she said, "that woman is far too young to have been my teacher. I started lessons when I was around your age, and that was a good seventy years ago." She laughed again, which made Clara feel like she should also laugh as well. Talking together in front of the television, the lesson became a fading nightmare in the cheerful dawn of Grandma's eyes. "I used to play in church every week, and in concerts and recitals, but I don't play anymore because of the arthritis."

"What's that?" Clara asked.

Grandma was looking back at the TV again, but it was clear that she wasn't watching the show. She looked like she had memories swirling around behind her old blue eyes. It must have been something sad because of the way her face changed. "When you're my age, everything hurts, right down to your bones."

"Oh," Clara said. "You should go in the jacuzzi in Mom and Dad's bathroom. It's your house anyway. That would probably help."

Grandma was just staring through the TV, straight out into nothing. "No, I don't think so, honey. Come over here and give me a kiss, would you?"

Clara climbed up on the couch and kneeled next to Grandma, puckering her lips like a fish and plopping them onto Grandma's powdery cheek. Her skin was dry and soft, and it smelled nice too, like baby powder. Then she sat next to her on the couch, and they watched TV together, but she didn't think Grandma was actually paying attention, because the young people on the show were kissing and she didn't turn it off.

Grandpa died almost two years earlier, but Clara hadn't cried because she'd only met him a few times. They went so long between visits that each time they saw Grandma and Grandpa, it was like meeting them all over again. Clara's parents had flown out to Grandpa's funeral without the kids, and Clara never really thought of him again.

She could see that Grandma still missed him, but she was probably a lot happier now, with the four of them living with her. Now she lived with four people instead of one, and that meant she had to be less lonely.

But Clara also understood that more people didn't always mean more happiness. She had to sit in a classroom with thirty-seven other kids every day, and not one of them made her feel happy. They weren't really mean to her, and no one beat her up or anything, but she felt lonelier in that cramped classroom of thirty-seven other kids than she did when it was just her and Grandma in her big, mostly empty house.

She started coming home excited to hang out with Grandma. They liked to talk and read books, and Grandma sat with her at the piano sometimes while she tried to practice. Lessons weren't going very well because it was hard for Clara to figure out where the little black dots on the page were supposed to go on the keys. Maybe she needed glasses, or maybe she was a little stupid. Grandma was never mad, though, and her presence at the bench almost made Clara enjoy practicing.

Clara felt a little jealous of the Tuesday bible study group that took her grandma away for an afternoon, already deep into their meeting when the bus dropped Clara off at home. Grandma said she could join them, but not all the ladies looked at her nicely, and she had a feeling that not all old ladies were as wonderful as her grandma. Besides, the bible wasn't a good book. Clara had been curious, so she looked in Grandma's, and the pages were thin and bleak, crammed front and back with small words. There weren't any pictures, which wasn't a big deal, but the story was boring, and Clara couldn't understand what any of it was supposed to be about.

Luckily, Grandma didn't push her to read the bible like she pushed the piano lessons. Instead, they read magnificent stories in Grandma's library: *Harry Potter* (but only books one, two, and three because Grandma said they started to get inappropriate after that) *The Hobbit*, *The Chronicles of Narnia*, *Charlotte's Web*, and *A Wrinkle in Time*. Grandma didn't really own any picture books, but she said they could visit the city library together if Clara wanted those sorts of books, but Clara liked Grandma's books better than the kinds she had read before. Besides, the library in Grandma's house was theirs and theirs alone. Going to the city library now would only feel like a punishment.

Grandma encouraged Clara to play outside, too. She said there was nothing out back that was dangerous, like Clara's mom was worried about. Clara thought she'd ask if she could go behind the fence, even though her mom had already given an answer.

Grandma seemed to think about it, which was a good sign. Then she shook her head. "No, I don't think that would be best. Not on your own, at least."

"We could go together," Clara suggested, and the idea filled her with excitement.

Grandma only smiled. "I can't walk out into the woods anymore, or even the grass after it's rained. It's hard for me to keep my balance, and I might fall. If you want to go back there, you'll have to get Cassandra to come along with you." Clara's heart sank. There was no point in asking her sister. They didn't do things together, and Cassie didn't like to go outside. Maybe it was because of the bugs and mud, but Cassie kept the blinds drawn in her room and wore hats and long sleeves outside, like she didn't want her skin to be touched by the sun. So, the answer was no.

Sometimes Grandma said strange things about outside, though, about the earth and the mud and the tall trees that surrounded the property like a cocoon. One night as Clara was drifting off, she thought she heard Grandma say, "You don't need to be afraid of her." It might have been a dream, though, and Clara let herself fall asleep.

NINE

March 2022, California

A few months before Grandma passed away, Clara received a strange call from her. They rarely talked on the phone, unless it was through her dad's phone to say hi, and Clara didn't have Grandma's contact in her phone. It rang at five fifty-seven in the evening as she was cooking a simple grilled chicken dinner, the blaring ringtone startling her over the hum of the stovetop. It was an unknown caller, but it wasn't labeled as spam risk and had a 770-area code. She picked up on the third ring.

"Hello?" she said, but there was no answer. "Grandma?"

"Where did she go?" Her grandma's voice came harsh and quickly, as if the phone was distorting it.

Clara turned the stovetop flame off, forgetting about the chicken. "Grandma, what are you talking about? Where are you right now?" No response. "Are you at home?"

There was a heavy sound coming from the other end of the phone, and the muted chirping of insects as if she was calling from outside. "What did you do to her, Clara?" Clara was suddenly afraid at the anger in her voice, something she had never heard from her grandma before. "She's gone. You made her go away. Why would you do something like that?"

It wasn't the first time she had felt like maybe she should be scared of Grandma. She used to say things back then when they lived together, things that didn't make any sense to Clara. It seemed like Grandma knew things that weren't meant to be known. Both of them had wild imaginations, Clara and her grandma, but when they lived together in that house, Grandma's imagination was sometimes more frightening than fun, like she wasn't trying to play with Clara, but tell her something important. Now that she was older, that they both were older, the moment felt crucial. "What are you talking about, Grandma?" She could hear the fear in her own voice.

The line went flat, and Clara was in a panic. She should probably call 911. She didn't even know how to call 911. But then the phone rang again like a horrible wail. "Grandma!" She didn't know what to say. "Please stay on the phone right now!"

All she said was, "We need to find her."

"Who!"

"She's still out there, somewhere. She needs me!" And then she hung up again.

After that, Clara called the same number four times, and they went straight to a voicemail box that hadn't been set up yet. She needed to call either the police or her dad, but she tried one more time.

She picked up. "Clara, dear, is this you?"

"Grandma!" She screamed. "Don't hang up again! You have to tell me what's going on! Are you at home right now? Are you okay?"

It was silent again and Clara thought she might lose her own mind. But then Grandma replied in her normal, if slightly confused voice, "What are you talking about, sweet? You're the one who called me, and please stop screaming. I'll need to take my hearing aids off, the way you're screeching!"

"But you called me first!" Clara said, aware that she was probably still shouting. "Just five minutes ago... twice!"

"Clara," Grandma sounded frustrated. "Are you taking drugs? I've always tried to tell Danny how California is no place to raise a family. People are *always* up to no good over there. In fact, I read a shocking story about that governor the other day. They need to do something about the homeless problem there, I tell you. It's out of control."

"No Grandma! I'm not doing drugs!" The words sounded ridiculous in her mouth, and she had an urge to laugh hysterically. She didn't. "It's just…" but the words died in her mouth. The old woman talking on the phone to her now was clearly a different woman than who was talking before. Maybe it hadn't been Grandma at all those first two times. Maybe someone had been prank calling. Or maybe it was *Clara* who was going crazy, not Grandma. With the phone still pressed to her face, Clara went to her bedroom and made sure she had taken her pills this morning. The MON AM slot was empty, so she had in fact taken them. Then she went back to the kitchen, barely listening to her grandma's usual ramblings about what a horrible place California was to live, that she should come out and visit her in Georgia, see the house again, all while Clara pulled her prescription bottles from the cabinet and checked the labels.

She should have felt relieved that Grandma seemed fine, but she felt horrible. Either she was crazy, or Grandma was, and it was impossible to tell which at the moment. Clara put a hand to her forehead, wiping at the perspiration. "Just… are you sure you didn't call me earlier Grandma? Everything's okay?"

"Why yes, Clara, what has gotten into you? Danny told me you have your own place out there now, so I hope you're eating and sleeping properly." She heard herself answering *Yes, Grandma, I am eating well and sleeping fine* and then said goodbye hollowly. It seemed like Grandma wanted to keep talking, but Clara needed time to think and recover.

She spent the next few hours almost in a trance, thinking herself into oblivion. The chicken went cold on the stove, completely abandoned. Petra rang the potty bell twice, and Clara took her out the second time, barely registering anything until she got back to her door and realized she had left her keys inside. "Damn you, Petra!" She said, kicking the locked door to their apartment. She hadn't even needed to go potty; it had just been her usual ring of the bell to go fool around outside.

Then she felt horrible and knelt to kiss Petra's little head with an apology. It wasn't the dog's fault that she forgot to bring the keys. She would have to call a locksmith. She sat down against the door, pulling Petra into her lap as she fished around for her phone in the pocket of her hoodie, but it wasn't there. Of course it wasn't. It was back in the apartment too. Today was an entire practical joke, and Clara was the fool. She cried like a baby, squeezing Petra against her until she squirmed away to look at a dead fly. She felt like a baby too, hungry, snot-faced, and incapable of living without her parents. She had no idea what had gotten into her today.

Petra ran at the echoing sound of someone coming up the steps, her tail wagging. Remembering that they were still outside, and that her door to the apartment was on level three above the parking lot, she tried to wipe her tears away quickly, but only succeeded in smearing snot onto her cheeks. "Oh, hey there little buddy!" came a voice from the stairway, and Clara looked up to see Petra trying to jump up on their neighbor, Ryan. She was painfully aware that 1) She was sitting on the ground wiping away her tears and snot 2) Ryan was her next-door neighbor from apt. 3401 and she had made little to no effort at introducing herself in the months since she'd moved in and 3) He was *super* hot, or at least, what Clara might have considered her type if she had enough confidence. She had only really seen him a few times before in passing, but today he was wearing a hoodie, thin framed glasses, and sandals with socks. He looked very normal bringing in the groceries. His sleeves were rolled up, and Clara could see his veins and forearm straining where four grocery bags swayed in one hand to pet Petra with the other. She wished she could disappear.

"Hey, hey!" He said, setting the grocery bags down to pet Petra properly. "Hi, by the way," he started, then looked down at Clara. "Oh, are you okay?"

"Sorry, yes I'm okay," Clara said, inwardly cursing herself for instinctually apologizing. She knew it was annoying.

"Um, I'm Clara. We're neighbors, I think," she said, even though she knew for a fact that they were neighbors. He was staring at her weirdly, and she fought the impulse to run inside, mostly because she literally couldn't, and stood up to be polite. He set his groceries down.

"Are you sure you're alright? What are you doing out here?" He said, with a slight laugh. Clara was surprised that it didn't make her feel bad, or like she was being weird, but it felt friendly and reassuring. He could help her.

"I locked myself out," she said, wiping the last of the tears from her face. "And left my phone inside, too. Would you mind if I borrowed yours to call a locksmith?"

He was already fumbling in his pocket, pulling out a small wallet, some stray tissues, a squashed pack of spearmint gum, and then his phone. Petra was still pawing at his ankles, begging for attention. He handed her his phone, and then a crumpled tissue, which Clara took gratefully. She didn't mind that it had just been floating around in his pocket; anything would do right now to get the mess off her face.

As she searched up the number on the internet, he picked up his groceries and unlocked the door to his apartment, then motioned for her to come inside. "You can wait in here while they're on their way," he said, but Petra had already dashed inside.

She followed him in as the number rang, and then told her information to the guy on the other end. He said that they should be there in half an hour. After hanging up, she felt a little better, but then she realized where she was. It wasn't that she had been unaware that she was in Ryan's apartment, but she had been so preoccupied with Grandma and getting locked out, that she had followed him right in without any reservations. Obviously, she wasn't worried about him being a serial killer or anything, but she had never been in a stranger's place before. And she rarely interacted with people outside of her family and work situations since she had finished college.

His apartment was identical to hers, structurally. Same

kitchen space, cabinets, window and off-white shutters. A generously roomy one-bedroom apartment. But while her apartment was still almost bare, devoid of any decor or personal touches, Ryan's place looked like a real home. There were modern-art pictures hanging on the walls: thin, aimless squiggles that he probably paid a lot for but looked surprisingly classy on the walls. Picture frames with family (a younger sister?), a small UCLA flag on the fridge, and a pretty cream bookshelf filled with paperbacks. A lot of Stephen King, Paul Coelho, and the entire collection of George R. R. Martin *Song of Fire and Ice* books.

He was unloading his groceries, and she went to give back his phone. Petra was running around with her leash dragging behind her, sniffing and exploring. Clara called her over and scooped her up, not wanting either of them to intrude any more in Ryan's space. For a little dog, Petra was quite heavy and compact. "Thank you," Clara said, as Petra wiggled to get free. "And thanks for letting us wait in here. It's nice to meet you," she said.

He laughed. "It's nice to finally meet you too," he said. "I'd seen you a couple times around here, walking your dog, but you guys are so quiet that I wasn't even sure if anyone lived next door."

"Oh, yeah," Clara said, trying to laugh. "She's not a barker." But that probably wasn't entirely what he meant. Sure, she had only settled in a few months ago, but she never had people over, didn't stay out late or play loud music. Over the years she had mastered how to live like a ghost, and her apartment gave her the space to disappear and recharge. Going through life quietly and unseen made things easier, and privacy suited her. If and when things went wrong, she had no one to blame but herself, and that meant she had the maximum amount of control over her life. Dr. Ashley stressed the importance of not allowing others to come in and turn her life upside down, and that she did by not letting anyone come into her life at all.

Ryan's laugh brought her back to focus. "She's a cutie. My aunt used to have one of those weenie dogs too when I was a kid. What are they called again?"

He was asking easy questions and Clara was grateful for that. "She's a doxon. Or dachshund. I don't actually know if there's a difference."

He smiled, reaching out to pet Petra. Clara was still holding her in her arms, and at the sight of his hand coming towards her, she quickly dropped Petra onto the floor again, heart racing. She wasn't afraid of him; she liked to think that she wasn't afraid of other people anymore; she simply chose to avoid them. But she was afraid of the new situation she was in, even though she was right next door to her own place. Thank God she had Petra to steal all the attention. "Have you lived here long?" He asked, crouching down to pet Petra's long body.

"Only a few months," Clara said. He was being nice, and she knew she should say more. "But I grew up around here, twenty minutes or so away. What about you?"

He stood back up and straightened his glasses, which had slipped from Petra jumping up on him. "I've lived here about eight months. My family's from the Bay Area but I've been down here for college."

"It's kind of a commute from here to UCLA," Clara said, and then hastily added, "Sorry, I'm just guessing from the flag." She pointed to the fridge, feeling blood rush to her face. She felt so out of practice... not that she had ever been particularly skilled at making small talk.

He didn't seem to think it was awkward, though, so maybe she was doing okay. "Oh, yeah. It's way too expensive to live in Westwood without roommates. I work around here, though, and I actually graduated last May, so now I don't have to drive all the way over there every day."

"Oh," she said, "That makes sense." Then she didn't know what to say, and the heat in her face still hadn't gone down. "Could I have a glass of water?" She didn't know why she had blurted that. She wasn't actually thirsty, but it had seemed like a fitting thing to say.

"Oh, yeah sure!" He said, turning around to get a glass from the cupboard. With his back finally to her, Clara tried to silently catch her breath, which was difficult because she felt like she really needed to pant or wheeze, like she had been swimming laps and was on the brink of drowning. Ryan turned back around with a plastic cup of tap water, and she tried to smile normally. A drop of water dribbled onto her hand from the side of the cup. "Are you sure you're okay, Clara? It's none of my business, but you seemed pretty shaken up back there."

Then, she started talking. It was entirely out of character for her. She hadn't even taken a sip of the water, and suddenly she was telling him about the crazy phone call, her grandma, Georgia, and how scared she felt. Ryan was a good listener, and she was not used to that. Even her own therapist talked over her, corrected her, and stopped her in her tracks. She didn't know why she was telling him these things, even as she was actively speaking, revealing more and more of herself. Maybe because he seemed so open, so kind. Maybe she had finally become lonely. Whatever it was, they were both saved when the locksmith called back on Ryan's phone, saying that they had arrived in the parking lot.

She remembered thanking him, scooping up a reluctant Petra, and seeing a smile that didn't make her want to look away. He had her to put her contact into his phone in case she needed anything in the future. They were neighbors, after all.

She met the locksmith, a very big, older man, and the whole thing was over in minutes. He was probably angry that he had to drive all the way over here just to unlock her door in a couple of minutes. But she thanked him and paid.

Back inside her apartment, she felt so light. She couldn't even hear the silence.

TEN

2012, California

The first person Clara started being afraid of might have been Cassie, but she was her sister and she loved her so that didn't really count. She wasn't horrible, she only yelled and threw tantrums and cursed. She often made their parents angry, and that made Clara scared.

Cassie wasn't like other kids or grown-ups that terrified her, though, because Clara really wanted to be like her. She was confident, loud, and had lots of friends. She was also beautiful and fit wonderfully into her body. How could two kids from the same parents turn out so different? They had the same features, but they were stunning on Cassie. Her dark hair made Clara glad of her own, until she started dyeing it, and then Clara didn't want boring black hair either. It couldn't change colors in the sun, and braids had no depth, they just looked like dark lumps on her shoulders. The first time Cassie dyed her hair at a real salon, the sun shone on her new hair, copper and golden strands like glittering flames around her face. She looked magnificent—like a wild animal, a lioness—and Clara understood why she did it. Even their mother marveled at her newfound beauty. Now she could do French braids, Dutch braids, fishtails, and each strand stood out with the new highlights and added depth.

Clara was afraid of Cassie the way humans feared their cruel, beautiful gods.

She understood that sometimes when Cassie was terrible, it was to protect the family. Like when she beat up their cousin for saying their mom ruined them by marrying a dad with such dark skin, or the time at the restaurant when she was defending them and Grandma, in her own way. Clara knew Cassie beat people up at school, she just knew. Even in high school, they got disciplinary calls home, which Clara never knew the contents of but usually heard the fighting with their parents when Cassie came home. She held grudges, too, sometimes for years. There was a time much later, after they had moved back to California and Cassie had her driver's license, where she took Clara with her to the old Japanese language school that their mom had tried and tried so hard to get them accepted into when they were younger, just to learn the language properly with other second, even third generation Japanese kids. They had not been accepted, as Clara was "too old to learn a new language" at only four years old. Clara learned the true reason they had been denied that day so many years later with Cassie. She barged right into their Saturday morning lesson like a gunman, words at the ready.

Everyone stared in silence, but Clara could feel the rage coming off her sister and knew she had something planned. The room was filled with full Japanese American children, all of them clearly older than four years old. There were even some teenagers. Clara was startled to hear something like a sentence come rushing out of Cassie's mouth; she had not been speaking in English. Had Cassie tried to learn Japanese? The old sensei looked scandalized, completely astounded to see someone like Cassie speaking Japanese, and Clara was astounded as well. Cassie must have been learning on her own all this time, after so many years. Looking around the room, Clara understood that four years old had not been too late to learn a language. She was, however, not the right kind of Japanese.

Cassie went on speaking, a rapid fire of sounds to Clara's untrained ears. Then, she grabbed Clara's hand, spun them

around, and promptly left. They didn't speak as they buck-
led their seatbelts and Cassie backed out of the parking lot.
They didn't speak on the drive, or when they stopped next
at H Mart to pick up Mom's grocery items. She didn't cook
Japanese food often, as the kids preferred American food, but
occasionally she would send Cassie to the store. There was
a little Japanese Market named Matsuda's just five minutes
from their house, but whenever Cassie was sent to get groceries, she only went to H Mart or 99 Ranch. Those stores were
massive, unaffiliated with any specific Asian country, and had
plenty of non-Asians browsing, so no one paid any attention
to the sisters. Clara trailed behind Cassie as she threw things
into their cart: jicama, ginger, persimmons, furikake rice sea-
soning, soba noodles. She hauled a bag of rice off the shelf,
and they finally spoke.

"Mom says it has to be the Nishiki brand," Clara said quietly. "That's Botan."

"I don't give a damn, Clara," she said. She started down
the aisle with the cart, making Clara chase after her. She
looked over her shoulder icily. "If Mom wanted specifics, she
should have come with us."

They didn't speak again until they got home, and Cassie
shut the engine off. "Who taught you to speak Japanese?"
Clara asked.

It was warm outside, but Cassie had a way of making the
air around her go cold. "I did." She paused for a moment. "I
did, because they wouldn't teach us. You know that, right?
They want to keep people like us out. Being back here again
almost makes me miss Georgia. They hated us there because
we were too different, but places like here they hate us because
we're not enough." Then they got out of the car and brought
the groceries in, and neither of them ever told a soul about
what Cassie did at the Japanese school that day.

With as many friends as Cassie always had, Clara never
would have thought that her sister also felt lonely sometimes.
She hung out with friends after school, both when they lived

in California and when they lived in Georgia. She seemed to acquire them quickly, new ones always coming and going. She didn't keep any of them for long, but there were always more, and Clara often wondered how many people Cassie knew. Important people knew lots of people, so it made sense.

Only a month into her new high school in Georgia, Cassie gave up soccer. Their mom had been trying to find a team for her since they moved, but one day at dinner she said she didn't want to do soccer anymore. She wasn't particularly good at it, so her parents let it go quickly. And then a week later, she came home and announced that she was going to try out for the cheerleading team.

Clara had been sitting at the kitchen counter eating her after school snack of sliced apples and pretzel sticks. She could feel the fight coming so she kept her eyes down, on her plate. "Cassie," their mom began. "Honey, you don't even know how to do a cartwheel."

"Don't worry, Mom," she said, already defensive. "I have friends who are also going to try out and they said they'll teach me." Clara wasn't worried; when Cassie wanted to do something, she did it, and she did it well. She was going to be marvelous at cheerleading. "It's like... a big thing here, you know?" Mom was still unsure, so Cassie dragged her over to Grandma in the sitting room. "Grandma, tell Mom how important cheerleading is here, that everyone does it!"

"Why yes," Grandma said, without looking away from the television. "Cheerleading is one of the best sports out there for young ladies like you, Cassandra. All my friend's granddaughters do it, and the ones that are too old for it now teach the little ones how to do it." So, it was settled, and having put the idea in Grandma's head, the two of them had never been closer. Grandma and Cassie watched YouTube videos together about the basics of tumbling and balance. Apparently in the summertime, the two most popular summer camps were

"Vacation Bible Study" and cheer camps. Grandma said they could sign up next summer.

They didn't know then, but by July next summer, they'd already be settling back into the barren suburbs of Los Angeles.

June 2022
Georgia

There were beetles on the roses.

Even after death, Grandma's roses flourished without a caretaker. That's how things were there, always growing. Flowers and vines grew strong and wild, and the only care they needed was trimming to keep from swallowing up a whole property.

Clara was sitting at the back porch, waiting for everyone else to arrive. It was nearly ten in the morning, and the day was already hot and sticky. Beneath the terrace was the lovely overgrowth of rosebushes, all speckled with iridescent beetles, emerald and copper bodies stuck to the petals like jewels, nestled in clusters at the center of every rose.

Now that Grandma was gone, who would deal with the beetles? Not Clara, at least not by hand. If it was to be her house now and her responsibilities, she would use pesticides and weed killer and bug sprays.

Of course not she mumbled. Who was she kidding? She didn't know the first thing about plants or gardens, pest control, or owning a house for that matter. She was in way over her head. In her death, Grandma had plucked Clara up from her predictable life and thrown her into this bucket of soap water.

The whole ludicrous investigation had been put to rest. For now, at least. Once Clara's dad brought in the lawyer, Miss Stacie seemed to sulk off. She wasn't sure who he'd talked to in the few days since they'd arrive, but they seemed to be getting a break for the time being.

Waiting this morning, alone on the property, it was Clara's

first time back with just her mind and the woods to keep her company. Maybe it was stress, the weight of knowing the house was in her hands now, but she couldn't see the magic. Beautiful, of course, but not like she remembered. Where photographs faded and yellowed over time, memories must work the opposite way because Grandma's backyard had remained so vibrant in her mind, maybe even grown over the years. Now that she was here and alone, it was different. Green and alive, yes, but somehow less wonderful. Maybe it was her, though, and not the house that had lost its magic.

She supposed that might have meant she had grown up. That part of her was lost in the years, probably unsalvageable. A small, childish part of her didn't want the house anymore, no longer shimmering behind the curtain of her childhood fantasies, but some things were not meant to be considered and she forced the selfish thought out of her mind. She was scared, and she knew it. Why why *why* was Grandma doing this to her?

Feeling overwhelmed, she habitually pulled out her phone and saw her fingers scrolling through her contacts to Dr. Ashley's number. She realized what she was doing and shoved her phone back into the bottom of her bag. She tried not to call unless it was an emergency, because she only paid for the forty-five-minute session once a week and calling outside of that felt like cheating. No matter what they talked about, she had to remember that her therapist was not her friend, she was a paid professional. No, she didn't need therapy right now, she just needed to breathe.

As she exhaled, the back door swung open. Dad, Cassie, and the fiancé. Her dad's jeans had dirt on the knees. She wasn't used to seeing him dirty, rarely seeing him wearing anything but his nice work clothes.

"I've thought all night about it and I just can't make rhyme or reason as to why she chose to do that!" Cassie said, plopping down on another patio seat. She was wearing a girly sundress, something that looked a little retro but knowing

Cassie, was probably highly fashionable. Tristan stood behind the chair, his hand on her shoulder. Clara wished he would go away. "I mean, what does she expect you to do with something this big?" Clara knew she wasn't angry or jealous, Cassie loved her life on the east coast. She was happy, or at least she seemed like it. She always did when caught up in a relationship, so energetic and enthusiastic until things went wrong. "I mean, who would want to be tied down to such a dowdy, old thing in this area, all the way across the country! It's lovely, of course, ginormous! But so unrealistic, isn't it, Clara?"

She was saved from answering when her dad's phone rang. He pulled it out of his pocket and stepped to the side to take the call. It was probably someone from work, never leaving him alone. Then she heard what Tristan was saying to Cassie.

"It makes you wonder what the point is," he said, gesturing broadly with his hands. He took up space so confidently, like he believed the world was created for him. But Clara reminded herself that there was no fault in having some confidence, and that she should be striving for that too. "All of this land, this mansion with no one to pass it down to." In another reality, Clara would have objected. Did she not count as someone that could inherit her grandma's house? He went on. "I mean, really, it makes me wonder what the point of this all was, using a fortune to build this house and then just throw it away."

Throw it away? How could her sister stand to listen to his prattling, Cassie who was so protective and vocal? Never mind that he was insulting Clara, he was criticizing their grandma. She wanted to say something, to stand up for them, but her lips felt stapled shut, like trying to open them would be torturous.

She wished it was just her and Cassie right now. Even when Cassie said things she didn't agree with, she could handle it because it wasn't coming from some outsider like Tristan. Why don't you get a job first and then you can question what people choose to do with their money, she wanted to shout. But she didn't.

Her dad got off the phone and was shaking his head

to himself like he did when he was deep in thought. Clara wondered who he'd been talking to. She knew that he could handle stress; he was good at it, hiding his thoughts from the family. Grandma's passing didn't seem to be taking too much out of him. He had never seemed to have any problems showing affection with Clara and Cassie, and even their mom, but she wondered if he had always been more removed from Grandma. He rarely talked about his upbringing, but she knew it must have been lonely. Not just because he was an only child in this great, empty house, but as himself in Georgian suburbs in the late seventies. She wondered if he had ever resented Grandma and Grandpa for bringing him here, even though he was brought up in wealth and comfort. He was not Indian in any way, and she wondered if he had ever wanted to be.

He came back over and put on his smile. "Well, what are you thinking, Clary?" he asked. "The funeral will be on Saturday, so we should probably sort through some things, make sure everything's right in the house before we go back."

Go back? It sounded like a nice dream. "Won't we—I have to come back at some point?"

"Yes," he said. "Mom or I can fly out with you later, if you want, depending on our work schedules." She nodded her head, barely listening. *What* was she going to do? What was she supposed to do? She couldn't live here, not when her one-bedroom apartment back in California was more than big enough. Not to mention the expenses of just keeping the house running, electricity and water bills, maintaining four acres of land? No way. Maybe it would be best to give it over to Mom and Dad. Maybe they should sell it. Without Grandma, they no longer had any ties to this place, nothing but an empty house and memories.

"Come on, let's go back inside," he said, a hand on Clara's shoulder. She hadn't realized that Cassie and Tristan weren't there anymore. She followed her dad back inside, her back to the woods.

ELEVEN

March 2010, Georgia

There was more to Georgia than just the people.

Terrifying things sometimes happened, and Clara learned that these kinds of things were bound to happen when you lived in a place with so much nature. There were strange insects, centipedes and millipedes worming around on Grandma's white tile, or big black ants with thick bodies. Carpenter ants, her dad said. He would call an exterminator. They were in the house by the back door, walking in lines, sometimes carrying little things in their fang-looking mandibles, or on their backs: food crumbs, carpet fuzz, dead ants or other bug carcasses. It was a sight to see, but Clara was glad for the exterminators. These weren't the kind of ants you could smear on the pavement with your finger.

The rain was another beast. The first time it poured, Clara cowered in fear, clutching at her mom's legs. It made her worry that maybe all of Grandma's bible stuff was actually real, and God was trying to drown them like in Noah's Arc for being bad. She hadn't been bad, but Cassie surely had. Would they all be punished because of her?

But it was just rain. Her dad explained that areas like Florida and Georgia sometimes got torrential rain, heavy downpours like someone was trying to dump the ocean from the sky. After the first couple of times, Clara began to love it. It was so loud that it sounded like the whole house was going to come down. One time, she was at Costco with her dad when it rained like that, and the rain against metal sounded like war drums, the rapid drumming before shots were fired.

Somehow, it never flooded after any of those rainstorms. There were storm drains everywhere, big gaping slots in the sidewalk that Clara never dared to walk near. Grandma said that if she ever got sucked into the drains during a storm, she would come out from the other end like a flopping fish, all the way down in Savannah by the ocean. Grandma seemed to find that funny, though, so Clara knew there would be no real danger there.

The real scare didn't come until months later, close to April. Clara had been trudging through fifth grade, waking up to get on the bus and sitting through the days like a zombie. It might have been the medicine—the little white pills she swallowed every morning. They made her feel tired, and her brain was slower than it used to be. She didn't notice a lot of things at school these days, not unless someone got right up in her face. But one day at recess, the sky turned green, and it was too horrible of a thing *not* to notice.

Clara didn't like recess. Three classes went out at once to the small play yard, which was a little under one hundred kids total. The teachers didn't pay attention, so bad things sometimes happened. Kids forced each other to eat leaves or grass. Others delighted in standing at the top of the jungle gym with fistfuls of woodchips, attacking anyone who was nearby. Clara didn't have anything to do at recess, so she usually brought a book from her desk, even if all she had was one of the school science or social studies textbooks. She read near the doors, always the first to bolt inside once the whistle was blown, but sometimes recess lasted much longer than twenty minutes. Clara always noted the time when they went outside, and the time once they were allowed back inside. One time, recess went for one hour and seventeen minutes instead of the allotted twenty. Clara had been so mad and tired that she wanted to cry. Mrs. Manning and the other teachers seemed to love recess as much as some of the kids, though, and that was probably why they let it go on for so long some days. The teachers always talked and laughed together every day at recess, behaving like Cassie and her friends. They didn't pay attention to anything during recess, especially not the time. Sometimes, they even disappeared for a while.

But on the day the sky turned green, recess was cut short. A horrible alarm sounded, and Clara had never heard anything like it—so loud that it seemed to be coming from everywhere all at once. It was a horrible wail, a high tone and then a lower one, and that went on for the next three hours. Mrs. Manning and the two other teachers hurried around the yard, their high heels sinking down in the mulch and mud, shooing everyone back inside. It was a disaster trying to funnel one hundred screaming fifth graders through one door, and Clara was almost separated from her left arm.

Clara pressed her hands flat against her ears. The other kids seemed excitable but unsurprised. "Tornado! Tornado!" said Daniel, jumping around in the chaos of the hallway. The heels of his shoes lit up blue and red when he jumped.

Before that day, Clara hadn't known that tornadoes were a real thing, real as earthquakes or tsunamis. She had only seen it before from The Wizard of Oz movie, a dark funnel of wind that swept up an entire town into the sky—houses, animals, bicyclers, maybe skyscrapers too. Amidst the mayhem, Mrs. Manning was calling roll and having the students line up in the hall in alphabetical order. She was only on Susie Deane when she had to pause. Kids were screaming and pointing because Clara peed her pants.

She hadn't ever done that before, and it was a shock to feel her own hot urine seeping through her pants and puddling beneath her. It looked very yellow on the white floor, and everyone had scampered away from her, laughing and screaming and falling over each other in the hallway to escape Clara's pee puddle. She began to cry. She couldn't hear a thing over

the sound of her own crying, the other kids' laughing, screaming, siren wailing, and the hailing that had started outside. She
could see it through the glass recess doors, white balls the size
of grapes smacking the pavement, covering the ground fast.

Then the Principal Nancy was there, and she took over so
that Mrs. Manning could drag Clara to the girls' bathroom.
Her grip was tight, and her hand wrapped all the way around
Clara's skinny little arm. It was a little quieter once they were
in the bathroom.

"Now what did you do that for?" Mrs. Manning said,
grabbing fistfuls of paper towels and roughly scrubbing at
Clara's stained leggings.

Clara knew she was embarrassing herself and making
Mrs. Manning angry, but she was too terrified to think about
how she was supposed to act. "I want to go home." The water
Mrs. Manning used to soak the paper towels was ice cold, and
Clara's lips trembled. She could taste the salt of her tears and
snot, and she didn't know which was which.

"Well so do I, Miss Clara." She was rubbing so hard that
the paper towels were falling apart, leaving wet little balls all
over her pants. "But there's a tornado watch out there right
now, so you'll have to stick it out like the rest of us until the
all-clear alarm comes on."

"I want to go home," Clara cried.

"You're going to have to wait like the rest of us," she said.
"Your momma's not going to be able to drive in this weather
anyway."

Clara almost peed again at the thought of her mom being
in the tornado. Grandma's house was big and heavy, but there
was no saying what a tornado might do. They might be up
in the air already, swirling around and around. What would
happen when it stopped—would they fall from the sky?

Mrs. Manning took Clara back into the hall where the
kids from every classroom had come out, lining up against
the walls and holding textbooks. Some students had different
ones, but most had either the math or the language arts books.

Hardback and heavy as bricks. The other teachers were making them get down on their knees and lean all the way forward with their heads against the walls of the hallway. Mrs. Manning shooed Clara over against the wall with the other kids, and she was given a language arts textbook. Her pee had been cleaned up by someone.

She just stood there, and Rebecca from her class tugged on Clara's socks. She was on the ground, motioning for Clara to get down as well. "What?" Clara asked. She hadn't quite stopped crying yet, and her nose was beginning to hurt from all the rubbing and sniffling.

"Get down and put the book on your head," Rebecca said. It sounded crazy, but Clara looked around and saw she was telling the truth. Kids were packed side to side, kneeling with their legs tucked under them, head against the walls, textbook on heads. The alarm was still wailing. Clara squeezed down next to Rebecca, uncomfortable in her damp pee pants, and tucked into a ball like everyone else. With the top of her head pressing up against the wall and the heavy book as a helmet, she grew uncomfortable quickly. After only a few minutes, her legs began to ache, folded beneath her curved body. There was some whispering, but mostly the sound of the alarm rang in her ears, and the howling of wind and rain outside.

Packed tight between the other kids, Clara stopped crying eventually. They were like sardines tucked against the wall, and although she was still scared, she felt less alone. Nobody was talking to her, but they were all the same that day, curled up on the dirty school floor, waiting for the storm to pass, wondering where the tornado was and where it was going. Clara wasn't the only one who had cried, but she had certainly been the only fifth grader to pee herself. She eventually dozed off to the drone of the alarms.

By the time parents were able to pick their kids up, it was past five. School had been over for almost two hours. Clara walked out the doors hand in hand with her dad, who had her backpack slung over his shoulder. No one had mentioned the pee incident to him, and she wasn't going to either.

Outside, the parking lot had become a forest floor, covered in tree branches and other debris. The flowers out front, pink tulips and yellow crocuses, were strewn in clumps across the pavement, uprooted and limp from the rain's brutal beating. There was dirt and mulch everywhere, along with some trash and papers still trying to take flight in the dying winds. "You must have been very scared, Clary-bug," her dad said once they were in the car, driving away from the school. "Mom and Cassie are back home already, and they're going to cook up a good hot meal for us all."

"Is the house okay?"

He took one hand off the wheel to pat Clara's leg. Luckily, her pants had dried after the three hours of waiting. "Yes, everything is fine. The tornado was small, and it actually passed closer to your school than Grandma's house. The yard's a mess, but everything else is fine." At least she got to ride home with her dad instead of taking the bus. She was eager to get back to the house, in fact, she wanted to go home and never leave again. Fifth grade was easy enough. There was nothing they did at school that she couldn't do at home.

They pulled into the driveway, and Clara took a timid look around. The damage wasn't as bad as it was over at the school, but it did look like a terrible mess. Tree branches were everywhere, entire limbs scattered on the lawn. Clara remembered the dead tree with the snakes that had to be cut down, and now she understood why. If a storm like this could rip up strong, living trees, she was surprised the everyday wind didn't push down dead trees like dominoes standing up. How could they still stand when the storm took a toll on even the strong, healthy trees?

Inside the house, though, all was as it should be. Mom was stirring something at the stove with one hand, the other holding the landline to her ear. She sometimes talked to her cousins on the phone for hours. Grandma was on the couch eating candied nuts and watching the local news. There were pictures of storm damage on the screen. Clara wondered if they would show the tornado, but the thought was too terrifying, so she made a conscious effort not to look at the television. Cassie was nowhere to be seen, but Clara could hear music playing upstairs.

Clara ran to her mom and threw her arms around her, smashing her face into her mom's back. "Oh—Clara!" She said, holding the phone away from her face. "Don't run up on me like that, especially when I'm in front of the stove." She turned the fire off and put the phone back to her ear. "Hana, I'll call you back tomorrow. Clara and Danny just got back."

Clara was overjoyed her mom had hung up the phone *and* stopped cooking to talk to her. She gave Clara a proper hug, and then pulled back with her nose scrunched. "Oh, you smell weird honey. Go up and change clothes and call your sister down for dinner while you're at it."

So, Clara ran up the stairs, going so fast that she had to use her hands to scamper up like a bear or some other animal. Back in her room, she changed clothes and chucked her pee pants and underwear into the trashcan. Having never been in a situation where she peed in her pants before, she wasn't sure what to do with her clothes, but she assumed they were to be thrown away. They were old pants, anyway, with a hole in the thigh and the seams coming undone at the ankles so that she always had to keep pulling the threads whenever she wore them. She was glad to be rid of them, and everything they had gone through today.

The house was so big that Cassie's room wasn't next to hers. She had to walk down the hall, past the floating staircase and up to a small little wing of upstairs, separate from the main hallway. When they had moved in, Grandma said the girls could choose any bedroom they liked. Cassie had chosen the bedroom farthest from everyone, even though it was small, and the walls were plain.

She knocked on the door many times, but Cassie didn't

answer. She probably couldn't hear over the music playing. She would have never done it on her own, but Mom had asked her to bring Cassie down, so she cracked open the door and peaked inside.

Cassie was at her desk with her back to the door. Clara stepped in, and then she realized that Cassie was talking to someone, despite the music playing. She wasn't just talking, though. She was Skyping on the computer, and there was a boy on the screen. Cassie was talking in a high, nice voice, not like the grumbling or snapping she used with the family. The boy was laughing and kept touching his hair. Clara didn't know how long she stood there, unable to leave but too afraid to speak, but eventually Cassie turned around and that nice, high voice left her mouth. "I have to go," she said to the boy, and hung up the Skype call. When she turned back to Clara, there was a cold light behind her eyes. Cassie didn't turn red when she got angry, but it always came out in her eyes, hard like ice. She shoved Clara out of her room so hard that she almost fell back on her butt. "What are you doing, you creep!"

Any other day, tears would have sprung up in Clara's eyes, but she had been through a lot today and her eyes were dry. She was all cried out for the day. "Mom says to come down for dinner."

"Tell her I'm not hungry," Cassie said, slamming the door in Clara's face so hard that the picture frames hanging on the walls vibrated. Behind her door, the music turned back on.

Dinner was always weird when Mom and Grandma cooked together. Mom didn't ever use enough salt, and Grandma always used too much. But tonight, Mom had made dinner and Grandma made dessert, which she was good at. When Grandma was living alone after Grandpa died, she probably only ate desserts for every meal.

Mom rarely made real Japanese meals, but she did make a lot of weird meals that were distinctly American but used the wrong ingredients. That night was particularly weird. Clara stared glumly at her plate of plain spaghetti noodles with sticky brown teriyaki sauce and chunks of bland salmon on top. She was hoping for a more triumphant meal after all the horrific experiences that day, but Mom already looked sad because Cassie wouldn't come down for dinner, so Clara sucked up a single noodle.

"Clara, what are you making that face for?" Mom asked.

No one else was complaining about the mutant spaghetti, not even Grandma. However, Grandma usually didn't eat much proper dinner. She was always saving room for dessert, and tonight she made two big trays of lemon bars. Clara didn't want to be the first to complain, but she said, "I don't think this is how it's supposed to be made."

"How what's supposed to be made?"

"Spaghetti."

Mom laughed a little. "Well, this isn't spaghetti, Clary. It's a special recipe." Clara stirred her fork around in the sticky mess of not-spaghetti, trying to make it look like she was eating. Her mom went on talking. "My mom made it this way, and your aunts and I always loved it when we were your age," she said. "In fact, she even used ketchup sometimes. Just noodles and ketchup. It's called Japanese ketchup spaghetti." Clara laughed and so did Grandma. Dad, as usual, was lost in his thoughts at dinnertime, mindlessly eating his food with unseeing eyes and unhearing ears. It was like his body was at the dinner table, but his mind was at the office, or wherever it was he went during the day. "So, eat up, and be glad that I didn't use ketchup. I don't think you would have liked that at all."

Grandma laughed, sitting back in her chair. There was a brown spot of teriyaki sauce on her old lips. "I don't think so either, Meg. Now, who's ready for dessert?"

Mom rolled her eyes but smiled, and Clara pushed her plate away happily as Grandma went to bring the lemon bars out.

TWELVE

June 2022, Georgia

Clara and her dad went through Grandma's room first. She had become very dirty and untidy in her old age, and there were four old glasses of water by her bed, one of which had a spiderweb strung across the rim. It was a dark, stuffy room, and the first thing Danny had done was push back the heavy curtains so light could come in.

Next, they gathered up all the trash. The bathroom trashcan was full of used tissues, so it seemed Grandma had started a new trashcan under the four poster bed. Clara felt the pressure of tears behind her eyes as she and her dad fished out all the trash from under the bed, everything from more tissues, clothes tags, cosmetics packaging, and two twinkie wrappers. "Why didn't we come back and visit her?" Clara said, unable to turn her face from the mess to look at her dad. She didn't want to see the look of shame on his face. "Or bring her over to California?"

Her dad was getting the way he did sometimes when he was stressed, when it seemed like only his body was left in the room with her. "She wouldn't leave this house," he said, as if someone else's voice was coming out through his mouth. Someone entirely detached from the situation. She wondered if he did it to himself on purpose, and if it worked. "She loved it too much. She couldn't part with it." *Maybe it was all she had left.*

So, she had let herself die here, in this dark, empty mansion. Clara couldn't imagine being alone in a space so big, when sometimes her little apartment back home felt like too much for just her and Petra. It probably drove her insane, if age hadn't already. How had she done it? How was it possible to live alone like this?

It was too awful to think about. Clara made herself focus on the work of cleaning, fishing out trash, clearing away the dust and cobwebs that filled the space Grandma lived and died in. In the end, she only had the spiders and other nasty bugs to keep her company.

Her hand touched a piece of paper, and she blindly pulled it from beneath the bed. Her dad had left the room to throw out the trash they'd already collected, and Clara held the small piece of paper up to the light.

It was a note, torn from one of Grandma's nice floral stationery pads, the edges embossed with a pretty design of roses. There were a few sentences written in her thin, looping handwriting, but the lines were wobbly as if her hands had been unsteady. But that wasn't out of the ordinary for a ninety-three year old woman with arthritis in her fingers. Clara held the note up in the sun. Written there was:

They took you away, but won't you come back home to me now?

Then she heard the sound of her dad coming up the stairs. She didn't have any pockets or sleeves, so she shoved it down her shirt right as her dad came through the doorway with a new trash bag and a vacuum in the other hand. They didn't speak for the next half hour, cleaning in silence, both lost in their own thoughts. Clara was repeating the note over and over in her head, trying to make sense of it. She was sure she could repeat the words in her sleep and would probably dream about it.

Who had Grandma been talking about? She thought back to the frantic phone call she'd gotten a few months before, where Grandma had asked where she had gone. Who was she? Did she mean Clara?

No, couldn't be. She would have addressed Clara directly, then. Besides, she knew where she was and how to contact her.

Maybe she'd had a friend in town who moved away. It was normal for people as old as she'd been to become confused or agitated. Distressed like she had been on the phone call. Clara put a hand against her chest, feeling the torn note against her skin. It felt scratchy like dust, but she was glad to keep it there for now. For some reason, she couldn't imagine showing it to her dad. It was too intimate, too fragile, a woman's secret. She needed time to think.

She cleared her throat, trying to break the silence. Danny looked over at her. "I was thinking," Clara began. "This house is filled with old stuff. Do you think we should try an estate sale?" She had been to a few before back in California, but they were in small apartments with a small number of belongings. Clara didn't know how they'd go about that here, especially in such a short period of time. With the funeral on Saturday, that would give them less than two days to set things aside and label prices. Would people even come? Clara needed to talk to people, preferably people who might have been around Grandma in the recent years, like neighbors or church friends. If she got the chance to talk to some people who were close with Grandma, she might be able to figure out who *she* was. Maybe Grandma had a friend other people in the community knew of who had moved away or died.

She bit her lip, waiting for her dad's answer. His brows were creased, and he looked old and tired. She wasn't sure what she wanted him to say; the thought of putting Grandma's old stuff up for sale and inviting strangers into her house left Clara with a gross, squirming feeling.

"I don't know, Clara," Danny finally said, and she felt both relief and disappointment at the same time. "There were some people in town, neighbors or church people, who weren't kind to your grandmother." He paused, clearing his throat. It was incredibly dingy and dusty in Grandma's room, as if the cleaning they were doing was only kicking up all the dust. "Some people didn't approve of our family, or my mother's choices."

Clara opened her mouth, but then closed it. Surely, he couldn't mean her choice to adopt?

"Clara, do you remember when I used to tell you and Cassie bedtime stories?" Danny laughed and set down the rag he had been using to wipe away the dust and cobwebs. "It was ages ago, when Cassie was young enough to still want to listen to things her parents had to say."

"Of course," Clara said, smiling slightly at the memory. When they were children, Danny used to tell them little bed-time stories. He told fairytales, folktales, and fables from around the world, strange little stories about wolves and pixies and firebirds.

"Do you remember the story of Chitranga the dog?"

The Dog That Went Abroad

There once lived a spotted dog called Chitranga, whose village experienced a famine. There was nothing to eat and dogs were starving and dying. Chitranga could not suffer the hunger any longer, so he decided to leave home in search of a better place fit to live, with proper food and opportunity. He left his country and traveled a long way. Eventually, he came upon a house in a town far away with its doors wide open. Inside, Chitranga feasted on all the good things left out. He ate and ate his fill because there was so much. Once he was tired and full, he decided to leave. Outside the house, there were other dogs from the foreign village, and from his spotted body they could tell he was not from their country. He could not outrun them since he was so full from eating, and the other dogs bit and attacked him. Somehow, he was able to escape, and he returned home. All the dogs at home were curious about his travels and findings. When they asked how it was, he responded, "There were many good things to eat, and I am no longer hungry. But there is one evil in a foreign country: You will be hated there because of who you are!"

"When I was a kid the neighbors and people at church used to treat me like a spotted dog," Danny said. He talked about his childhood so little that Clara couldn't imagine him as a kid, and it made her feel uncomfortable. It was strange to think that her dad had a previous life alone with Grandma and Grandpa. "Except that your grandmother raised me as her child, so I felt no different from anyone else in town until they made me see it. And some people thought she did the wrong thing."

Clara wasn't following. "Grandma? You mean by adopting you?" Were people still that openly racist? "I thought you were first connected to her and Grandpa through the church, anyway."

"It's true, we were," he said. "My biological family in India was connected to your grandparents through a church program that matched families in the church with impoverished families in Asia, Africa, and South America. Families like Grandma and Grandpa sent money to their 'other' family monthly, supposedly until each child per family turned eighteen." Clara had known that much, but he wasn't finished. "Your grandma, my mother, sent handwritten letters to us, and we wrote back, but only my oldest sister could write back in English. Still, the money through the program wasn't enough. I had four other siblings, and I was the youngest. My father died." He paused, as if trying to remember. He didn't look sad, just thoughtful. "They say he was hit by a train walking home from work one night," he said. "My oldest sister turned eighteen and that meant the funding from the church dropped for her. It wasn't much but we weren't well off. My mother in India was always sick, and she couldn't take care of me. We were starving."

He told Clara about the poverty and begging Grandma had seen when she went to adopt him, to bring Danny over to the states for a new life. He was four at the time and had no memory of living in the slums of Calcutta, the "disaster of India." That if Grandma hadn't come to get him, he might have died, or worse. "She saw child beggars with their fingers cut off," he said. "Waiting by the trains from five in the morning until past dark, standing all day long with their hands out, exhausted and sick."

"So, she just… took you away?"

"Yes," he said.

"What about your sisters?" Clara asked. Weak sunlight was coming in from behind the drawn curtains, and she could see dust floating in the air where the light shone through. "Your mother?"

He shrugged, but suddenly it seemed like there was a lot of weight on his shoulders. "I don't know. Better off with one less mouth to feed. Maybe not."

Clara's mind was muddled with all the new information. She wondered how her dad could have kept all this from them for so long, all to himself. She thought about Grandma, her grandma who loved them so much. Maybe too much, in her own way. Did people do everything just because they loved you?

"She just took you."

"Yes," he said, *and paid them off* went unspoken.

"Do you ever wonder about them?" Clara asked.

He didn't speak for what felt like a long time. "It's hard to wonder about what you can't remember." He finally said. "How can I care for something I have no memory of?"

Clara's phone buzzed on the ground where she had left off cleaning, a text from Mom. She was back at the house and had picked up late breakfast for them. The house was so big, Clara hadn't even heard her come in. She clicked her phone off and looked over at her dad, feeling unable to simply get up and walk downstairs as if he hadn't just revealed so much about himself and Grandma. She wished for a moment that the conversation had never happened. But he smiled as if he was untroubled and patted her on the shoulder. "It's okay, Clary-bug. Don't have that look on your face. It all turned out okay, didn't it? I don't resent her for making that choice for me. She was a good mom to me. She really did love me."

They got up and left the bedroom, dust particles suspended in the air like they might stay there, frozen forever. Clara closed the door behind them, breathing in the cool, fresh air of the hallway. *I don't resent her for making that choice for me.*

But should he? Clara chewed her bottom lip, thinking. She could taste blood by the time they met Mom downstairs in the kitchen.

Tristan had gone back to the hotel, and finally it was just Clara and Cassie, Mom and Dad. Sometimes she felt embarrassed, ashamed of how much she wished it could always be the just four of them together. Mom and Dad wouldn't get any older, Cassie wouldn't get married to someone who might make her miserable. Clara could have her family back the way it was meant to be.

She knew, in a sense, that it wasn't supposed to be like that, though, that things were not meant to go like that for a healthy life. Dr. Ashley drilled it into her head, always with the example of concentric circles: Clara's life, as most, began as one circle with Mom, Dad, and Cassie. As she grew older and more people came into her life, she would gain more circles, like Grandma or friends, coworkers, partners. Dr. Ashley said that she needed to let herself gain more circles, the way tree trunks gain rings with age. It was the only way to grow into a great big tree, and Clara was preventing that from happening. She was a twig, and she knew she wasn't allowing herself to grow. She felt comfortable where she was, even if that meant she might stay a twig forever.

Her mom had brought sandwiches, and they ate them as they went over the schedule for the next day and the funeral plans. Only she and Clara were sitting at the table. Danny was eating standing in front of the granite island countertop, and Cassie was over by the window, not on her phone but also not paying attention. Her hair, currently a milky brown color, had a few millimeters of black roots growing in. Clara thought she was probably thinking about what color to dye it next, and when.

Eleven a.m. on Saturday. About a half an hour service in the church, and then the burial would follow in the church affiliated cemetery. Refreshments at the house after. Then Danny asked Clara if she would speak.

"It would be brief," he said gently, as if he already knew her answer and was imploring her to reconsider. "Just something about Grandma, a small anecdote or story to remember her by."

Even Cassie had broken out of her daydreaming to look over at Clara. She realized she was picking the dry skin of her cuticles and put both hands under her butt, forcing herself to stop fidgeting by sitting on them. "I don't know," she said.

"I can do it, of course," Danny said. "But I think it would be extra special coming from you."

She saw her Grandma as she had been twelve years ago, bright lipstick and too much blush on her cheeks, powdery, perfumed old skin that Clara could smell when she sat next to her on the couch. She wanted to be brave, the way Grandma had made her feel when she was ten years old.

"I'll... try," Clara said, expelling the words that were suffocating her in one big breath.

He nodded, seeming satisfied with the answer for now, and they went back to finishing their sandwiches.

Late in the evening, Clara sat at the hotel room desk in her room with a pen in her hand and a blank paper in front of her.

It had been that way for nearly an hour, and she felt frozen with no idea of where to start.

She really had no idea of what was expected for this sort of thing. What was she supposed to say? The last funeral she had attended was her great uncle Takumi, and that was when she was in late middle school and she and Cassie had both gotten real phones. Thinking back on it, Clara realized that she couldn't remember any of her great uncle's funeral. If she could remember so much from living in Georgia years before that, there was no good reason why she couldn't recall what his funeral had been like. Of course, she knew the reason, but it wasn't good—she and Cassie had been enamored with their new iPhones, and while she couldn't remember something as significant as a relative's funeral, she could still remember her highest score on Angry Birds.

Yeah, she knew why she couldn't remember that funeral.

Frustrated, she scribbled a beginning onto the hotel-branded notepad. It was stuck to the desk, tethered by the back cover so that people wouldn't take it home with them. She wrote "Debbie Graham was a wonderful grandmother."

No, too ordinary. She scribbled through the words and started again.

"She was my favorite grandma."

No, that was a horrible thing to say when her other grandma died of breast cancer before Clara was born. She scribbled it out again, but then tore out the page and ripped it up, starting fresh again.

She took a deep breath. "Debbie Graham was a wonderful lady."

After a moment, she cursed and raked her hands through her hair, wincing as her fingers snagged a tangle. No, none of these were good enough. She needed to say something special, something that could encapsulate how magical her memories of her grandma were, but for as much as she loved to read, Clara was a horrible writer. She got up from the desk and walked over to the bed where she had laid out the strange note from underneath the bed. It was a small piece of paper, so little and delicate that Clara worried it would disintegrate before she could figure out its meaning. Thinking up all the ways she might lose it or ruin it, she took out her phone and snapped a quick picture of it. Then she read it again, though she didn't need to look at the words to remember what it said. *They took you away, but won't you come back home to me now?* She repeated it like a mantra, whispering, shaping her mouth around the words in the silence of the hotel room.

Taking the note with her, she sat down again at the desk, pen in hand. She started again. "Grandma was my first real friend. She made this place my home when I lived here twelve years ago." She started, letting the story sweep her away.

THIRTEEN

Things at school got a lot worse for Clara after the tornado day. Kids usually ignored her, but now they laughed and taunted. At lunch, they formed a ring around her, even though everyone had assigned seats. "Don't drink too much apple juice Clara!" They reminded, snickering and hollering. At lunch, kids accidentally spilled their drinks onto her, and several times she suffered through the rest of the school day with sticky pants from juice or sodas or strawberry milk that got knocked into her lap. She started to fear lunchtime, and one day she had the idea to go to the nurse's office before lunch had started.

She figured she could wait it out there, even if it meant she had to skip eating her own lunch. A grumbling stomach until she got home was better than sticky pants and the sound of laughter ringing in her ears for the rest of the day. But the nurse looked up at her when she walked in, lowering her reading glasses to narrow her eyes at Clara. "What do you need?"

Clara had to think for a moment. "My stomach hurts." Truthfully, it did. A combination of hunger and fear usually did that to her.

"Did you eat breakfast this morning?" The nurse asked. Her nametag said "Ms. Jones" and it was decorated with stickers.

"Yes," Clara shifted on her feet, worried that she might say the wrong thing and Ms. Jones would send her back.

"Have you gone to the bathroom today? Besides peeing?"

Clara didn't know the correct answer for this one. "No?"

The nurse sighed, and Clara knew she had answered wrong. "You're probably constipated. Skinny kids like you usually have a problem with that." Clara didn't understand what she meant by that, but her heart was beating fast. She knew she had to say something else and say it quick.

"I think I might throw up," Clara said. Her heart was hammering, trying to escape.

The nurse looked at her for a long moment, and then sighed. "Okay, you can lay down on the bed for a bit." Clara sat down on the cot and the nurse got up from behind the desk. There was a mini fridge on the other side of the small office, and she got a juice box from it to give to Clara. "Drink this."

So, Clara sat with her legs dangling over the side of the cot, knocking her sneakers together when she swung her legs. She chewed the little straw that came with the juice box and watched the clock. It moved so slowly, the second hand barely struggling to make its circular laps for every minute. She wondered how long the nurse would let her stay…

Not long enough. According to her clock watching, less than thirty minutes. The nurse looked up from her computer, peering at Clara over the top of the screen. "Okay kid," she said. "I think it's time to go back to class."

Hearing those words, Clara's stomach began to hurt more. It was only 11:14. Lunch didn't end until 11:30. Panicked, she said the first thing that came to mind. "I'm not done with the Juicebox."

"You can take it with you," the nurse said.

Clara squirmed on the cot. "I think I need to go home." The nurse looked at her, eyes narrowed, as if she could look right through Clara and see the lie. "I'm not feeling well at all." It wasn't really a lie—she didn't feel well at all. In the coming years and into early adulthood, Clara would learn that "anxious" was not a temporary feeling, like happy, or excited, or bored. She would come to know that it was a sickness real enough to explain the stomach aches, the tiredness, or the feeling of her heart beating too fast when people looked at her. These things she would come to understand, but for now she just felt like a big fat liar.

She and Miss Nurse were locked in a silent battle of wills. Would Clara stay, or would she go? She couldn't think of another thing to say if it depended on her life. If she had to speak again, to open her mouth, she truly might throw up, and although the nurse might finally send her home for that, she would have to go back to the classroom to get her backpack, and if everyone saw then would be the pee girl *and* the barf girl. What would they do to her then? Better to keep her mouth shut and cross her fingers instead. It didn't usually work but it she was at her last resort.

At last, the nurse looked away and picked up the telephone. "Alright. Go sit out in the lobby and I'll call a parent to pick you up." Overjoyed, Clara had to remember to walk out of the office glumly. She was going home sick, after all.

If Mom was the one to come pick her up, though, she was not going to be happy with Clara. It was important to go to school. Clara was used to hearing her mom and Cassie argue about her grades. Mom was always saying that Cassie was very smart but wasn't applying herself, too focused on her hair, makeup, friends, boys, even the cheerleading, which had only lasted a few months of after school practice before Cassie said she didn't like it. She wasn't lazy; Clara knew it wasn't all the practices that made Cassie quit. She must have either truly not liked it or been very bad at it. No, Cassie wasn't lazy by far. She was a hard worker, almost obsessive to become the best—but only at the things she was already good at.

Clara was still thinking about Cassie when the front doors of the school parted, and not Mom or Dad but Grandma stepped inside! It truly was a lucky day. Grandma rarely drove on her own, but she had come to bring Clara home, to save her from school. Her low heels tapped on the shiny floors as she went to sign out for Clara, putting her signature on the clipboard. The floors were always clean in the front lobby, but rarely anywhere in the rest of the school.

"Okay Clara, I'm here," Grandma said, and Clara felt wonderful. Her stomachache was gone, and she put her backpack on, put her hand in Grandma's, and they walked out the doors together. Outside, the sun was shining, and a breeze stirred Clara's wispy hair. She could hear birds chirping, and water droplets from the sprinklers tickled her ankles when she walked on the grass to get to the car. The school was beautiful now that Grandma was with her.

In the car, before she turned the engine on, Grandma said, "Were those kids being mean to you again?"

It caught Clara off guard. She had only prepared for a scolding, or perhaps a questioning the truth about her "sickness." "No," she said. "Not really." But she didn't need to lie. Not to Grandma. She didn't need to feel embarrassed that the other kids didn't like her. "Yes."

Grandma started the engine. It was weird to see her driving, and she had her seat scooted all the way up so that she was almost pressed against the steering wheel. "They don't like me at all," Clara continued, but she didn't want to tell Grandma about the pee story. "I just wanted to come home today."

Grandma had successfully backed out of the parking spot, although it took her a few tries. Her thin lips were pressed together, a little bit of fuchsia pink lipstick smudged at the corner. "That makes me so sad," she said. "I'm sorry you're not having a good time at school. And I won't tell your mom and dad about today." Clara hadn't realized that her parents didn't know yet, that Grandma had been the one to answer the phone call at the house.

"Did you miss your lunchtime?" Grandma asked.

"Yes," Clara said.

They were out of the school parking lot now and on the main road, driving too slowly. That's probably why Clara had waited in the lobby so long for Grandma to get to school. "Let's go get you some lunch then."

They drove for about ten minutes, the car jerking with Grandma's uneven, inconsistent pressure on the pedal, until they reached historic downtown, which was really just a single street. Clara had a strange feeling in her chest, something like happiness and wonder. Grandma was so good. Maybe church really did make people be good. Grandma had saved Clara today. And her dad too, she thought, since Grandma adopted him. As a fifth grader, Clara hadn't known yet that sometimes it was wrong of people to try to save other people all the time. That sometimes, people like her grandma were saving other people for the wrong reasons.

But that day, Clara had really needed it, and her entire day had been turned around. Grandma parked the car crookedly, right in front of a little old diner. It had a blue neon sign that said OK Café! and lit up, but the light flickered in the letter A of café. But the light of the sign was faint under the light of the noon sun.

A bell at the top of the door tinkled when Clara pushed it open. The lady taking orders behind the cash register looked almost as old as Grandma, small and hunched over, her hair all frizzled white. Grandma ordered for both of them and Clara went to go sit down, basking in the awesome turn of events: clean pants, free from the tireless teasing of the other kids, lunch with just her and Grandma, and a break from school. Until tomorrow. Today was only Wednesday, after all.

After ordering, Grandma sat across from Clara in the booth she'd chosen by the window. They were the only customers in the diner besides an older man sitting in the back, with only a glass of orange juice and a newspaper laid out on the table in front of him. "Now, my dear," Grandma said. "Why don't you tell me what happened today."

But Clara didn't want to talk about it. She didn't want

to reveal anything more than the fact that she wasn't getting along with the other kids in the class. She didn't have an arch-nemesis or anything, but she didn't have any friends either. Not one.

At her silence, Grandma began again. "Okay. Why don't you tell me about a different day."

"Which day?" Clara asked, confused as to what Grandma wanted.

"Any day," she replied, stopping as the old cashier lady came out from the back with their drinks on a tray. A cherry coke and a lemonade.

After the old lady shuffled away, Grandma looked across the table at Clara with sparkling eyes. "You can tell me anything," she said. "How about a day that hasn't happened yet. Tell me a story, Clara."

"Make up something?"

"Yes," Grandma said. "Why don't you tell me a story about what Clara will do tomorrow at school when the other kids are mean to her."

Clara didn't tell stories. She liked to read them or have them told to her. She didn't know if she knew how to tell a story, but the light behind Grandma's eyes made her want to see if she could. She could try.

School was always difficult for me, but even more so that year we lived in Georgia. It was a hard transition. Things didn't go well with the other kids, and I wanted to stay home every day. But I was also very lonely. My grandma understood that. She always knew too many things. She wasn't just my first friend in Georgia, she was my first friend ever. I wish it had stayed that way, that we would have visited and kept in touch more after we moved back. She left me with some of my best childhood memories, and I only wish we had more.

By the time Clara put the pen down, it was past midnight. Looking up from her scrawled letters on the notepad, it felt like she had returned to the present after traveling back in time. It was draining, the feeling of trying to grasp fragmented memories that were so quickly retreating like a tide crawling back from her consciousness.

Clara didn't know much about relationships or how to socialize with unfamiliar people, but she knew about love. Especially as she had grown older, from teen years to her early twenties, she had fought a gnawing fear that she wasn't capable of connecting with other people. That maybe she had nursed her introverted tendencies into a thing of its own, an uncontrollable fear that had taken over every aspect of her life. She was used to living like she was helpless, and as uncomfortable as it was, that felt safe.

But looking down at the paper in front of her, she realized she had grown tired of herself. She had a strange feeling rising from her stomach, up into her chest and into her throat. She was an adult, with a job and an apartment of her own, and a completed college degree, but had she really changed since those days with her grandma? Had she changed at all?

Her phone buzzed once. Lit up briefly with a notification to update her software, and then winked off. She saw her face reflected in the black screen, staring back at her like some creature peering up from underneath a dark water. *You don't need to be afraid of her.* Hadn't Grandma once said something like that to her as she drifted off to sleep?

I'm not Clara whispered to the empty hotel room, with only herself to tell, only herself to listen. She was going to speak at the funeral because she was going to brave for her grandma one last time.

INTERLUDE

a story

Listen: let's start again.

When Clara was ten, she met the devil, and they became friends.

The devil is a girl her age, with horns and yellow eyes and sharp little teeth who lives in the forest behind her grandma's backyard. She is Grandma's guest because she has no home of her own, nor any creatures of her own kind.

Clara is frightened at first because she has never seen a girl like this before. She might have been a monster, except there is nothing so different about her aside from her horns, eyes, and teeth. She is alone and afraid too.

It takes time, as friendships usually do. Clara tells her mother and is sent to a child psychiatrist who doesn't understand or try to listen because she is an adult. Clara takes some pills and does worse in school because now her brain is messed up. She starts to hate school, dread it, fear it.

But Grandma knows about The Girl in the woods behind the fence.

The Girl needs a name, by the way. We'll call her…

Lucinda.

Little Clara and Lucinda begin a slow friendship. It takes so long that it's nearly over by the time it has begun.

At the end of their story, Lucinda saves Clara's life.

120

FOURTEEN

June 2022, Georgia

Today she wore the plain black dress that she had packed what felt like ages ago. It was a modest, long-sleeved garment, velvety black with a high neck. Her grandma would have hated it. She had always loved colorful, fashionable clothes, and above that, buying pretty things for Clara and Cassie.

It really did feel like an age since they flew over for the funeral, even though it had been less than a week since they'd arrived back in Georgia. Nothing much had happened aside from hanging around the house, cleaning, some meals as a family plus Tristan, and the nasty business with nosey Miss Stacie and the detectives, but that felt settled and over. At least Clara hoped so. How could something so frivolous as an accusation—no, a rumor, really, be anything more than short-lived?

After the funeral today, Clara and her parents would spend one more day at the house and then fly back early Monday morning. It wasn't over for Clara though. She'd have to come back eventually because of what Grandma chose for her. She felt like a tethered bird, chained around the ankle: she could only escape so far before feeling the heavy pull back to this place. The feeling made her skin crawl, and she scrubbed at her arms to make it go away.

She slipped her feet into the black flats she'd borrowed

from her mom. She didn't own the proper kind of clothes for this event. The dress she had found in her closet, hidden away between other dresses on hangers, but she couldn't remember where she'd even gotten it. It seemed to have just resurfaced when she needed it.

She realized she hadn't brought a bag other than the old backpack she used to travel. For now, she picked up the speech she'd written the night before and folded into a tiny square. Maybe too tiny. When she opened it up to read at the funeral, it would probably have deep creases like a rubix cube because of how many times she folded it. She undid the folding and opted for a simple fold in half. She didn't know why, but she tucked the strange note from under the bed inside the crease of her speech. She wanted that piece of Grandma with her today, creepy as the note itself was.

She checked her phone for the time and weather. It was just past nine in the morning, so they would be leaving soon to get there ahead of time. When she saw the temperature on the weather app, she cursed herself for bringing such a heavy, long sleeved dress. It was already seventy degrees outside, with a humidity of eighty two percent for today. She'd be drowning in her own sweat before the funeral started. There was nothing she could do about it at this point, so she gathered her things and stepped out into the hallway.

She opened her phone again and texted Cassie.

do you have a purse I can borrow?

Cassie texted back three minutes later.

U didn't bring a bag??

A few seconds later, Cassie sent over a picture with three bags on the bed. Judging by the size of the bed and the smooth white sheets, Clara could tell the hotel was nice. Tristan had probably paid for it.

*which one do u want? Im probably using the middle one
tho*

Clara zoomed in on the picture. None of them were black,
but they were all better options than her own dirty backpack.
The middle one that Cassie wanted was one of those classic
Louis Vuitton purses, a pretty chocolate brown with the LV
and four pointed star design in beige. As cute as the small
cream tote bag on the left was, it said "THE TOTE BAG MARC
JACOBS" in big bold letters on the front, which would probably be inappropriate. Clara texted back, opting for the bag on
the right: a small maroon clutch shaped like a heart. It was the
smallest option, but she didn't have much to bring anyway.

With that settled, Clara knocked on the door of her parents' hotel room. The walls were not soundproof, and she
could distinctly hear her mom's voice and the drone of a hair-
dryer. Her dad answered the door.

He was wearing a somber black suit, but Clara was used
to seeing him in nice clothes. His face was closed off, but he
had on his usual mask of a tight, distracted smile. "Danny,
who was that?" Her mom asked from the bathroom where the
blow-dryer was still whirring.

"Just me, Mom," Clara replied, knocking on the bathroom
door.

"Oh, good. Come help me with my necklace, will you?"
The door swung open, and Clara stepped inside the small
bathroom, taking the necklace that her mom held out to her.
It was a medium sized gold cross, small enough to be tasteful,
perfect for the occasion. Grandma had worn crosses just like
it, except hers had usually been large silver pieces studded
with gems and decorative cut-outs. Clara fumbled with the
little golden clasps of her mother's necklace, her short nails
slipping against the metal.

"How are you feeling this morning?" she asked after Clara
had finished with the necklace.

Clara felt a little blank. Passive. She felt like she should be feeling more, but for now she felt disconnected. Maybe once the funeral began, or when she saw the casket cradling Grandma's body, maybe then she would feel more.

"I'm okay," Clara responded. She was standing next to her mom in front of the bathroom mirror, looking at their reflections together. To her surprise, they looked quite similar. As a child Clara had been a bit darker than she was now, and people always said she looked like her dad because of that, even though they really didn't look alike at all. Cassie had always been the one that resembled their dad, with her thick wavy hair and big eyes. She had her dad's stronger features, and her mom's coloring. Clara, like her mom, had a squishy nose that she had never quite grown out of, wider cheekbones, and hair so straight and black that it looked limp. They were an unusual blend, Clara and her sister, and she sometimes wondered if there was anyone else in the world who was like them, besides each other.

She didn't think about these things much now as an adult, especially living in California. However, she was prepared to be blatantly reminded of it again today at the funeral. Who would be there? Mostly church folk, Clara assumed. She would likely recognize very few of the attendees, and that didn't exactly ease her nerves.

"You look as pale as a ghost," her mom said, drawing Clara back into the little bathroom they were standing in. Her mom was vigorously swirling a poofy brush in a circular blush compact. "Here, let me," she said, setting the brush to Clara's face. Pink powder went everywhere, and Clara had to keep from inhaling the stray particles that floated in the air afterward. The color was all wrong for her—too pink, like twin circles of bubblegum on her tawny skin. She resisted complaining, making a mental note to wipe it off in the backseat on the car ride over to the church.

It was unsettling, the three of them in black funeral attire. It almost felt like they were about to attend Cassie's funeral, not Grandma's. Clara always felt Cassie's absence, ever since she moved to the east coast and started her own life. Then, she thought more darkly, that Cassie's funeral would be soon, in the guise of a wedding. Instead of black, Clara might wear a bridesmaid dress and watch her sister be taken by Tristan, leaving them forever.

But first, Grandma. It felt like the beginning of the end.

Clara's dad didn't ask to read the eulogy she'd prepared, only if she was ready. She nodded, clutching the folded paper in her hands. She was grateful for that.

In the rental car, Clara was trying to set up the car's GPS, painstakingly moving the dashboard cursor to type out the letters and numbers of Northcrest Church's address. Her parents were loading the trunk with bushels of white lilies and long stemmed irises to decorate the casket. They were also quarreling over the free continental breakfast, which was driving Clara nuts.

"I'll just pick up coffees if you're worried about the time," Megumi said.

"No, we don't need it. We should get going." Danny said.

"It's still free though! Plus, Clara will get hungry. I'll just go run in quickly and see what they have."

"Clara's fine. Please Meg, let's just get going."

Once they had finished packing up and the GPS was all set, they made it out of the parking lot without pausing for the free breakfast. Maybe it was the nerves, but Clara felt on edge and quick to irritate. She was already regretting the heavy dress like she knew she would and was engaged in a futile attempt to smooth down the frizz of baby hairs around her face. She was glad that her dad had argued against grabbing the free breakfast. Her mom had always loved free things, even if they were of no use to her. She had been dragging Clara down to the lobby almost every morning since they'd arrived, sitting down at the sticky tables as early as seven a.m. to use their meal coupons. The breakfast was shitty, but Clara's mom had been making sure to go down every morning before they left the hotel. Even for a watered down coffee or artificially flavored yogurt to-go. Frankly, Clara was surprised the hotel they were staying at even had a continental breakfast; it was one step up from a motel.

Then she thought of Cassie and her luxurious room with Tristan. She was sitting in the backseat of the rental car, still clutching the eulogy in both hands as they drove, clutching it too tightly as she worked herself up into unwarranted anger over Tristan. It was easier to put all of her negative energy there, toward him. Did he feel big, staying with Cassie in a nice place while the rest of her family had been cooped up in that dark, dingy hotel by the side of the road?

The paper was becoming limp and warm, almost soggy where she worried at it. She was aware of her nerves and the weight of this day, and she was also aware that she was getting into useless, imaginary fights with Tristan to avoid thinking about anything else. Pushing those petty, projective thoughts out of her mind, she allowed herself to think of Grandma. According to the GPS, they were only fourteen minutes away from the church, but Clara closed her eyes and fell into a memory-dream.

She didn't dream of Grandma, though.

The air was wet and warm from the rain. Lying on her back in the grass, rainwater was seeping through her clothes, crawling to her skin. She could feel her own warmth in the ground, held by the mud, steam rising from the earth like the pavement after spring rain. When the mud was moist and warm like this, Clara liked to get on her hands and knees and dig, tearing away rich grass and scraping away layers of brown dirt and mud until finally, her hands came away stained red, gritty dirt under her nails and hearty lumps of red Georgia clay, ready for her hands to mold into whatever she pleased. That day she made little earthy bowls, the center pressed in with her thumbs to hold rainwater, acorns, weeds, and all the other grubby things she came upon in the backyard. She lined the little clay bowls up against the back fence, some of them already melting back into mud from the warmth of her hands. She put them there in a line and sat back, admiring her work. Then she waited, she didn't know why. There was nothing out there behind the back fence except for bugs, snakes, and other dangerous little creatures. And endless forest, wild, foreign land. When the clouds started to gather above her again, heavy with fresh rain, she got up and made her way back to the house, mud on her clothes and hands, face and hair. Back inside the safety of the house, she never saw the small, pale hands digging at the other side of the fence, burrowing and clawing beneath the rough wood of the fence, making enough room for her arms to squeeze beneath and grab the bowls, one by one. She never saw those hands, but the next day when she went back to check, she saw the beautiful blue mugs that had been left in place of her misshapen mud bowls. Cornflower blue, hand painted with yellow and purple pansies. Mugs she had used only a week ago. Mugs that had come straight from her grandma's kitchen cupboards.

Her eyes flew open when the car stopped. They had arrived at the church parking lot, but it felt like Clara was awakening from a decade of slumber. She couldn't remember what she had been dreaming of, but the way the June heat made her clothes cling to her, the funeral dress smothering like a second skin, it felt like she had opened her eyes at the gates of Hell. She rubbed at her face, tugged at the suffocating high neck of her dress, and felt around blindly for the eulogy. As the sounds and sights of her present surroundings came back to her, she saw the folded piece of paper on the floor of the car. She reached to pick it up, not noticing that the strange little note from under her grandma's bed was no longer tucked inside the eulogy where she had placed it earlier that morning.

She helped carry the casket flowers in, but the bushels felt like something much heavier than petals and stems. She looked up at the church entrance and dropped all the flowers she was carrying, hitting the parking lot ground with a resonant thud.

"Mom?" She called, her voice quavering.

"What, Clara?"

"This isn't Northcrest Church."

It had been a good twelve years since she had seen Grandma's chosen place of worship, but no amount of time could have mistaken the place they were not at. Northcrest Church had been a huge, semi-modern establishment, a place so happening that it could take up to an hour to get out of the parking lot after Sunday morning service. They had a cool pastor that had become as famous as a non-denominational Christian pastor from the suburbs could become, granted that his fame and appearance on the Today Show had come from being well-liked, not some racist old man that became famous on the internet for his backward evangelist messages. No, Chris Pruitt, whose picture Grandma had shown Clara on the internet so many years back, was a cool person by anyone's standards, and he had most definitely not been a pastor here.

No, this place was all wrong. It was a small, red brick thing, scarcely bigger than a house, with a deep triangular roof and a skinny steeple that rose into the air like a needle. Clara shuddered, Grandma's flowers on the ground completely forgotten.

"Clara, we already went over this," came her mother's voice. "Northcrest didn't have any reschedule bookings, since we had to cancel the original date last-minute for all that witchcraft nonsense."

No, no no. Clara was shaking her head. Surely, she would have remembered that conversation. She could have sworn she had specifically typed in the address to Northcrest Church in the car's GPS only a half hour ago.

Nearly stumbling over the flowers, she dashed back to the car and looked at the GPS screen from the front seat. It read "Destination, arrived: Stonecross Church." If Clara's parents were talking at her then, she couldn't hear them over the sound of her own frantic heartbeat, blood rushing in her ears. It shouldn't have been a big deal, and her mom had given a somewhat logical reason, but something felt off. Clara's stomach started to hurt so badly that she forgot about how much she was sweating.

Her mom came from around the car, her arms full. "Clara, come finish helping, there's still a lot—Oh!" She shrieked, nearly dropping her own flowers. "What happened? Why are the flowers on the ground? Clara, look at them," she said, rushing over to nurse the flowers, oblivious to Clara's sickly pallor. "These ones are ruined!"

Her dad came around next, hearing all the commotion. "What's going on?"

It wasn't right. Clara knew she was making things difficult, and she didn't want to ruin the funeral, but she couldn't shake the crawling paranoia that something was very wrong. She just couldn't let it go.

"This isn't Grandma's church," she said again, but her words felt hollow.

"I know, Clara, but the original plans were disrupted and we had to put together something else."

"What about the burial?" Would she still be buried next to Grandpa?

Her parents looked at each other, worry and exasperation showing in both of their knowing looks. *Here she goes again* Clara could imagine they were thinking. *Getting all riled up at an important event. Remember last Christmas? Or two Easter Sunday's ago with my mom's side of the family?* Clara's legs felt wobbly. She really did ruin everything. She was probably going to ruin Cassie's wedding too, having some sort of anxious fit or meltdown. *We should up her therapy to twice a week.* She hated herself.

Her mom stepped over the broken flowers and made her way into the church. With one last worried look at Clara, her dad followed. The heel of his dress shoes crushed a white lily by the church entrance that had blown away from the pile she dropped.

Clara kneeled down and gathered what flowers she could salvage. Tears burned hot in her eyes. Everything was burning.

FIFTEEN

Funeral Day

"We are a Jesus-church, a Jesus-people, trying to tell everyone the Jesus-story. For us, everything is secondary to Jesus. We elevate Jesus' name, live life Jesus' way, and won't stop until Jesus' fame is over everything!"

For such a small, plain church, their pamphlets were loud and gaudy. Clara was standing in the hall next to the restrooms, trying to catch her breath and collect herself. Her parents were going over things with the funeral officiant in the altar room. Luckily, no guests had arrived yet.

The Stonecross Church pamphlet she held in her hands was tacky, or maybe she was just in a bad mood. On the front panel was white Jesus with golden-tanned skin, on his knees, arms outstretched over his head to the glowing cloud that read "Come worship with us! Jesus accepts You!" Clara slid the pamphlet back into its acrylic slot on the wall. Didn't they know that Jesus wasn't white?

Clara hadn't been inside a church in many years. As kids in California, their mom only dragged the family out for Easter service, and sometimes Christmas. After she graduated high school, even that stopped, although Megumi Graham still

131

went to church every Sunday by herself. Clara didn't know how she could take it, all those perfect Japanese families with their full-blooded Japanese children.

The inside of this one was plain and unassuming. Aside from the few bulletin boards, the walls were mostly bare. There was a drinking fountain on the wall across from the bathrooms. The carpet was a horrible tan color that was tinged gray from years of people walking through. Clara had never been to those kinds of churches with tall domed ceilings and glistening stained glass windows. As big and popular as Northcrest Church was, it was also a modern building, and the place of worship was a huge auditorium with a black stage and band kit, as if it was also used for theater productions or a small concert venue during the weekdays.

She checked her phone. The funeral would start in less than an hour. Cassie and Tristan still hadn't arrived, and Clara needed that purse before the eulogy completely disintegrated in her restless, sweaty hands. She was deliberately trying to shut off her brain, lest she conspiracize herself into a panic. She was already feeling exhausted, and the day had only just begun.

Right on time, Cassie emerged through the front entrance, Tristan a step behind her. Clara peeled herself away from the wall, subconsciously tugging at the neck of her dress. Cassie was stunning, as always. She made it look like she was born to wear funeral attire. The dress was modest, for Cassie, but so effortlessly chic. Tristan looked sharp, too—they looked beautiful together, but Clara barely saw him next to the beauty of her sister. With a pang in her chest, she wished she looked like her. No, she wished she *was* her.

Cassie strode forward, gave Clara a side hug, and held out the heart-shaped bag she had chosen from the picture. It was even cuter in real life. "Thanks," Clara said, stuffing her phone and the eulogy into the bag.

Clara could tell the exact moment when Cassie took in her appearance, because her mouth twisted like she was about to bite into a lemon. "What are you wearing? Clara, you're sweating like a pig! And you look... unwell."

"I'm fine," Clara said, a bit breathlessly. But if she had looked into a mirror that moment, she would have seen a sick, ugly creature looking back at herself. Whatever had come to the funeral that day was not her, not quite. Or maybe it was only the worst parts of her. Jealousy, fear, and paranoia, consumed with anxiety that made her legs weak. Yes, she did feel unwell.

"Well," Cassie said, with one last glance up and down at Clara, "should we go in?"

Tristan was saying something, but Clara heard her voice talk over his. "I need a breath first. I'll meet you inside in a bit."

She watched Cassie and Tristan turn away from her and walk toward the sanctuary. Then she spun around and dashed into the bathroom behind her, but it felt like her body was moving in slow motion. She saw her feet in front of her body, taking her forward, one foot blurring in front of the other. Sweat trickled from her forehead and temples, stinging her eyes and making her vision swim. She wasn't sure if it was her anxiety or heat stroke that was making her feel so physically sick. It could have been both.

She stumbled into the bathroom, the soles of her mom's flat shoes slipping on the watery floor. Water, she thought. Unbalanced, Clara flung herself at the nearest porcelain sink, turning the nobs on both sides. A strong spray came from the tap, so fast and forceful that the stream looked white instead of clear. She stuck her head under the faucet, drowning her face underwater. It wasn't very cold, but it would do.

She stayed like that, awkwardly crouched with her face in the bathroom sink until she choked and sputtered from inhaling the water. She broke free from the spray, staggering away from the sink, coughing and hunched over until her body stilled. The sink was still running when she heard someone enter the bathroom.

Clara heard a woman's harsh voice muttering in annoyance in a foreign language. Sink water still dripping down her face, Clara saw the pointed tips of snakeskin patterned shoes first. An old memory came to the front of her mind, a mixture of childish fear and discordant, black and white keys. "You," the woman said, and Clara looked up into her face.

Miss Mischa looked less like herself, or at least what Clara remembered of her from those weekly piano lessons twelve years ago. Her hair, once so neat and sharp, now fell in brittle wisps around her head, carefully arranged to cover sparse areas and bald spots where her scalp, spotted with age, was bare. Her eyes had a milky sheen, cloudy blue like a blind, walking corpse. Her lips were thin and drawn, sticky with bright red lipstick. She looked more ancient than Grandma.

"Which one are you?" Miss Mischa said again, one long, bony finger pointed at Clara's chest.

"Clara," she said, surprised that Miss Mischa remembered who she was. "The younger one." But then, how many people at the service today would look like Clara and her sister? How many people had Miss Mischa ever met that had the sisters' unplaceable blend of Megumi and Danny Graham's features?

Miss Mischa grumbled. "You still play?"

"No," Clara said. "Ma'am."

"What about your sister?"

"No," Clara said, all too aware of the sink water dripping down her face, trickling beneath her dress and mixing with her sweat. She was so uncomfortable. "No. We didn't have a piano after we moved back."

She grumbled again. "A waste." Of time, she must have meant. Surely not talent, as both Cassie and Clara were about as musically gifted as worms.

Clara didn't know what else to say, but she knew she should say something. "Thank you for coming today."

Miss Mischa muttered something unintelligible. Then she said, "I knew her longer than you've been alive, girl. I should be the one thanking you for coming back after leaving your old woman alone in that house for years. Do you know what it can do to a person to be alone for so long?"

Visions of settled dust and cobwebs came to Clara's mind. The handwritten note hidden amongst trash and junk underneath Grandma's bed. Processed and packaged food, old water glasses, Grandma, all alone in that empty house for over a decade. And the sound of her panicked, rough voice coming from that strange phone call a few months ago. Yes, Clara had some idea of what isolation could do to a person, and it horrified her.

Clara opened her mouth to defend herself. Or her family, her dad, her Grandma. Miss Mischa took one last indignant look at her, and then went into the nearest stall, closing the door in Clara's face. Clara closed her mouth, defeated. What was there to say, anyway? She was right. How had they been content knowing that Grandma was spending the end of her life alone.

She tore a brown paper towel from the dispenser and scrubbed at her face, wiping away sweat, water, and makeup. Then she left the restroom and walked into the sanctuary without looking back.

Stonecross Church had no organ. A feeble old lady played the piano, but it sounded wrong, like it was in need of tuning. This day felt like disgrace on top of disgrace to her grandma's memory. Northcrest would have had it all. It didn't mean much to Clara, unfamiliar as she was with a church setting, but she knew it would have meant everything to Grandma for her service to take place at the church she'd been going to for upwards of forty years. This place they were at meant nothing to Grandma. It had nothing to do with her except that plain steeple on the roof and her picture displayed on an easel next to her dark cherry casket. Besides that, it was just a room with her dead body. It wasn't anything special, not like it should have been for her. Even the flowers that they had placed on her closed casket looked skimpy because of the ones Clara had dropped and ruined.

A traditional hymn began, and guests raised from the pews to sing. Clara didn't recognize the tune, but it was slow and droning, starting soft and dull with reluctant voices from the crowd. Clara's eyes traced over the words to the hymn on the small slips of paper everyone had been given. *The night is dark, and I am far from home.* She closed her eyes and tried to still her mind by focusing on the words. *Lead thou me on, amid the encircling gloom.*

She had recognized almost no one as the guests arrived, floating in through the doors donned in black. Her dad had separated from them to greet a few people, and Clara looked around, wondering who all these people were and who they had been to her grandma. She wondered how many years it had been since they might have seen her, or if any of them had been a friend to Debbie Graham in her last years of life. She wondered, guiltily, what her grandma had done to fill her last lonely days.

By the time the music stopped, Clara's mind had been lulled to slow, and she watched and listened to the event before her, feeling disconnected as if she was watching something tragic but far away on the evening news channel. There were words spoken by the unfamiliar officiate, prayers read that Clara did not know, and then the call for her eulogy to be read. Perhaps it was a blessing that her mind was moving slowly, all thoughts and feelings as uninspired as gray slugs. She pulled the piece of paper from Cassie's heart-shaped purse and stood on surprisingly steady feet. The officiate left the podium for her, and Clara found herself there, standing behind her grandmother's casket, faced with an unrecognizable audience. She couldn't even spot Miss Mischa.

She held the wrinkled paper out before her and spoke into the little padded microphone attached to the podium, sticking out like an antenna. Her lips brushed the microphone when she spoke. "Good morning. My name is Clara Graham, and Debbie Graham was my grandmother." She looked down at the words and swallowed, trying to moisten her dry throat. Why hadn't she practiced beforehand?

She looked down, past Grandma's casket, at her family, sitting in the first row, directly in front of her and Grandma. Her dad nodded at her, and she looked down at the paper and spoke again. "Our time together was brief, but she was and always will be my first friend. School was always difficult for me, but even more so that year we moved to Georgia." In her mind's eye she saw herself standing at the front door of that house with her family and their suitcases, and her little, fashionable grandma opening the door of that magical house. She always wore bright colored skirts and matching bright lipstick. The casket in front of her now was giant for such a small woman. It seemed so big that she wondered if Grandma was lying in there with half the belongings of her house.

"School was hard," Clara said again, dragging herself back into the bleak room. "I wanted to stay home every day. But I think I was also very lonely." She was ashamed to hear herself read those words, and immediately wished she could suck them back in. Who was she to speak of loneliness? While she'd been hiding herself away in her one-bedroom apartment back in California, her grandma had been wasting away, alone in her crumbling mansion.

Clara cleared her throat, feeling an intense heat in her face, and continued to read. "My grandma understood that. She always knew too many things."

There it was. Gone was her detachment and passivity. Clara tried to keep reading, knowing that the sooner she finished, the sooner she could sit back down, but she felt an overwhelming sense of sadness, anger, and shame. She looked up, willing the wetness to stay in her eyes. If she looked down at the paper again, she feared it would all come flooding out.

Looking out into the crowd, her tears blurred everyone into a sea of strangers. It was burning her, keeping everything in. Then, all at once, her face went slack.

Nobody else at the service saw what she saw, and they would never guess what it was that stole the color right out of Clara Graham's face. Some people were nodding off, others were checking their phones, whispering to their partners, staring blankly at the floor, or trying to figure out what kind of ethnic background Debbie Graham's granddaughter had. For the most part, people were in their own heads.

The funeral officiant stood off to the side, watching the eulogy delivery with some distress. The girl was obviously having a hard time, and she was taking a while to get her words out. She kept pausing and looking out into space, seeming lost in her own personal memories. None of this was surprising, though. He had officiated many funerals, both for people and families he knew, as well as complete strangers like this particular funeral. They would get through it. He had observed many such occasions.

Cassie Graham, who considered it a particular talent of hers to make people squirm, was almost desperate enough to squirm herself right now. It hadn't been that surprising that Dad had chosen Clara to prepare the eulogy. She'd spent a lot of time with their grandma when they lived in her house, and Cassie knew that her poor sister didn't have a lot going on in her life at the moment. She was an antisocial, nervous wreck with a dead-end job and no prospects of ever getting married and starting a family of her own. Her little sister was attached to the idea of their "family" and obsessed with keeping things the same. If she could, she knew Clara would probably live with their parents forever, stuck as a child. This moment, with Clara flubbing at the microphone, staring into space like a lunatic, was mortifying for Cassie to endure with Tristan sitting beside her. She couldn't bear to look at him. She hadn't made any time for her fiancé to get to know her sister before their wedding, in fact, she had been specifically keeping Clara from him this whole time for exactly this sort of reason. She was strange. And yet Cassie couldn't look away.

Danny Graham was watching his daughter with pain. She had been a lonely child and that affliction had carried on into her adulthood, the way she shut herself away from everyone and everything. It had warmed his heart to see her as a child with his mother, giving her the love and adoration she craved where he could not. If not for that year in Georgia, he wondered how Clara might have turned out for the worse. Danny had a lot to be grateful to his adoptive mother for, and perhaps her friendship and comfort to his young child was one of the greatest things. Poor Clara. If he had known the reading would take such a toll on her, he would have read it in her place. She must have been in so much pain.

No, they would never know what Clara saw in that moment. Even she couldn't believe her own eyes. She rubbed at her eyes, clearing the gathering tears away. There, in the back row, occupying an empty bench all to herself, was The Girl. Horns and all.

She locked eyes with those terrifying, golden eyes at the back of the room. The devil was real, and she was *here*. She looked the same, after all these years, and her presence was tearing open all of Clara's obscured memories like talons on tissue paper.

Clara let out a small noise of fear, which the audience interpreted as a sob. She knew she had to finish reading the eulogy, but she couldn't tear her eyes away from that Girl sitting in the back row. She didn't smile, but Clara knew that those sharp little teeth were waiting inside her closed mouth.

Clara tried to finish the speech. But her hands were trembling, and the eulogy ripped in her sweaty hands. Her mind was completely blank now, emptied out of shock and fear. "I'm sorry!" Clara said at last, rushing from the podium, but it came out like a squeak.

SIXTEEN

Nobody spoke to Clara about what happened, and that was a mercy. She could feel Cassie giving her looks throughout the rest of the ceremony, and then again at the burial site as the casket was lowered into the ground and their grandma's body went down into the earth forever. Cassie was giving her a heavy stare, like she knew what Clara knew. But what was there to know? After the train wreck of her speech, she had sat down in the pews again and looked back over her shoulder. The Girl was gone. Of course she was. She had never been there in the first place. Clara knew she always had to find ways to mess things up, and if there wasn't anything around to fear, her mind would conjure up something. For someone who dreaded being the center of any attention, Clara felt like she had been a horrible attention hog. Then maybe that's how those kinds of people were, she thought bitterly. The kinds of people who claimed, even believed on the surface level that they hated attention, but always did something to make themselves the center of it.

She had done a terrible job and made a big loud mess of it too. In fact, she should probably go ahead and ask Cassie to live stream her wedding so that Clara could watch from afar, lock herself up in her apartment and not ruin anything else for anyone in her life. But there was still the refreshment hour back at the house, and on the car ride back, Clara vowed to keep it together.

She had been a quiet, timid child for the most part, with the extent of her troublemaking being soft crying or clinginess to her parents. There had been several occasions in her life, however, that had turned into huge meltdowns on her end, sometimes publicly, and two incidents that had landed her in short psychiatric hospitalizations. One had been in Georgia, late May when school had almost ended, and perhaps it had been the catalyst for the Graham's moving back to California. The other instance had been more recently, when she was nineteen. It had only solidified her lifelong (nineteen years) belief that the best way to not let bad people into your life was to not let anyone in at all.

Yes, Clara Graham was a private person, and she liked feeling like she could occupy zero space in the world. But she knew that that in itself held its own consequences, and that she had a pattern of exploding every few years in order to reset. Although it seemed like Cassie had mini explosions daily when they were teenagers and lived together at home, she had never had debilitating meltdowns like Clara. Cassie could bounce back, but Clara took time to recover. She knew all this about herself, and she was keenly, shamefully aware of it in that moment. She needed to do better. She *wanted* to do better. She was getting too old for these kinds of fits. Somewhere on the road between the church and Grandma's house, she pulled out her phone and logged into her client portal on Dr. Ashley's website, upping her weekly sessions to twice a week.

When their car pulled into the driveway and the house loomed above them, Clara remembered her seventeen-thousand square foot inheritance and almost relapsed into another panic. It was too much; it was too damn much. She wanted to go home. She missed her dog. She needed to get out of this dreadful dress that was melting into her skin.

But the funeral guests would all be arriving within the

next half hour, bringing along home-cooked food and old sentiments. The day continued to charge ahead at her, and Clara was losing her grip. She needed a break. She had done well with changes in her schedule or routine, and this past week of being back at the house was pushing her into an uncomfortable mental space. It felt like day-to-day surprises, from the initial witchcraft rumors to finding out the contents of her grandma's will, all of which was further aggravated by her own memories attached to the house and the people she lived in it with: Mom, Dad, Cassie, Grandma.

And those were the only people she felt belonged in this house. Clara knew every room and staircase and window like she knew her own body, but now, if only for this afternoon, the house would be opened to a world of strangers. They were people who knew her grandma, but they were nonetheless strangers to Clara. She thought back to Miss Mischa's words in the bathroom: *I knew her longer than you've been alive.* Maybe all the guests would think of Clara and her family as the strangers. That was more than likely the case, and the realization filled Clara with a sick chill. How foolish of her to think that Grandma's life and livelihood had revolved around Clara and Cassie and their parents. How could it have, when they had been so unabashedly absent from her life except for that one year they lived together, and then only short, inconsistent meetings for the holidays in the years after. In twelve years, they had only spent about a week's worth of days altogether. It felt despicable for Clara to be given the house when she felt she had done close to nothing to be a part of her grandmother's life.

Oh, and what a life. As the day progressed and funeral service finished, Clara learned things about her grandma that she had never had the curiosity to think about. After she had spoken disgracefully and fled from the podium, a slideshow had played. There had been pictures of her, old black and white photos with yellowing edges, scanned into a slideshow and displayed on a screen with a flash drive and church projector. There were pictures of her as a baby in a long white gown on the day of her baptism, all the way up to her high school graduation in 1948. There were her wedding pictures from 1952, beachside on the Florida Gulf Coast, standing barefoot in the sand with Clayton Graham, a grandfather that Clara only had the faintest memories of.

And there were pictures of Clara's dad as a child. It was so strange, almost uncanny to see the little brown boy in her grandma's arms, rich ebony hair and large eyes, sitting on a retro floral-print sofa that was still in the house to this day, only it had been moved to the basement because the style was so outdated, replaced with those pretty cream couches in the sitting room. Yes, that was her dad in those pictures, slides rolling on the church projector of him toddling around in rooms out of Clara's own childhood memories. It was hard to imagine the house before she and her family had moved in with Grandma back in 2010, hard to imagine that life in that house didn't just start when Clara stepped into it for the first time, but decades before. Before the idea of Clara had even existed. It was hard to imagine Grandma or her dad as any other way besides how she knew them.

Her mind was flooded with memories of the past and anxiety about the future, so Clara felt out of touch with the event unfolding before her. The front entrance had been propped open, allowing guests to come in an out on their own time. A warm afternoon breeze floated in with the arriving guests, coming in slowly at first, and then all at once, flooding the front entrance with bodies. The house had always been too big for its own good, but now that it was filling with guests and loud voices, Clara wished for it to be empty again.

It had only been two days since she proposed the idea of an estate sale to her dad, in hopes that maybe some of her grandma's old friends would stop by and maybe tell her something, anything, about the last few months of her life. Now, however, she felt so far away from that version of herself from two days ago, the one who was curious and motivated to figure out her grandma's strange behavior to the degree that she had even considered talking to people she didn't know. She had gone so far as to *suggest* people come over for an estate sale. Today, she felt very far away from that outgoing prospect.

Somehow, it seemed like there were more people here at the house than there were at the funeral service. Clara was standing as far off to the side in the main foyer as she could without going into another room entirely, and she watched the steady stream of guests arriving. Few guests arrived alone; most brought a spouse or arrived in groups as if this whole affair was an evening gala. At twenty minutes past two in the afternoon, Clara guessed there might have been upwards of seventy people that had entered through the front doors. She wondered, angrily, if some people were showing up for an "open house" and not because they knew her grandma or had attended the church service at eleven. At least everyone had the sense to bring food.

The night before, Clara's mom had been stressed out about how much food to prepare for the funeral guests at the house afterward. "I don't know what kind of funerals you've been to," her dad had said to her mom, "but over here, the food will take care of itself." So, Clara's mom had settled on putting out an electric kettle and an assortment of teas, and the rest of it did take care of itself.

It was like the twelve days of Christmas, but with each new party of guests that arrived, four, five, six, seven more dishes of casserole appeared. Tupperware covered with tin foil, each with a different type of casserole. Green bean, corn, chicken, tuna noodle, cauliflower, squash, broccoli, and a whole host of unidentifiable ones. With the kitchen island covered, Clara didn't even know what a casserole was anymore. But there wasn't anything that *wasn't* a casserole, either. Food was always a good thing at social gatherings, though, because she could look busy with a full plate in her hands.

The incoming flood of guests seemed to be slowing, so Clara filled her plate until it was warm and heavy in her hands. Then, she looked around. Truly, the only familiar faces were her family and Tristan, and it looked like her parents were busy talking with guests and introducing themselves. At social gatherings like these, Clara grew more uncomfortable with every year that passed, and she was painfully aware of her dependency on her parents. She wouldn't embarrass herself or her parents any further today, so she set off towards Cassie and Tristan, who were standing together against the wall. Her sister's back was to her, but Tristan locked eyes with Clara and snaked his hand around her waist, resting low enough on her backside to make Clara shrink away. She felt his eyes still on her as she hurried away, the plate of casseroles still warm and heavy in her hands. She no longer felt able to eat. She felt like a child today, constantly on the verge of a fit. What was Tristan's deal? Was he purposely trying to steal her sister away? Or maybe, had Cassie warned him about her? Maybe she had told him about how Clara had issues. Or maybe he had observed that from her performance today.

She couldn't take it. Clara found herself locked in the bathroom, sitting on the toilet. Except the lid was down, and she was using it as a seat. The warm plate of food was balanced across her knees, and the plastic fork was clenched in her hand like a weapon. She sat in there for a while, passing the time by tasting the casseroles, but eventually someone tugged at the locked doorknob, and she knew her time was up. To keep up the act, she flushed the empty toilet and washed her hands. When she exited the bathroom with her plate of food, the lady waiting gave her a strange look. That was reasonable, Clara thought, because it was definitely gross to bring a plate of food into the bathroom, but as she tried to walk past, the lady grabbed her arm.

"You're the little one, weren't you?" She said, but it wasn't so much of a question as an accusation. Clara paused, studying the woman's face. She was old, as most of Grandma's friends were, but not quite as old as the rest of them. Her skin was dull and wrinkled, but there was a clearness in her eyes that made Clara wonder who she was, and when they had met before.

Clara forgot to reply, but the lady went on. "Yes, you are. I can see it in your coloring. Strange little family." It was a rude thing to say, but the lady didn't seem aware of that. "I remember when you moved here."

Clara finally spoke up. "I'm sorry, who are you?"

She didn't look offended. "I'm Lacey Bristol, your neighbor a few houses down. I'm not surprised you don't remember me. I only saw you a few times. You used to peer down at us from your little perch in the stairs during our weekly Bible Study."

Clara didn't know what to say, so she just stood there with the plate in her hands. Miss Bristol kept talking. "She was always going on about you, the littler one, even after you packed up and left. Said you were shy as a bunny but such a sweet thing. I'm glad it was you who ended up reading her eulogy, even if it was short. She was a good one, Debbie. It's a shame to hear all the rumors."

Clara didn't need to ask which ones. But she did say, "Why did they start saying those kinds of things about her? Where did the rumors come from?"

Miss Bristol was shaking her head. Gray pearl earrings bobbed at her sagging earlobes. "Oh, that bitch across the street was always throwing hissy fits about your grandmother," she said, catching Clara off guard with the change of tone in her voice. She was talking about Miss Stacie, of course. "But rumors don't always start from nothing."

She paused then, shooting Clara a knowing look as if she expected her to put the rest together herself. "What do you mean?" Clara asked, finding herself leaning in closer to the older lady.

Miss Bristol sighed, shifting her weight on her feet and looking around as if people might be listening, even though they were standing in the hallway in front of the bathroom. "Well, maybe I shouldn't. It won't do any good to go spreading things after the fact."

"No, it wouldn't," Clara found herself saying. It was one of the things that had made her the angriest with the situation, hearing such blatant lies being spread about her grandma after her death, poisoning the memory of Debbie Graham. But after being back for a week, Clara felt she was getting a taste of something strange going on, something from the past that was spilling into the present that she couldn't make sense of yet, not without more information. "It would not be good... to spread tales," Clara repeated, "but indulge me, if you would." It felt gross to be whispering like this only hours after the funeral, but Clara needed information and Miss Bristol didn't need any more convincing. It was only human nature to gossip.

The woman looked around one more time, eyes darting around the empty hallway, before leaning in closer and putting a hand up to the side of her face, shielding the world from what she was about to whisper to Clara. "Well, I *heard* that she was spending a lot of time out there in that deep backyard," Miss Bristol whispered, and her breath was hot on Clara's face. Still, Clara didn't move away, feeling like she was on the edge of hearing something terrible.

"You know, old women like us just don't do that, no matter how nice a day it is. Sit out front, yes, but not wander around out back for hours in the mud and wood. There's ticks and bats and poisonous vines."

"You mean, she was going behind the fence?" Clara asked.

"Yes," Miss Bristol said, and there was an excited edge to her voice that made Clara sick. People really did love to gossip. But Clara had a feeling that there was something real about this, something that might start to explain everything.

"Did anyone actually see her out there?" Clara said.

"Yes, yes. Word travels fast, and folk get nervous."

"Okay, but did *you* ever see her out there? Doing any-thing... strange."

"Well, no," the Miss Bristol admitted, and she had the decency to at least look ashamed. "But... well, there was this one night, maybe a few months ago," she said, and then paused. "But listen, honey, I don't want to make you get all nervous. It's just that one night, when my youngest daughter was visiting home, she found your grandmother in our front lawn. She had wandered all the way over in the dark, barefoot and in her nightgown. It was, I don't know, maybe eight or so in the evening, but who could say how long she'd been out there?" Miss Bristol was speaking in a fast, low voice. "When me and my husband came out, she didn't seem to recognize us, wouldn't come sit in our car and let us take her home. Said she was looking for someone. But as far as anyone here knew, she'd been living all alone in that house for over a decade since Clayton passed and your family moved back west."

They took you away, but won't you come back home to me now?

Clara thought of the little note from under the bed that she'd been carrying around, and suddenly realized she didn't know where it was. "I have to go," she blurted, too embarrassed to look Miss Bristol in the face after what she'd just heard. It scared her, and it made her angry. They should have been there with her. What kind of people leave a ninety year old woman alone in a house across the country? And where was that goddamned note?

She hurried out into the main room where all the guests were. The sounds of so many people in one place, plates and glassware clinking was all a blur in her ears. She needed to find that heart shaped purse.

There were so many people in her grandma's house.

Her house. Filled with bodies, she barely recognized the place. A house this big and yet it wasn't meant to be filled with people. It didn't feel right. Clara wouldn't do anything about it, though. She never did do anything important, and she hated herself for that.

The information Miss Bristol had shared with her in the bathroom hallway was too chilling to digest at the moment. An old woman, wandering barefoot hours past sundown. An old woman that was her grandma, the grandma who had been her first friend and saving grace as a child. Clara was so angry with herself; she could feel the emotion curling up inside like a piece of paper blackening in a fireplace. She should have taken that phone call back in March more seriously. She should have been more terrified by it. She should have told her dad, and they should have flown down immediately. Maybe things would have turned out different.

She felt hot and angry and sick. She shouldn't have eaten those casseroles in the bathroom. Her stomach was churning, and she needed fresh air, away from the noise and heat of all the bodies. She set down her plate and left the main area. In the back hallway it was quieter, with only a few people lingering, and Clara made her way up the staircase to the upstairs floor. She didn't know where she was going, but she wasn't in the correct state to talk to anyone else, or to hear any more rumors that were possible truths.

Once she reached the top of the stairs, the noise had diminished to a hum below. Their old bedrooms were up here, hers and Cassie's, still furnished as they'd left them. Clara floated into her old bedroom. When they'd moved in, Grandma had let them choose a color to paint their new bedrooms. Hers was still baby blue, after all these years. The white shelves on the walls were lined with those beautiful porcelain dolls that Grandma had given her when they first moved in, the ones that her dad had not let her bring back to California when they left. Clara ran her fingertips lightly over the delicate fabrics of their dresses, disturbing a layer of dust. The curtains were drawn back, and afternoon sunlight poured into the room, illuminating the particles of dust in the air. Clara realized for the first time that day how beautiful it was outside. She walked to the window that faced the backyard, pulled the latch, and pushed the window open. She could see all the back property from here, almost all the way out to the back fence. From this window upstairs, she had that feeling again that she'd had as a child, like this place was an entire planet away from their home in California.

Then, a small movement caught her eye on the patio down below. Someone had opened the back kitchen door and was standing on the patio, looking out into the deep woods behind the house.

Ever since she had come back to Georgia, to this old house from her past, a part of her mind that had been sleeping for twelve years had been stirring. There was something in her, a small crack that had formed on the neat, predictable surface of her adult life. And now, staring down at the little horned girl on the patio, that thing in Clara shattered like glass.

She climbed out onto the windowsill, sweat trickling down her face. The edge of her funeral dress snagged and ripped as she jumped from her childhood bedroom window to follow after that devil girl into the woods.

PART 2

What She Found There

SEVENTEEN

May 1952

Debbie Jean Compton hated her parents. When she had kids of her own, she was going to do it all different. For starters, any daughter of hers would be allowed to begin dating once they reached sixteen years of age. Like anything, girls and boys needed practice with each other, and Debbie wouldn't stand to have her daughter turn out like she had: nearly twenty-three years old and desperately seeking an engagement.

Melinda, her old friend from school, had gotten married to her high-school sweetheart last year at twenty years old. Even that was late; many people, including Debbie, had thought that they would marry right out of high school. But Debbie wasn't so lucky as that. Her parents had always been incredibly strict about everything concerning their only daughter, only child. She had never had a boyfriend up until six months ago. Dashing and handsome as he was, Alan Whitney wasn't quite what she had always dreamed of. He hadn't introduced her to his parents yet. He hardly cared to meet hers. But he was nice enough, in other ways, and despite her inexperience, Debbie knew she had a lot to offer. She was beautiful, always well dressed in the height of feminine fashion, coming from a wealthy and established family. The Compton's had been long-time residents of Georgia, and members of America's

South even farther back. And, as the cherry on top, she played the piano wonderfully. Surely Alan's parents would have seen and heard her playing at Sunday service. They'd meet properly soon enough, she expected.

Tonight, his car was waiting on the street for her, a few houses down for extra measure. He drove a tan Chevy Bel Air, the newest model. It was so fast and sleek, and Debbie loved to go around in it with him. Sitting in the passenger seat, windows rolled down, she felt she finally bore some semblance of her age.

So tonight, like most nights recently, she went out through her childhood bedroom window. She still lived with her parents because she didn't have a husband. She prayed every week, as her last prayer before bed, that her life would change soon. She was ready for it.

It was not a far drop. All she had to do was throw down her heels first (landing in wet grass in heels was no good) and then be careful not to snag her skirt as she climbed out the window. It was a large window, made for sneaking out in the night.

She hadn't known that this was the last time she would ever go through that window to sneak out. At least, not as the same person.

She landed nicely in the grass, carefully balanced to remain upright while also absorbing the fall in her knees. She wondered how much longer she'd have to do this. Her body was only getting older and soon she feared she wouldn't be landing as nicely. Alan would have to propose. Either that or agree to meet her parents over dinner if this sneaking out was ever to be rid of. Desperate as she was, she wasn't going to do it forever. No well-bred lady should.

She hadn't known how final one night could be.

The summer heat was already creeping in mid-May. These were the months for spying lightning bugs, going to the lake, bright patterned dresses, and leaving windows open for the breeze and for lovers. Beneath her carefully curled hair,

Debbie could feel beads of sweat forming on the back of her neck. She slipped her feet into her shoes and hurried away from her own house, furtive like a thief in the night. She told herself there was no reason to feel guilty. Even though her parents didn't know, God did, and that brought her comfort. He saw everything, and she wasn't doing anything *wrong*.

Alan was parked two houses down as usual, in front of 957 Evergreen Lane. Nobody lived there since the previous family had moved out, so nobody minded the tan chevy parked out in front of the house, engine running and headlights blazing like two eyes in the dark. They blinded her as she came closer, and she had to put her arm over her eyes.

She opened the car door, swooping up her skirt as she stepped in. She could smell his citrusy soap, the leather of the car, and the dizzying air of gasoline. It was an aroma that drew a smile from her lips.

He greeted her with a kiss on the cheek. "Hey Dolly."

She laughed and leaned into him, even though he'd said it a hundred times before. "It's *Debbie*, you flutter-bum."

"My Debbie Dolly," he said, and put his hands on the steering wheel.

Alan wasn't a planner. Some girls might have thought that rude, even presumptuous, but Debbie felt exhilarated. She never knew what they'd do, where they'd go. Sometimes they'd drive into town and get a soda, maybe go dancing. Other times they might drive aimlessly, stopping on a quiet road, a park, or a lake here and there. There weren't any proper lakes in the nearby area, not unless you went east, or west for that matter. But there were some still, murky bodies of water with docks to sit by. Swamps, if anything. At least it meant privacy.

Debbie hoped they weren't headed for one of those "lakes" tonight. She had chosen her blouse and skirt carefully, as well as arranged her hair and powdered her face. She hoped they might go somewhere well-lit and clean, where he might look upon her and notice her loveliness.

They rode a while in silence, which she didn't mind. They'd been seeing each nearly every other day like this, and she liked to lean out against the window and hear the rush of wind in her ears. The summer night was coming alive as it always did at this time of year, and if she paid attention, she could hear the bullfrogs crying and the hum of cricket-song, thrumming like a chant against the warm night air.

They were spending so much time together recently— surely, he was planning *something*, whether he was a planner or not. "Where to tonight?" She said, growing curious as they drove farther into the night. They were away from her neighborhood and the town, the car speeding steadily past empty farmland and coming upon the quiet backwoods.

"It's a surprise," he said, throwing Debbie a cheeky smile. "A surprise place for something special."

Her heart leapt up beneath her breastbone. He was going to propose. She looked away from him and out her side of the open window to hide her smile. She knew that something important was going to happen tonight. She had known it from the pit in her stomach as she climbed from her window and walked down the dark street to his car.

A surprise location. For something special.

Slyly, she peered down at her hands. Her nails weren't painted, but they were shaped neatly, filed into a pleasing almond shape that was classy and fitting enough to sport a new diamond ring.

Alan slowed the car at the traffic light. They were riding again in silence, and Debbie was too giddy and nervous and excited to speak. There was no one else on the road, so Alan looked both ways and then blew past the stoplight. *He must be just as nervous as me*, Debbie thought.

When she was lost in her daydreaming, Debbie sometimes felt that the world went on without her while she was painting beautiful fantasies in her mind. She had always loved stories, especially those of her own fiction. Now, as they drove, she was imagining the ring, the shape, the cut of the diamond, and how it might look on her left hand. She was creating her wedding dress with her mind's eye. She wanted puff sleeves and a cinched waist. Small, creamy pearls stitched onto the sleeves and bodice. Would it be an autumn wedding, then? Or perhaps a winter one, if they were to have a long engagement. A long engagement might be best. She still had to meet his parents, and he hers.

The road flew beneath her as she imagined these beautiful things, Alan speeding them along through the darkness. She had no idea where they were or what direction they were going. In the dark of night, everything looked different. Unrecognizable. But she felt safe because she was with Alan.

She woke up from her fantasies when the car stopped. Alan turned off the engine, and suddenly the world seemed to have gone silent. The road had ended.

"What happened?" Debbie asked, wrapping her arms around herself. Her skin was standing up in goosebumps, but she wasn't cold.

All he said was, "Follow me, my lady," and extended his arm to her gallantly.

Now Debbie felt a little afraid, but sometimes people will do stupid things when they think they are in love.

Nobody saw what Debbie Jean Compton did that night. Nobody except God, and that especially brought no comfort to her in the months and years after.

You can't climb back into a window as the same person you were when you first jumped from it. Three short weeks later, Debbie knew she was pregnant. A woman knows her body, and she always knows what's hers.

She was not engaged to Alan Whitney. They did not even live in the same state anymore. It turned out he *was* a planner after all. Debbie had never been over by his house in the time that they saw each other, so she had never seen the real-estate signs in his parents' front yard from months ago, and certainly not the moving trucks that packed up all the Whitney family's furniture and belongings the morning after he took her into the woods. They were off before she had woken up the next morning, her skin feeling sticky and shameful with the previous night's sweat. She couldn't rinse the feelings from her skin, no matter how hard she scrubbed, no matter how hot she turned up the water.

There wasn't a thing to do except tell her parents the truth of it all. Before, she would have trembled at the thought of admitting to sneaking out at night, but now she had to tell her mother and father the unspeakable. She was ruined, and she would be bringing the Compton name down with her.

Her mother wailed for a week, seven days and seven nights without reprieve. Her father struck her so hard that she fell to the ground, and he shook her mother by the shoulders and told her to listen. *Listen*, he said. *We have money*.

It was the same thing he told the physician in North Carolina.

On the day of, Debbie and her mother were driven out to an empty road where they met the middleman. She was blindfolded and taken to the destination by car ride. The blindfold was not to be removed, not even during the operation. She didn't know where she was, or who was with her in that room. She remembered feeling cold and vulnerable, the way the open air touched her thighs and between her legs. The blindfold was soaked through with tears.

She knew that many women suffered from this procedure, often permanently. She knew that many women also died. She felt like she had cheated some system and would never be rid of the guilt. It wasn't considered a therapeutic abortion because her life had never been in danger. Pre-marital sex was a crime, almost as much as the afterward procedure itself. If they were found out now, the consequences would be more severe than just tainting the Compton family name.

So, it was never spoken of again between Debbie and her parents, but she knew without being told that she had been able to get it *and* live because of her parents and their money and the kind of people that they were. *It* might have been gone, but she would still live with it for the rest of her life—both the guilt and the ghost of what could have been, if only things had turned out differently. But nothing could cure that, not even magic.

Less than a year later, she was wed to a son of their family friends, the Grahams.

Clayton Graham was everything that Alan had not been—quiet, plain, thoughtful, and unchanging. His body was big and soft all over and he wore thick glasses that obscured most of his face. Most of all, though, he was kind. There was no doubt in his sincerity, however mousy and boring he was. Quickly, she had come to appreciate him for these things, even come to love him after some time. There were no adventures and there likely never would be, but Debbie was okay with that. She felt she had gotten enough of that for the time being, and it had not been a good time.

In the beginning they had a small house together, hardly more than a cottage. It was just the two of them, though, so space wasn't an issue. Clayton was incredibly smart and dedicated to his work. He was one of the top engineers at his company and made a modest salary. She hadn't anticipated, though, that one day his company would be bought over, and her husband and the other chief-level employees would be rewarded with so much money. An engineer!

He had enough money to buy them a new house. Quiet as he was, Clayton was a sweet and observant husband. He was always attentive when Debbie seemed quiet or sad, but he did not have the courage to ask why. He asked other pointed questions, like if she missed her parents, and if moving to a new house closer to them would raise her spirits.

Her answer had not been what he expected. Strange, almost. "I want to go north," she had said over dinner. "Past Atlanta, maybe." North was away from her parents and their hometown. Would they be okay up there, just the two of them?

159

Clayton had an uncle living up in Marietta. Eventually, he and Debbie took a trip up north and settled on a plot of land east of Marietta. It was just a plot of land, though, nothing but trees and dirt. It took them two years to build the house, but it was worth the wait. When Debbie stepped though the grand front entrance for the first time, she felt a little bit lighter. It was all so new that maybe one day she would forget who she had been. Building the house had been about creating something new, and it turned out wonderful. In their new house, far away with Clayton, Debbie's view of love had shifted. Love was not always passionate and desperate. Sometimes, it was quiet and steady, constant and comforting as a shadow. She was comfortable, and she wanted to feel that way for the rest of her life.

But even if Clayton was constant and steady, the world around them still moved. Her mother-in-law wanted grandchildren. People at their new church, Northcrest, were wary of the newcomers. The neighbors scowled at their big house, for they had no children to fill it with.

They had tried with no success. Clayton feared it was him, but Debbie knew otherwise. Her womb had been scraped away and now nothing would grow there.

Ten years of comfortable life passed, but children never came. In the eighth year, Debbie's mother passed from a stroke. They drove down for the funeral, and Debbie knew it was she who put her mother in that grave. Some memories could never be buried, not even by time.

Still, she could not speak a word of it to Clayton. They would go to a doctor and discuss their options, but he could never know why she could bear no more children. It would kill him too, she feared, if it did not kill her first.

She understood that she would never carry her own child again unless God blessed her with a miracle. Which He wouldn't, she knew, because of the things she had done. It was hard to mourn the existence of something that never was, but she did it anyway.

Their life went on. Debbie especially had grown into the church community, with time, of course, the way kudzu eats up covering everything in its path, no matter how foreign the object. They went to church every Sunday at eleven a.m. service, but Debbie also joined other communities to keep herself from being lonely. There was her group bible study on Wednesday evenings at Tracy Anderson's house down the end of their street, where Debbie became slowly acquainted with the other women in the neighborhood. They had been sickly sweet on the surface from the moment Debbie first met them, but it took years before she felt something like friendship from the group.

The church also hosted many community events, from luncheons and Tupperware parties to volunteering and service projects. Some women had their children to keep them busy, but Debbie had the church. It brought her enough work and happiness where she supposed a child might have filled that space if her life turned out differently.

Eventually, she and Clayton decided to go on their first service mission trip.

She had heard the testimonies of other women from bible study and speakers at the church every so often. One time, Chrissie from bible study threw a dinner and party at her house the week after she and her husband returned from their service mission to Kenya. They were only gone for seven days, but Chrissie said it felt like she had been gone a lifetime. She went on all evening about how they had assisted a rural, underdeveloped community by building schools, hospitals, churches, and houses with clean drinking water. Debbie had no idea how that much physical labor could be accomplished in one short week, but Chrissie seemed so happy and excited, she was glowing. It was as if Jesus was shining through her, entreating Debbie and the other dinner guests to follow her example. The next mission trip with Northcrest church was in eight months, to India. The rest of the evening was spent pouring over the trinkets and treasures Chrissie brought from

Africa. She had a whole table set with things she was offering to sell and give the money back to the church. Debbie bought a little green beaded elephant that fit in the palm of her hand, as well as a wooden soup spoon with its handle fashioned into the shape of a zebra. The magic of Jesus had worked. On Chrissie. Debbie was properly enthralled.

Eight months later, Debbie and Clayton sat side by side on a plane to Calcutta, India. She had never been out of the country before. In fact, she had never been anywhere out of the south. She might have tried visiting somewhere like California first, but she felt inspired and filled with purpose. She thought it might be good for her to see people whose lives were much, much worse than hers. Only a year before, the queen of England had visited India, and before that, the first lady, and now it was Debbie's turn! She felt an adventure in her heart, and that was something she had not felt in the years since she had buried Debbie Compton and started life as Debbie Graham. The more she submerged herself in this new life, the farther away she felt from the agony of that past.

Twice in her life now, Debbie had experienced the anticipation of something she knew would change the course of her life. The first had been that evening in May of 1952, although it had been a much different event than she had expected it to be, with an outcome far worse than she could have dreamed. Now she felt the same anticipation, except she was ten years older and wiser. She knew that life changing events could go both ways: good, or very, very bad.

The total flight time was nineteen hours. There were eleven other people in their group, which consisted of five other couples and one university student. Thirteen people total. Debbie had four diet colas from Atlanta to London, and then there was a five hour layover. Waiting in the terminal, she pecked at the bag of salted almonds she had collected on the flight, eating just enough to settle her stomach. Clayton urged her to eat more, at least during the layover, but she claimed she was too tired. She couldn't even wander the airport with him. In truth, her stomach was turning with uncertainty. One step closer to India, she couldn't shake the anxiety that she was about to step into something much bigger than she was prepared for.

It did, in the end, lead her to something much bigger than she had expected. But that wasn't to come for several years later, and by then Debbie would be ready for it. In fact, she'd welcome it when the time came. But for now, and after this trip concluded, it would remain dormant. She was still astonished by the way that life can turn paths, even after what happened in May of 1952, and now again unsuspecting as she looks into the baby's eyes in the slums of Calcutta. Not all life-changing events went very, very bad. Some things would change her life for the better.

In India, Debbie saw, heard, smelled, and tasted things she had never imagined before. There were more people bustling around one city than she expected there probably were in the whole state of Georgia. There were street markets with rows of curries and fried doughs, vendors peddling their booths and wares, musicians, labor unions and protests, children and animals wandering alike. Every street was overcrowded and bustling; there was no order to the way cars and taxis moved around each other, bicyclists swerving and flitting around busses, and yet there seemed to be no accidents. It was beautiful and messy—unlike anything she'd seen before. At times she looked around and wondered if the human eye was meant for so much visual stimulation, if there was such thing as seeing too much color and movement. She ate dishes of rice and meat and sauces with flavors so unknown to her that she had no words to describe them. Spicy wasn't enough of a description—it was like calling a rainbow colorful. There were spices like seed pods and stars and leaves in each dish. They drank hot teas made fresh in a pot of milk with crushed spices and almonds, but no sweet, iced tea like she was used to drinking at home. Ice was not even used for water here. She heard so many different voices and words that couldn't all possibly be one language. Later, she learned that there were over twenty official Indian languages, as well as a vast array of regional dialects and mother tongues and languages so old you could only find them in books.

Truth be told, there wasn't much that could be done in five days in terms of the service mission they had come for. Many from the crew, including Debbie, were sick from travel, waking and sleeping at the wrong hours for the first two days, so she and the others who needed time to rest missed out on some of the beginning activities. The whole point of the trip was to spread the love of Jesus through acts of good service, though, so she did what she could. They visited a clinic and helped around, passing out cloths or water and sanitizing the tables, sometimes helping bathe patients or holding their hands. Like any city, there were parts that were well off and parts that were in a much worse state. She knew that they were not taking the group to any areas that might shock or distress them, though, and a small part of her nagged that maybe she didn't need to fly all the way out to India to do community work where she could be just as useful in her own state.

It bothered her, the thought that they weren't doing much of anything to help here. In fact, it sometimes felt like they were only getting in the way. What could they really do in five days that would make a difference? There was a nasty image that she kept pushing down, one where instead of being like Mother Teresa, she was just another hungry eyed tourist making a spectacle out of poverty.

Because when the group traveled in cars or vans, they were instructed to keep all the windows rolled up and the doors locked. And especially, they were told not to make eye contact with the beggars that clawed at the sides of their vehicles. Not even the ones that were children.

"If you give to them," their guide had said, "you're feeding the system. They use children for a reason. If you give in, it only affirms that child beggars work best to get what they want. I mean, look at them." There was a girl, no more than ten, barefoot and covered in a dried film of mud. From the side of the road, she outstretched her arms to the cars passing by. Many of her fingers were missing. "They do that on purpose," the guide said. "Cut off their children's fingers so they'll look more pitiful." Debbie felt sick, but she was unsure if her revulsion was toward what she saw, or if it was also the way their guide spoke about those children.

On the morning of the fifth day, the last day before their flight back, the group was taken to one last place: a shanty-town south of the heart of the city. There were rows upon rows of dwellings in the shape of houses, but not quite houses. They looked almost like patchwork quilts from the outside, constructed out of different materials like plastic, corrugated metal, plywood, cardboard, and whatever other scraps that had been discarded and thrown together. Some of the dwellings had meager access to electricity and drinking water. Others looked as if one gust of wind might scatter them to the ground.

Debbie thought of her own house, all seventeen thousand square feet for two people. A backyard pool, even though Clayton didn't know how to swim. A library so big, they had needed to buy more books just so they could fill up the beautiful mahogany shelves. There were eleven bathrooms in the house. What did they need eleven bathrooms for? Looking around her now, Debbie felt she had to do something, anything to atone for her own extravagance.

She knew she couldn't change anything. It felt like there was nothing she could do in this one morning that could help the people who lived here. Not for the first time on this trip, she felt a great sense of embarrassment and shame. She and Clayton had spent so much money on the tickets for the trip; what if they had donated that money instead? It probably would have done a lot more good.

So, on this last morning of the trip, Debbie Graham did

the only thing she felt she could do in the moment: give herself completely, if only for a few short hours, to the people in front of her. There were hundreds of people compacted into this one town, but she went along and talked to as many as she could. She learned the names of every mother and child she talked to. Not all of them spoke English, but just talking with them, if only sitting down with them to exchange a few words, she finally felt a small bit of purpose to this whole mission trip.

There was one family she met near the end, with four daughters and one newborn baby boy. The two older daughters spoke English well, and the eldest who was sixteen years old could read and write it too. Her name was Joyeeta, and her hair was long and dull. Their mother was always sick, she said, and their father worked by the railroads. It was a dangerous job, and far away, too. Sometimes he could not come back for a week at a time. Joyeeta talked about her baby brother, as well. His name was Debesh, and his name meant "favorite of the gods." Debbie smiled, because she thought it sounded a bit like her own name. Joyeeta said she feared he would not live, that he was born sick like his mother. Debbie didn't know why, but she promised Joyeeta that her brother would live. If she could do one thing, she would somehow save this child, this baby boy.

She wrote down her address from a pad of paper in her purse and pressed it into Joyeeta's hand. The girl looked down at the scrap of paper blankly. "Write to me," Debbie said. "I will make sure that my church keeps us connected."

Three months after Debbie and Clayton had arrived back in Georgia, she received her first letter from Joyeeta. She had felt the weight of it among the pile of other letters in the mailbox, sifting through the junk mail until she came upon it. She ran her hands over the envelope in wonder. It was bent and wrinkled and smudged with something gray, looking as if it had been through years of travel to get to her. She had never received mail from out of the country before, and the front was decorated with postal stampings. It was such a precious piece of mail to her that she used her thin, cow-patterned letter opener so not to disturb any part of the envelope. She saw Joyeeta's wiggly letters and smiled, clutching the paper to her chest.

The next morning, she had Clayton drive her to church, even though it was only Thursday. She had arranged a meeting with the board of volunteer services and community outreach. She had a lot on her agenda that she wanted to discuss, including connecting families in their church to families like Joyeeta's.

It took close to a year in the making, but finally Debbie helped start Northcrest Church's first sponsorship program. Through an outside organization, the church helped pair families with each other. Those who chose to participate would agree to send a set amount of money to the family per child each year until that child was eighteen.

By this time, Joyeeta was already seventeen, but she still had four other siblings, and the baby boy was only a year old. They exchanged correspondences for three years after this, until one day Debbie received a distressing note.

Now twenty years old, Joyeeta was married and about to move away. She wrote in the month of February to tell the Grahams that their father had died. *It is a dangerous job,* the note read. *He was hit on the tracks and lay in the hospital for two days before he died. Please, help my family. My mother is ill and cannot get up. My other sisters are old and well enough to look after themselves, but not our baby Debesh. He is only four. You promised he will not die. Please, save him.*

Debbie and Clayton took the same flight they had taken four years ago, Georgia to London, London to Calcutta. They had been on two mission trips since Debbie had helped reform the program and planning of the church's service mission trips. Debbie was now thirty-eight years old and barren. But she was going to save this child. She would.

They named him Daniel. The two younger sisters wept

to see him go, but Joyeeta wept and kissed Debbie's hands. She was leaving their town in a week, and there would be no one left of her family who could read or write in English. The Grahams would continue to send money, of course, but the hand-written correspondences would now be put to rest. Their baby boy wailed all the way back to Georgia, all nineteen hours. Only outside of the airport, in the car ride back to the house, did he finally stop.

He didn't speak a word of English, but he was only four. They knew he would learn quickly, as young kids always did with language. Later, his first words in English were his own name, "Da-nny. Da-nny."

He had never slept away from his family before, and Debbie sure as hell wasn't going to make him sleep in a room by himself the first night, perhaps not even in the first month. She had Clayton set up a small trundle next to their bed, on her side so she could watch him all night, hold his hand if he cried. He was happy to run around the hallways, she thought, even if he had no idea where he was right now. He was young, she told herself. He would learn, and he would also forget.

When she tucked him in that first night, pulling the softest blanket she could find up to his chin, he stared at her with big, black eyes. He had babbled, sometimes, on the plane ride, but now he was silent.

"Your home is here now. Goodnight, our sweet Daniel."

Afterward, as she had turned off the lights and changed into her nightclothes, something moved outside the master bedroom window. Slowly, like a ghost, she drifted over to see what was moving outside. There were deer that wandered through their property sometimes.

This was no deer, though.

Debbie's body didn't let her scream—it would be bad for Daniel. She didn't want to shock him anymore than what they'd already done in the past forty-eight hours of traveling. But outside, shrouded in the evening fog, was a child, maybe thirteen or fourteen years old.

It was a girl, with horns like the devil, watching Debbie across the yard with piercing yellow eyes. When she opened her mouth, it was filled with sharp little teeth. Debbie bit down on her bottom lip so hard that she felt the warm trickle of blood on her chin, smelled the metallic tang of her own fear in the air.

It was the first time she had ever seen her, but somehow, Debbie felt like she knew who the girl was. She had finally appeared, that child she had given to the devil so many years ago. And now she was here to take her mother.

EIGHTEEN

Clara woke from a troubled dream of her grandma, wandering the grounds of her property at dusk in only a nightgown.

She reached out to the table beside her, grabbing for the cup of water. Green and red buttons beeped and shone in the dark room. It was her last night in Georgia, and she was in a standard hospital bed. Tomorrow, they were flying back to California.

She was fine, truly. Only she didn't remember jumping from her old bedroom window the day of the funeral, which was, according to the date on her phone, only yesterday afternoon, fewer than twelve hours ago. She did, however, remember seeing The Girl. Nobody believed Clara, of course. She had jumped out of a window for God's sake, so naturally she had lost all credibility for anything. She even had a nasty bump on her forehead, purplish-blue, to alert everyone who saw her.

Clara knew her parents were furious, or maybe she was projecting her own self-hatred onto them. She had stolen her beloved grandma's last day above earth, snatched it up in her grubby, greedy hands to turn it into a catastrophe all about her. Guests had screamed at the sound of her body thumping on the ground below, fallen from the second floor.

And she had made the mistake of describing it the way she did, just like she had as a child: a girl, with horns and yellow eyes and sharp little teeth. When she had become coherent again after a few hours at the hospital, a social worker had come in to talk to her about an inpatient psychiatric stay, perhaps somewhere back in California if she preferred to do it back at home.

She begged her parents not to send her away. She pleaded with them, and it made her feel like a child again. After the social worker came and talked with her, Clara could hear the conversation with her parents outside her door.

"She doesn't check off as suicidal," the social worker was saying Clara's parents. She had curly red hair, so stuck in place with hair product that it looked crunchy. Her ID badge said her name was Sara, and she asked a series of questions so basic that Clara could have found a quiz online to diagnose herself instead of having Sara read from a list and have her services charged to the hospital bill.

"However, she is still a danger to herself," Sara's voice came from outside the room. "Her delusions are so strong that she's acting on them. It would be irresponsible, reckless even, to allow her to immediately resume daily life without some form of psychiatric treatment."

"Something has to be done," agreed her dad's voice.

"It's a cry for help, I think," said the social worker. "I saw the history of anti-psychotics in her charts."

"Yes," Clara's mom's voice said. "A long time ago, back when she was in elementary school. It was when we lived here, actually. She was seeing things then, too."

Nobody will listen, Clara thought. *Nobody will hear me.* If she was still a child, Grandma would have taken her for ice cream and listened to everything. But she wasn't a child, and Grandma was gone.

Her parents came into the room a moment later. Clara couldn't look at them; she was too frustrated and embarrassed. She was starting to become confused, too. Yesterday, she was so sure of what she saw. Now, she was beginning to doubt herself. She had to ask the important questions.

For example: why had she grown up and the girl from the woods hadn't? It looked as if no time had passed for her. Somewhere around thirteen years old, for how many years? She looked just as she had been all those years ago, watching Clara as a child from the backyard.

Another question: Why didn't she ever come inside the house? Clara thought maybe she only appeared in Grandma's backyard and the forest behind it, but then she'd showed up at the church for the funeral! She had sat in the pews when Clara stood to read the eulogy, sitting like a solemn statue with glittering eyes.

And finally: what was the connection between Grandma and this devil child? Clara knew the two were related somehow. At first, back when she was a child in Grandma's house, she had thought that little girl was some magical, special thing, like an elf or fairy that only she could see. A secret friendship. But she had come to understand that Grandma knew things about everything. And in all twelve subsequent years that Clara had lived in California, the girl had never appeared. In fact, it was as if she had been erased from Clara's mind completely. But now she was back, and Clara knew that adults didn't have imaginary friends. She knew what she saw.

But that was the thing about crazy. Did crazy people know that they were crazy? Could they even know? *Lucinda*, she mouthed, tracing the shape of the word, the name, with hollow lips.

"Clara?" Said her mom. "Clara, did you hear me?"

She didn't know when her mom had started talking. They just stared at each other. Then, Clara's dad spoke. "They said you'll be discharged in the next couple of hours. Our flight is pretty early tomorrow morning. Mom packed your stuff earlier today so you should be all set to go home."

Home. It seemed like some faraway place across space and time, more immeasurable than a six hour flight from Atlanta to Los Angeles. Somehow, she felt as if this trip had taken her back in time and now there was no way to return to her present. She might be back in that one-bedroom apartment tomorrow evening, but she feared she would also still be *here*.

Nothing had changed, really, and yet it felt like everything had. From the look on her parents' faces, it seemed that they were worried she was falling back into an old pattern. Her crazy was dormant like a volcano. Then one "blow up" and it was a pause on her life until she could become emotionally rehabilitated again.

Her mom was talking about some facility down in Long Beach for emotionally volatile adults that she had been researching and making calls to, but Clara was only partly listening. "It might be a good time to go in," her mom said. "Stay for a few months, while things are slow in your life right now, with your career…" She trailed off. Why did her parents always talk about her library job like it was a volunteer position, or a steppingstone to a real job?

"Mom," Clara said, "what about the house?"

There was something about the way both of her parents moved, almost imperceptible, like the shift of her dad's foot or the twitch of her mom's finger. "What about it?" Her dad responded.

"Will there be time to go back before we leave tomorrow?" Clara asked.

Her parents shared a tense look, as if daring the other to speak first. "Your dad and I don't think that would be best," her mom said at last. She looked uncomfortable, and old. Stress seemed to wrinkle her face in on itself. Clara felt a strange sense of shame under the gaze of her concerned, old parents. They were all old, Clara too. Too old to be like this.

That's not how it is this time, though! Clara wanted to say. *I saw her right there!* If she was losing her mind, she knew it wasn't without good reason. She thought that if she could just go back to the house, just one more time, then maybe she might find some answers.

She had to pick her battles, though, and right now it felt most pressing to keep herself out of some psychiatric facility of her parents' choosing. So, she killed the fight inside her, squashed the writhing need for answers and willed herself into passivity. It was easier than she'd imagined, and she soon fell back into a troubled sleep.

There was no sunrise the next morning. The new day rose without preamble, slate gray skies promising an early summer storm. Clara wished they could stay to see it.

As their flight took off, a strong wind blew the first drops of rain against the tiny airplane windows. But Clara was in an aisle seat and didn't have much of a view. She stared at the back of the seat in front of her, waiting in silence for the plane to take off.

There were ants on the ceiling, which Clara found herself thinking about as their plane was speeding down the runway. Big red fire-ants, each sculpture as large as a grown man making a trail on the ceiling at the entrance of the airport, right by the Delta check-in. It was something she had remembered from when she was a child and was still equally baffled by the creative choice as an adult. Who had decided to put fire-ants on the ceiling for decoration? Clara enjoyed art that was beautiful, or whimsical… the ants on the ceiling of Hartsfield-Jackson Atlanta International Airport made her squirm. She closed her eyes as she walked under them, surprised that they were still there after all these years.

The plane was getting up in the air now, and as Clara closed her eyes, a different memory about ants came to her. She felt she had no choice but to indulge it.

She had been playing in the flower beds in grandma's front yard, leaping over small shrubbery and hopping from stone to stone. Remembering it now, she had almost perfect clarity of when it had been. Their time spent living in Georgia with Grandma was short, barely over a year long, so Clara often found that she could remember even the smallest events chronologically, like a storybook in her mind about that one strange year at the house. She had been barefoot, because it was late summer after they'd arrived, and she hadn't yet learned how many little crawling creatures there were in the lush earth. In California, the grass was either so parched and yellow that it felt like walking in sand, or it was the sprite-bottle green turf, plasticky smelling, neat and sterile. So, the summer they moved to Georgia, she had relished the sensation of her bare feet in the grass, cool as water in the heat of the day. She delighted in the feeling of her toes squelching in soft mud. But she had been in for a nasty surprise that one time, hopping around in the front yard and landing barefoot in a red ant's nest.

Thinking about the hundreds of red bodies that rose from the pile of dirt in mere moments, swarming her bare feet, made Clara's stomach turn. She opened her eyes. Perhaps it was only the sinking-rising feeling of the plane climbing into the sky that was unsettling her. After all, the memory was so long ago that she couldn't remember the sharp pain of their bites or the sting of her swollen feet afterward. Frightening as it was, it was only a faraway memory, so far away that it could only be reached in her mind now.

But memories were potent. Once they decided to turn up, even memories as small as ants could not be denied.

A bright, two-toned *ding* drew Clara's mind back into the airplane seat. The seatbelt light above her head had gone off, signaling that they'd reached cruising altitude. It was surprisingly dark in the cabin, and for a moment Clara wondered if she had fallen asleep. She realized she had been daydreaming for a while, perhaps half an hour, and now other passengers were unbuckling their seatbelts, getting up to use the restroom, and pulling the tray tables down in front of them.

To her left at the window seat was her mom, fast asleep. There was a half opened magazine in her lap that she had bought before the flight along with a single tray of Red Vines.

The more she looked at her parents these days, the older they seemed to get. What was she going to do when they kept getting older and she kept getting older, forever straying from the parent and child relationship she longed to stay in. It felt like she had already lost Cassie to the inevitable path of growing up. Cassie didn't need them anymore. She was her own person now and she lived her own life. Soon, she would have her own, new family with Tristan. But Clara didn't feel ready for anything like that, and the older she became, the more ashamed she felt about these feelings. People her age were supposed to *want* to spread their own wings, if they hadn't already done so. Clara felt sorely out of touch with her age group. She hadn't been a happy child, and she wasn't exactly a happy adult either. But sometimes she thought she preferred childhood.

Lonely and terrifying, but she knew how things ended. As an adult now, she also felt lonely and terrified, but this time she didn't know how her story was going to end.

In fact, she had no idea where she was supposed to go from here.

The first step was to evade psychiatric hospitalization. Then, she would be expected back at work. That would be easy enough since her job behind the front desk of the children's book section didn't require much interaction with anyone. Because if for some reason she had to explain the bruise on her forehead, her boss would hear about it, and she would be asked to take some personal time off from work. No, that wouldn't do. She would have to call it a fall. It wasn't a lie, just a half truth. After she climbed out of the window, she did fall. And they didn't need to know *where* she fell from, or how.

She would pick up Petra from the sitter's house, and they would go back to her quiet apartment. Hopefully Petra would be happy to be back at home with Clara and not whine by the door the first night, missing the sitter and her kids. They would go on their walks, the usual route, of course, and life would eventually go back to normal. Clara was looking forward to getting back to the way things used to be, however boring seeming those days were. It was comfortable, and she would gladly welcome a life of unspecial days if it meant she didn't have to go back to that house. Goddamn it, that cursed house!

Remembering her obligation to it, Clara felt all her boring, safe plans dissolve like smoke. She had almost forgotten the enormous matter of her grandma's house. Her stomach started to hurt, and she squirmed in the seat, which suddenly felt unbearably uncomfortable.

A figure towered over her, and Clara looked up into the eyes of the flight attendant. "What would you like to drink?" She said, scooping ice into a cup.

"Ginger ale, please," Clara said, hoping it would calm her stomach. The woman nodded her head to Clara's mom. "Oh," Clara thought, not wanting to wake her. "I think she'll have a Dr. Pepper."

"We don't have that," the flight attendant said, passing Clara her ginger ale.

"Um, just a water then."

She poured water from a bottle and handed it down to Clara, but Clara's nervous hands fumbled, and the ice water poured over her shirt and lap. It seeped quickly through her clothes to her skin. The soft plastic cups were so small, so she was shocked by how much water one little cup could contain. "Oh, I'm so sorry," the flight attendant said, reaching for napkins stored away in the cart. Clara moved to clean herself up, but as she shifted, her knee knocked against the tray table and her ginger ale went to the ground too. She burst into tears.

The flight attendant stood frozen in shock, and the nearby passengers started peering over at all the noise. Clara was crying, loudly, shockingly, like a child that fell of a bicycle and skinned their knees.

Her mom woke up. Her dad got out of his seat from two rows behind and came over. There was a big commotion and other passengers looked around awkwardly because they couldn't understand what was happening. Clara couldn't really understand either. As the sobs were heaving out of her, she tried to reason with herself. It wasn't a big deal. It was only water. And the sticky ginger ale had gone to the ground and not her clothes. She woke her mom up. Other people were giving her strange looks. She was scaring the flight attendant. She was doing a poor job of proving to her parents that she was fine.

Her mom's hand was on Clara's arm. "It's okay," Clara's dad was saying to the flight attendant. "We've got it."

Without a word, she wheeled the beverage cart away, down the aisle. Clara's dad kneeled down in the aisle to be level with Clara, the knees of his nice pants soaking up the spilled ginger ale. "Clara," he said. He didn't sound angry. "What's wrong?"

What was wrong? She knew it by a feeling in her chest and stomach, but she feared trying to say it out loud would only sound babyish and trivial. She shook her head, eyes closed to keep the tears in. She was too embarrassed to open her eyes and look at her parents, to take in the reality of things.

There wasn't really anything wrong, but for some reason she felt like she was barely keeping it together. "What am I doing?" She thought, but then realized that she had spoken it out loud.

She felt so small, so far from an adult. She wanted to hold her parents' hands. She wanted to go home and lay under the covers of her bed for months and months. She wanted to go backwards in time. "What am I supposed to do?" She asked again.

She felt her dad's hand in hers, and her mom's hand on her back. "It's okay, Clary," her dad said. "We'll help you. You don't have to do it all by yourself."

NINETEEN

One Week Later

Clara sat up in bed in the early hours of the morning, as if startled awake by some unseen force. She reached blindly toward the nightstand to her left until her hand found the stale glass of water it was looking for. Blinking red across the room, her digital clock read 3:39 AM. She had been having the same dream every night since she'd gotten back to her apartment. Yellow eyes watching her in the dark, seeing through space and time. *My name is Lucinda, don't you remember me?* she said, and her voice was all wrong.

Now that she was back in California, away from the house, Clara only saw the girl, *Lucinda*, she called herself, through dreams. She was beginning to understand that the girl was tied to the house and to her grandma, so Clara felt more or less at ease in her apartment until she shut her eyes to go to sleep. Then, she was haunted by nightmares, relentlessly pursued by memories until she startled herself awake. Some were memories of her own, dreams of playing in the backyard until the sky darkened and Lucinda came out from her haunt in the trees. Others were unfamiliar scenes, old pains that she seemed to have no connection to. Memories, somehow, that did not belong to her.

Now, she could feel the sleep falling away with each passing moment, and she tried to shrug it back on like a coat. It was still too early to get up, and she hadn't been getting good sleep in the past week because of the nightmares. Even though she wouldn't be starting back at work until next Monday, she hated the restless nights and dreaded the half-awake days that followed. It didn't help that she had been mostly sedentary since they returned. Days of doing nothing made it hard to get to sleep at night, she had learned. She felt groggy during the day and restless at night. Only Petra slept well, lounging in spots where the sun came in for her daytime naps and buried under a mound of blankets on the other side of Clara's bed at night. But even Petra seemed a bit dejected, likely missing the dog sitter and their old routine of walks around the block. Clara hadn't been able to bring herself to do even that.

She lay back down and tried to fall back asleep. Her hair would be matted by morning from tossing and turning, and trying without success to get comfortable.

After half an hour without results, Clara reached over to the nightstand and grabbed her phone. At this point, she was wide awake and itching to get out of bed, so she figured she might as well check any social medias that she wouldn't mind forgetting by morning. She might have used this time to read any unopened texts if she actually had any texts her besides an automated CVS prescription refill. Instead, she opened up Instagram.

At the very top of her feed appeared a post two days ago from Cassie Graham-Becker. Clara thought it was weird that her sister had already changed her username to add Tristan's name when they were still only engaged. She double tapped the picture but didn't scroll past. It was a picture of Cassie and Tristan at a rooftop dinner in New York, the smile on her face so incredibly happy that it looked almost maniacal. Perhaps Cassie changed her name already because she felt threatened. Terrified, maybe, of things going south like Clara knew they did with many of her relationships. Friend or boyfriend, it made no difference. Clara knew that much about her sister's life. She had witnessed enough of Cassie's screaming fights back in high school. When they were younger, Clara thought

Cassie was a typical drama-attracting diva, but now that they were both older, Clara had to wonder if things weren't as they seemed, that maybe she had misjudged her own sister. Maybe Cassie was just scared. Maybe now she was digging her claws into Tristan, terrified he might leave.

She looked at the post for a long time before finally scrolling past, uncomfortably aware of her own desire for connection with her sister. They had never been close, but Clara wished it could change. She didn't like the idea of Tristan, but a part of her wished that Cassie would tell her about him, what she liked about him. If she could see him the way Cassie saw him, then maybe Clara wouldn't need to dislike him so much.

Always, the most uncomfortable thoughts came in the early hours of the morning.

More scrolling on her phone showed her things she didn't want to see. Old classmates from high school with significant others, master's degree programs on the east coast, or starting high-profile careers. With each window into her old acquaintances' lives, she felt angry and sad. Part of it, she suspected, was self-pity, but another part of her felt so angry with herself. What was she doing? *Nothing.* Her head began to throb.

She clicked her phone off angrily, letting the room fall into darkness again. She lay thinking with her eyes open long enough that they adjusted to the dark and she could see all the way to the empty corners of her room. Somewhere by her right knee, Petra was twitching and kicking her paws in a dream. She envied the pup's ability to sleep so easily and think of nothing. She wondered if she'd be happy if she were a dog instead of a human with complicated memories and emotions.

When at last she fell back asleep, she dreamed not quite of nothing. Her dream-self was back in the house, standing still enough to collect dust, haunted by the empty sound of silence.

The next morning, Clara's mom drove over to her apartment to bring groceries. Clara went down in the elevator to meet her in the parking lot, and they both went back up to the apartment. Her mom insisted on escorting her, as if she worried that Clara might fall again. But when the elevator doors sprung open and her neighbor Ryan was waiting on the other side, Clara's face heated with shame. She began to wish she had been splattered dead on her grandma's lawn after the fall instead of right here in front of him. His hair had grown out since she'd last seen him, and he was in gym clothes, and she could hardly think of anything besides how much she hated herself.

Clearly, Ryan did not know where to start. Excitement, then confusion, disturbed curiosity, then shyness danced over his face. He settled on saying, "Let me help you with the groceries!" He plucked the brown paper bags out of Clara's lap and yanked the other bags away from Clara's mom so that both of them were carrying nothing. He looked like he was going to say something, but then decided against it and went back down their hall to Clara's door. Clara glanced over at her mom who was grinning like she had just found a new son-in-law.

Clara shook her head, silently communicating, "As if we were that lucky." Clara knew her mom feared as much as Clara did, if not more, that she would be alone forever. A modern spinster with an apartment full of dachshund siblings for Petra.

At her door, Clara fished the key from the pocket of her sweatpants and handed it to Ryan. He unlocked her door with one hand in one smooth motion. Clara almost frowned, thinking of how she always had to twist and fight and bother at the lock until it yielded.

Inside was a disaster, but Clara only realized it the moment Ryan entered her apartment carrying all her groceries. The air was stale, the curtains were drawn, the sink was full of dishes, and the couch was buried under a mound of blankets, books, and unfolded laundry. Ryan pretended like he didn't notice the mess as he set the bags down on the counter, and only seconds later, Petra came flying at his ankles, barking growling, seeming both scared and excited. She was probably overwhelmed, Clara thought, considering there had never been this many people in their apartment before.

As Clara's mom began unbagging the groceries, Ryan looked her up and down, clenching and unclenching his fists. Clara felt herself shrink under the weight of his eyes, and she wondered if it was possible for her to shrink so much that she disappeared entirely.

"I didn't know you had gotten back," he said, as if they were friends. Clara wished that they were. "How was your... vacation?" He asked, seeming to question the words that had already escaped his mouth.

Actually, it was a funeral Clara might have said, but she didn't have it in her to make the situation any more uncomfortable. "It's good to be back," was all she said.

He nodded, and his eyes wavered to a spot above her eyes where the bruise had grown and darkened in the past few days to a greenish purple.

Well actually, my grandma's funeral was postponed because the neighbors said she was practicing witchcraft. I inherited a multi-million dollar estate in Georgia. I saw a ghost from my past and it drove me so crazy that I threw myself out my childhood bedroom window.

"Clara had a really bad *fall*," her mom answered for her, emphasizing the word like it had been nothing more than a freak accident. "She fell and hit her head."

"Oh, man," Ryan said, rubbing the top of his head. "I'm sorry about that."

Clara didn't know what else to say, so she just nodded.

Sensing danger, her mom jumped in again. "Clara didn't tell me she had such a nice friend! I'm her mother, by the way." She stuck out her hand, smiling. She probably thought she was helping the situation. "Megumi. But most people just call me Meg."

Clara almost winced as they shook hands. "I'm Ryan," he said. "I live next door." Then, after seeming to consider something, he said, "You never told me you were Japanese, Clara."

When have I ever told you anything about myself? Clara wondered, but then thought back to that day she locked herself out and waited inside Ryan's apartment. She vaguely remembered holding a glass of water and the feeling of telling him many things, and the feeling came back to her now, unpleasant like remembering the feeling of vomiting.

Her mom kicked the back of her shoe.

"Oh, yeah..." Clara said. "But I'm only half."

"So am I," he said, and he gave her a smile that made her want to smile back. She could see it now, the Japanese side, like it had been hidden in plain sight. She could see it in the brown of his hair and the softer features in his face. The spattering of freckles below both of his eyes that would one day bleed into each other to become the sunspots that Clara's mom and elderly aunts and uncles had.

"How wonderful!" Clara's mom said, reminding Clara that she was not alone with this beautiful boy. Somehow, she had drifted away from the reality of the situation, and when it hit her, she came crashing back into herself that she so hated.

"You'll have to come over for dinner with Clara one of these days!" Her mom said. Clara's heart was pounding; this situation was getting so out of hand. "Her dad and I only live half an hour away, so we like to have her back home for dinner a lot," she said.

"That sounds great," Ryan said, and Clara couldn't tell if her heart was jumping because of the anxiety or a secret excitement. "My dad doesn't know how to make any Japanese food, so I only really get it at restaurants."

"Oh, yes," Clara's mom said with a sigh. "We're a dying race. I've only recently been getting back into my Japanese recipes. Clara and her sister despised anything besides, well, mac n cheese or hot dogs when they were kids."

"Mom..." Clara said, but she felt a little sad because she knew how true it was.

"In fact," she continued, "why don't you two come for dinner this Saturday? Clara might need someone to drive her, anyway. In case her head is not fully recovered."

"Mom!" Clara shouted, feeling so embarrassed that she was close to tears. "He's not an uber driver!"

But Ryan was laughing. He was leaning a little on the counter, looking comfortable. In fact, he looked like he was having a good time. "Sure, that sounds great," he said. I would love to come to dinner, if that's okay with Clara."

Four eyes were on her, each pair looking like they were trying to tell her something. *Come on!* She imagined her mom was trying to say through her eyes. *I'm only trying to help you!*

In Ryan's eyes, there was a different look. Not frantic like her mom, but something calm and grounded. There was a kindness in his eyes that Clara was not used to seeing, and when she recognized it, she was hit with the devastating blow of realizing how deep down she craved friendship. He seemed to be saying *let's be friends, Clara*. Was it possible for someone to reach out a hand with just one look?

"Okay," Clara found herself saying. She took a big breath. "Sure. That sounds fun."

TWENTY

That evening, her mom decided to stay and make dinner for Clara with the groceries she'd brought back. Clara felt revived, whether it was from the interaction with Ryan, the afternoon spent with her mom, or both. In fact, she was feeling better than she had in a long while. Perhaps her mom did know what she was doing. It felt nice to be taken care of by her mom like she was sick, Clara thought, like she was a child again.

Her mom made steak, claiming she was worried about Clara's iron levels. "You're too tired these days," she said, setting two plates for Clara and herself. "You need to eat better."

Maybe that was partly true, but Clara couldn't tell her mom the other reason why she was feeling so tired and half-alive. She had evaded the hospital, making the excuse that she told those fairy-stories about the girl in Grandma's backyard because her head had probably been messed up from the fall. Her parents believed it all too easily, as if they were looking for something to believe in that made sense to them.

No, she couldn't tell her mom about the dreams as they sat down together for dinner. Clara still spent a lot of time with her parents. Probably more than most people her age. She was close with them, but close didn't mean she could tell them things they couldn't understand. She knew that this kind of talk would only scare her parents. Grandma was the only one who might have believed in this kind of stuff, but she was gone now. And that made her feel all alone with her dreams.

She wasn't exactly scared of the devil girl. The desire to understand what was going on was greater than her fear. In fact, Clara felt more afraid of the upcoming Saturday dinner with her parents and Ryan than the prospect of seeing Lucinda again in her dreams. Clara had been doing a lot of thinking about that name. Had she named herself? Or was it a name that was given to her? Lucinda sounded an awful lot like Lucifer, the devil himself.

Is that truly where she came from? The devil?

And if Grandma had been a good, devout Christian, what did it mean that she had the devil stowed away in her backyard?

"So that neighbor of yours," her mom said, cutting into the hunk of steak on her plate. "He's very handsome, don't you think? And he has such nice manners. When did you become friends with him, Clara?"

Clara stared down at the steak on her plate. It was weeping blood-juice. Her mom said that it was better for her tiredness this way, but Clara thought that might need to be fact checked. She poked at the meat with her fork. "He's not my friend, mom. I don't even really know him."

Her mom looked wounded, as if this was a personal slight against her. "Well, don't you *want* to know him? I think it would be good for you to have a friend."

"He might not want to be friends, Mom," Clara said, fighting to keep the glumness out of her voice.

Her mom gasped ridiculously. "You mean…?"

Clara looked up from her steak. Her fork was stuck in it, standing straight up. "What?"

She set her for down and started again. "Do you mean that he's *interested* in you?"

Luckily, there was no food in Clara's mouth, because it would have flown out in disbelief. "No Mom! That's not what I meant at all!"

*   *   *

After dinner, Clara and her mom took care of the heap of unfolded laundry that had overrun her couch. Then, they sat and watched the news. "You don't have to stay, Mom," Clara thought she should say, but she seemed to be enjoying herself, as if she wasn't noticing the world's state of crisis on the television—gasoline prices were at a record high in the United States, and there was a war in Ukraine, where missiles had been launched into Kyiv only weeks before. There was a looping replay of the president falling off a bike, footage that seemed ridiculously funny and inappropriate to be showed alongside the grimmer news in the world. Clara thought her mom looked to be enjoying herself, though, not because of the news program but maybe because of the evening spent together.

When at last they said goodnight and her mom left the apartment, Clara sat in silence for a while, replaying the events of the afternoon and evening. She always knew she was anxious when she found herself doing that, replaying the day and its conversations and all the smallest interactions as if she could sort through the fresh memories and pick out the good moments, the bad moments, or moments where she thought she had messed up in the day.

From her phone, the time read 9:17 PM, but Clara's mind was buzzing. Even if she could walk, or run, she probably wouldn't have. At times like this, she felt like she couldn't move an inch. She knew a lot of people exercised to help themselves feel better, but when she got like this, the only thing that felt feasible to do was to try to go to sleep. But she hadn't been having much luck with that recently, and now she worried that laying down would only make her more awake.

Despite the day's events, Grandma was still lurking in the back of Clara's mind. Back at home, she was far away from the house and its history, but Clara had a growing sense of fear that it was all waiting for her back at in Georgia, unseen but certainly felt, like the presence of some cold ghost.

She sat down at the kitchen table and opened her laptop. After nearly forty-five minutes of searching the internet, she gave up. It turned out there were a lot of Debbie Grahams in the world, and her grandma seemed to have close to no online record. Clara had found only two mentions of her on the Northcrest Church website listing their high donors. Aside from that, the internet didn't know *her* Debbie Graham. Not unusual, perhaps, for a woman of her age, but then again, she hadn't always been ninety-three. Clara had an idea to search her up by her maiden name, but then quickly realized she had no idea what that name was. She was stunned with how little she knew about her own grandmother. Then, she wondered if her dad knew what it was. Surely, he knew…

Unless, Clara began to theorize, there was something hiding in her grandma's past. Maybe it was something so far back that it was buried with her old name. It just didn't make sense. She knew her maternal grandmother's maiden name (Hatanaka, and later Kitayama when Clara's mom's mom married Clara's mom's dad). She knew these things and she had never lived with her maternal grandparents before. So why was something that should have been basic so mysterious?

Maybe she would call her dad tomorrow morning and ask what her grandma's maiden name was. But for now, the trail was empty, and Clara had nothing to do but think. And the mind was perhaps the least reliable source of all.

Friday morning came after another sleepless night. When her eyes opened to the morning sunlight lighting up her room, Clara couldn't remember when she'd even fallen asleep. It seemed like she had been awake all night, tossing and turning and thinking. But now, blinking dry eyes, she remembered Lucinda walking into her dreams and accepted that she must have been asleep at some point during the night.

She didn't get out of bed for another two hours, though.

Time seemed to warp, hours folding into what felt like mere minutes.

When her room was fully lit by the morning light, Clara knew it was time to get up. It might have been noon already, she couldn't have said. Days of doing nothing had made her body feel stiff, as if she was turning into stone and she would turn into a human statue if she spent another day like this. She looked forward to going back to work on Monday, although she was both afraid and eager to go back into the world. It would be good for her spirits to get back into a routine, even if her typical workdays often passed in silence. Her position as a children's library assistant wasn't usually very eventful when most children came in with their parents. She just hoped the library wouldn't realize that any time soon and fire her.

At last, she got up and busied herself in the bathroom. The bruise on her forehead was slowly fading, but it had now ripened to a sickly yellow. She dressed herself in a sweater and kept a blanket across her lap. People always talked about California sunshine, but after returning from the deep south in June, Southern California felt cool and breezy in comparison. Something about the humidity there had been stifling, like each breath of the air there was slowly suffocating her. It made her think about a headline she'd seen on the news many years ago about a very old man who had choked on a pea and swallowed it the wrong way so that it went into his lungs and eventually grew into a little pod living on his lung like a plant in a greenhouse.

Back in California now, it seemed unlikely. But in Georgia, it seemed like anything could grow there. The land and the air had something about it, more than humidity and good soil. There was something about it that made Clara believe even the dead could grow there.

Then, another possibility came to Clara's mind, one that almost seemed too real: Were she and Grandma being haunted? She shook her head, muttering under her breath even though she was alone in the apartment. It was stupid,

stupid, stupid. If she wanted to return to work on Monday, or at the very least not freak Ryan and her parents out at their dinner tomorrow, she needed to keep her thoughts in check. There could be no theorizing or letting her mind wander for hours until times like this, when she was home alone. Yet as she tried to fight against it, she could feel herself succumbing to obsession about this girl, and the more she tried to forget it, the more impossible it felt, like an iciness in her limbs that was slowly creeping into her body. She knew it probably wasn't real, but didn't the bump on her head say otherwise?

No, she thought. It didn't matter if it was real or not. Whatever it was, whatever *she* was, Clara would put it out of her mind. She would make herself forget.

In the main room, she went to the fridge and pulled out her mom's leftovers from last night to heat up. It wasn't like her to have a steak for breakfast, but she was feeling strangely hungry, and it would be hard to make herself a proper breakfast in this state. As she peeled back the plastic saran wrap covering, the sound of frantic footsteps made her pause, but it was only Petra who had come running from the bedroom at the smell of the meat. She laughed but ignored the begging and whining. Petra had a weak stomach and couldn't eat human food without having accidents in the house, but Clara swore the little dog always came running at the first sound or smell of food, even if she was dead asleep.

She placed a paper towel over the steak before putting it into the microwave so that it wouldn't make the microwave messy, and then she closed the door and set the time to one minute and thirty seconds. Pressing START, the lightbulb inside turned on and the plate began to spin in slow circles, spinning around and around to the deafening hum of the microwave.

But the truth is that you can't really forget something. You just forget to think about it.

TWENTY ONE

Georgia, 2010

There were hospitals for children who hated either themselves or the world. Clara hadn't known which one she was, but it had been enough to put her in a bare room with a small bed that was nailed to the floor and not be let outside or see her parents for two whole weeks in the last month of fifth grade.

The other kids didn't like her, but she didn't need to be *liked*. She wanted to be left alone. But because she acted different, looked different, she stood out. And the first thing that all kids learn to be is a bully.

It only got worse as the school year progressed. Things happened every day that made Clara cry, and eventually she cried so much that the teachers took no notice.

At recess, she hovered near the gossiping teachers so other kids would avoid coming near her. Earlier on in the year, before she understood her part in the fifth grade community, she had been excited when a group of boys in her class invited her to play a game with them at recess. They gathered wood-chips and gravel, holding their shirts up from their bellies to store it all, and instructed Clara to wait at the bottom of the jungle gym with her eyes closed. So, she closed her eyes, smiling, as the they scrambled up into the jungle gym. Their names were Anthony, John, and Christian, and she wondered if they would soon become friends. With her eyes closed, she could hear them laughing and sniveling as they climbed up the ladders into the area above ground.

Then, something *hard* hit her in the face. It was small, no bigger than a cherry tomato, but it smacked into her cheek so hard that the inside of her mouth got cut on her teeth. She opened her eyes just as a whole hoard of woodchips, rocks, and muddy gravel was hurled at her face. It stung a thousand times where it hit, and when it was over, she had dirt on her face and in her hair, blood in her mouth, and a gritty feeling between her teeth.

"Why did you smile like that?" One of the boys said. She couldn't see who; the tears in her eyes blurred their faces together.

"Yeah," said another voice. "Don't smile at us, it's ugly!"

"She's like Medusa!" someone else said, and they started to laugh. They had been learning ancient Greek mythology in the social studies hour before recess that day.

"Medusa!" They screamed as she ran away. "Medusa, Medusa! So ugly she'll make you die!" In the bathroom after recess, Clara wondered what it had been. Her teeth? The two front ones were squished and crooked, folding into each other like an opening book. Or maybe her tangled hair looked like snarling black snakes. It could have been her eyes, so black they looked like two coat buttons. Standing in front of the dirty bathroom mirror, she thought she looked like some nasty goblin-creature, dirt on her face and blood in the corner of her mouth.

She hated herself for it, and she hated them too.

Another time, the whole school had recess indoors because it was pouring outside. Rain was okay to play in, but whenever the lightning and thunder started, whistles were blown and recess for the day had to be conducted inside. Some kids played card games or drew with markers on the board. Even Mrs. Manning sat at her desk, playing some game of stacked cards on her computer screen. Others sat in circles and talked because they were big kids, going to be in middle school next year.

Clara loved indoor recess because she could sit at her desk and stick her nose in a book. That day she had been reading a big fat book about the wizard Merlin that she'd brought from home. Sometimes, her dad took her to the bookstore and let her pick out as many books as she liked. Because he bought them for her and they were hers, not some library copy, she wrote her name in careful letters with a black sharpie on the inside cover of ever book she owned. Clara Graham, often written in her cursive letters.

That afternoon, as the rain and thunder sounded outside, Clara held the book close to her face, so close her eyes almost went cross-eyed, her hands gripping at the book's the smooth front and back cover. There was a wonderful image on the cover of a dark haired boy whose face was mostly hidden behind a blue flame. Even so, she imagined him to be very handsome, and just having the book near her, inside her desk during the school day felt like her own exciting secret. Now, she was reading a part where the young wizard was learning how to transform himself into a great stag, running in an open field until his legs changed. As a boy, he was called Emrys, and he lived with his mother who was Branwen. Clara didn't know if this was the way it had actually been, but this was the story in her book, and she adored the idea of Merlin as a boy her age rather than an old man with a white beard so long it brushed the floor. This way, he felt like a friend, and having the book with her at school felt like having a friend with her during the day.

She looked up at a movement in front of her. It was Monica and Laurie, standing over her, both with their arms crossed. She had no idea how long they'd been there, or what they might want. They had been part of the group sitting in a circle and talking, and she was almost certain they wouldn't want her to join. Fear, bright and cold, rushed into Clara's chest.

It was Laurie who spoke. "Why did you steal Monica's

book." But it wasn't a question any more than a statement of accusation.

Clara had no idea what to say. She was confused. Her mouth opened a little, trying desperately to find the meaning in their words.

"Hey, did you hear us?" Monica said, stepping forward. Clara began to tremble.

"Monica says that's her book," Laurie said. "And now the whole class knows you're a liar and a thief."

It made no sense. Clara had picked the book off her shelf this morning to bring to school. It had come from her room in Grandma's house.

"That's *my* book." Monica said. "Give it to me."

Clare knew it wasn't Monica's book. It was like they were trying to convince her that the sky was made of jellybeans when everyone could see that it was not. Clara's hands trembled as she flipped to the front cover, scrambling to show the girls her name that she had written in thick sharpie. Maybe Monica had a book like this and was confused. "It's mine," Clara whispered. "See? It has my name."

The girls were silent for a moment, staring hard at the book and then at Clara. Then, Laurie said, "Why did you do that to Monica's book? Just because your name's in it doesn't make it yours."

They were smiling, and then Clara knew it wasn't some mix-up. She had never even seen Monica with a book, much less this exact one. "Give it to me," Monica said, as Laurie ripped the book from her hands. The cover tore as Clara tried to grab onto it.

They were laughing, holding her broken book. Despite her best efforts, Clara burst into tears, big fat ones spilling from her eyes that turned into a loud wail. She couldn't keep it in. It was loud in the room, though, the sounds of indoor recess swallowing up her crying. Mrs. Manning had earphones in, listening to the background music of her game to drown out the loud kids. *Clara the Cry-Baby,* they called her.

Monica and Laurie walked away with her book, and Clara cried for the rest of recess, which lasted almost an hour because Mrs. Manning liked recess a lot. By the time they began class again, Clara was hiccupping and heaving, her upper lip messy with snot and tears.

At the end of the day, as they lined up to leave for the busses, Clara found her beautiful book in the trash with its cover torn almost completely off.

In the last few months before summer break, Clara tried everything she could to stay out of school. She could only say she was sick so many times before her parents became angry with her lies, so she tried things like getting into a steaming hot shower until she couldn't bear it any longer, and then quickly toweling herself off and jumping back in bed so that her parents could find her shivering with heat sickness and feigned fever under the covers. Or a different time, she stuck her toothbrush so far down her throat that she choked a little and coughed a mixture of toothpaste and spit into the toilet. Then she called her mom upstairs to show her, but she looked skeptical, and it only worked that one time. Hot water stung her skin and the rough bristles of her toothbrush made scratches in her throat, but these things were more bearable than having to go to school every day.

Then one day in early May, after an entire month of faking illnesses, Clara woke with a glob of dark blood in her underwear and rejoiced. She didn't care why it was there or what it could mean. All that mattered was that it looked serious, and her parents would be so worried they might not make her go to school for a few days. It was a good thing, and Clara didn't even care if it meant she was dying.

She screamed like she was in pain, but really it was a secret scream of happiness. Grandma came hurrying into her room, looking startled. But when Clara showed her the blood in her underwear, Grandma smiled and congratulated her. "Welcome to womanhood, my dear," she said. She looked proud. She suggested they throw a party. The confusion was enough to keep Clara's mind busy at least for that one day, as she was still made to go to school. Only she didn't trust Grandma's medical opinion and went to the school nurse's office halfway through the day. At home, she had put a band-aid on the spot, a part of her body which she had never examined or been curious about before. But the band-aid had not been sufficient, and by lunch time she finally started to become frightened by the bleeding that hadn't stopped.

For all that she visited the nurse's office, neither of them ever acted familiar with one another. When Clara waddled in that day, the nurse didn't look up from the computer she was typing at. Clara stood there in uncomfortable silence until the nurse raised her head and said flatly, "What is it."

"I have a cut," Clara said. "It doesn't hurt, but it won't stop bleeding."

The nurse looked her up and down. "Well? I don't see where."

Clara looked around, nervously. She was glad there were no other kids in the office right now. "It's down there," she whispered.

The nurse was silent for a moment. Then, a sort of smile broke across her face, if Clara had ever seen one from her before. She shook her head as if in disbelief. "Does your own mama not tell you anything?"

She gave Clara a little purple wrapped square and instructed her on what to do with it, then sent her on her way. As she was ushered out the door, Clara finally yelped, "But am I okay?"

The nurse just said, "When you get home tonight, go show your mama."

According to her mom, the "period" wasn't reason enough to stay home from school. "You only have a month left of school," she said. "Less than that, actually. Just hang in there, Clara." But Clara couldn't hang in there much longer.

One Thursday at lunch, only two weeks before the end of school, Clara did something that got her in a lot of trouble.

Mrs. Manning's class was so big that they had two designated tables in the lunchroom, two long tables with room for thirty-four seats per table. That meant that only four people needed to sit at the overflow table, since there were thirty-eight kids total in Clara's class. Whenever she could help it, she sat at the overflow table, since she could sit anywhere at the long table, spread out far away from the other kids who sat there. Usually, the other quiet kids sat there, as most of the class wanted to sit where all the action was. At the main table, it was a constant food fight. That was where her classmates had poured strawberry milk on Clara's pants after the pee-incident, but things like that happened every day on the main table and many of her classmates seemed to enjoy it. There would be pea-flinging contests, won by whoever could bend their plastic spoon back and catapult the school's frozen peas the farthest. Other popular lunchtime festivities included mixing every single condiment into their trays of applesauce, bouncing the cafeteria's horrible hot-dogs on the ground, or making trades between kids who brought home-lunches. Lunchtime was a daytime nightmare for shy kids like Clara, almost as bad as recess, so the overflow table was usually the closest thing to a safe haven for her.

But starting on the Monday before the last two weeks of school, Monica, Laurie, and their other friend Chloe decided that they wanted the privacy of the overflow table. Except it couldn't have been only that, because each day they sat right in front of Clara, lined up on the opposite side of the table three in a row. The rest of the table, all thirty seats, were left wide open, but they sat right in front of Clara. They didn't speak a word to her, though. In fact, every day, the three of them built up their lunchboxes to form a wall between them and Clara, and they spent all lunch whispering and peeking over at her. The first day, she tried to move, but they moved with her. The next day, she tried to race to the main table, but the seats were all full by the time she had waited in the lunch line (somehow, she always ended up at the end of the line). The third day, she cried, right there in front of them. And on the fourth day, Thursday, Clara couldn't stand it a moment longer. She did something big, and it resulted in the premature last day of fifth grade for her.

To be fair, she had tried sticking it out. Just hang in there, Clara, she told herself, trying to hear her mom's voice saying it to her in her head. But their whispering was growing louder by the minute, eventually loud enough that it drowned out Clara's own thoughts. Clara felt like she couldn't last another second. A thought started to form in her head.

It was an escape plan.

The table they were sitting at was right next to a set of doors that led to the school bus drop-off lot. From her seat in the cafeteria, it was no more than a few steps to the door. She was so close. Just a few steps and she didn't have to be here. She could go anywhere, as far as her legs could take her. Anywhere but here.

Clara had never been very good at bravery, and it would take a lot of that to get up from her seat and run out the doors. But then, it was also something like the opposite, wasn't it? Getting up and running out of the school at that moment seemed more doable for Clara than sitting for another second in the lunchroom behind a wall of her classmates' lunchboxes. Maybe instead of bravery, it was cowardice.

Because at the root of it, Clara wanted to run away from the monsters.

She didn't really have a plan. Part of her knew she had to stay; they weren't allowed to get up during lunch, not even for the bathroom unless they got permission from the lunchroom staff. But another part of her begged her legs to get up and *run*. That was all she had to do—run. There was no plan besides that because that was the plan. Where would she run?

It didn't matter to her. All that mattered was that she ran until she was far away.

She shouldn't do it, but she could. In fact, she had to.

In a split second, overcome with bravery or cowardice, Clara stood up from her seat. She had nothing with her, no backpack or sweater. She didn't bring her lunchbox as she made the dash from her table to the doors. It was a small distance, and almost in the blink of an eye she was throwing herself against the doors to outside, which sprung open for her. Those doors were only ever opened before and after school, when kids from the busses came scuttling in like mice. There was a little bit of commotion in the lunchroom behind her, but Clara couldn't hear anything over the sound of her heart pounding and the blood rushing in her ears and her own frantic, reptilian-brain thoughts. She was completely overpowered by a primitive fear and instinct of survival, and these things powered her little legs, taking her body fast and far away.

It was mid-May and there was no trace left of the April chill, but the burst of warm, humid air on Clara's face felt liberating compared to the suffocating stink of the cafeteria and all its noise. Having taken flight, it seemed to all fall away from her now. Surrounded now by the open world, the sound of bugs and birds chirping, grass and trees swaying in the wind all came together like a wild symphony of music. Tears from the lunchroom were still drying on her face, but now she almost laughed because of the sheer relief she felt of not still being there, sitting behind that wall of lunchboxes and whispers.

A part of her had not thought herself able to do something like this. But now that she'd made the first great leap, she felt emboldened to continue.

She ran straight forward without thinking of direction, although her course would eventually lead her past the empty field they used to play capture the flag and kickball and into the wooded area behind. It felt like she had never run so fast before, which was probably true. She was surprised by her own speed and endurance. In PE class, she lagged during laps and failed miserably at the pacer test, but now it felt like she would never run out of breath. She couldn't imagine slowing down. It felt so easy to just run and keep running, impossibly easy. It was as if the earth herself, the ground and wind that loved her, were all working together to propel her forward, far away from the school.

All those weeks of faking illness had been a game of luck that she was losing at. But this was *real*, and it was working. She did this, all on her own.

Halfway into the field, she still wasn't slowing down. Dry, overgrown grass scratched at her ankles, and the smell of weeds and crumbly dirt was in her nose. Memories from the school year of being made to run around and chase after balls in that field now felt like nothing more than memories. Whoever that girl was, who lurked meekly at the sidelines of field games and tripped over her own feet when chased…she couldn't have been the same Clara that was running away from school so fast it felt like flying. Where only minutes ago in the cafeteria she had been filled with uncontrollable emotions, now she felt something exhilarating. Equally emotional, somehow, but this was deliberate and hers. If she was scared now, it was from her own actions and not because of anything her classmates could do to her anymore.

It felt like the end of times, like she was holding the apocalypse in her own two hands.

Clara thought she was free, but that moment only existed for as long as she ran. But while she was so lost in this state of frenzy she called freedom, she missed several important things.

On the other side of the field, just outside of the wooded area, there was a big street with two-lane traffic. Too busy trying to stay afloat the great wave of relief she felt, she forgot about the world around her. The street. The cars. And the people inside of them. The state of California had a law that prohibited talking on the phone and driving without a Bluetooth device, but the state of Georgia did not have such a law yet.

Her feet understood first, from the moment they felt stark change from grass to road. Then, several things happened at once.

A car honked, loud and angry like someone had slammed down hard on the wheel and not let go. Car tires screeched as they tried to come to a halt, rubber burning as it tried to grasp the road. Clara felt the breath knocked from the bottom of her belly as something hit her and sent her flying. It was painful, and the impact left her heaving on the ground, but not as painful as it would have been if it were the car that hit her instead of the body of a girl about her age.

What was a monster, if not this girl, this *creature* that came to Clara in her last hour of need? How could it be that the children inside the cafeteria, with their pink and white hair-bows and cartooned lunchboxes, were more monstrous than the wild girl hovering over Clara, with her horns and yellow eyes and sharp little teeth.

After that moment, and perhaps many years later, Clara began to understand that monsters were not some universal evil that existed, but rather the evil that was *created* in every individual story. This devil in her grandma's backyard, Lucinda, might have been someone's monster, but she was not Clara's monster.

She had saved Clara's life. But by the time people had gotten out of their cars and the lunch staff had finally caught up, she was gone without having uttered a word, vanished into thin air like a spirit, and nobody saw a thing except a little girl huddled on the road, miraculously unhurt.

"How did this happen?" Somebody was yelling. "Call the police, now!"

"It's a child!"

"Where the hell did she come from?"

Someone else was touching her arm. "Are you hurt?"

But when Clara tried to speak, all she could do was cry for the girl.

"Lucinda, Lucinda!"

Caught somewhere between a dream and a memory, she woke up sobbing with the shape of that name still fresh on her lips. She had no idea at what point she'd dozed off, but it felt like it had been hours. The microwave had long since finished its minute and thirty seconds and now it was dark and still inside. She took the plate out and discovered that her leftovers, the steak her mom had made the night before, had gone cold. She wasn't hungry anymore, and she felt groggy and utterly exhausted.

Worst of all, she remembered everything.

TWENTY TWO

Friday morning passed to evening, but Clara couldn't get it out of her head. Over and over, she saw her fifth grade body lying dead on the road behind Blue Ridge Elementary. Except things never came to that because Lucinda had saved her. Lucinda. Not the horned girl, the monster in the woods, the devil in Grandma's backyard. She was those things, maybe, but now Clara knew that she was also as real as the daylight, real as a memory could be. Clara's twenty-two year old body, alive and walking, was proof enough. She knew it to be true.

Her mother, or a doctor, for that matter, would have said that it was her head injury that was conjuring these day-time dreams and late-night paranoias. Or mental illness. "A healthy person does not live in a state of paranoia." Hadn't Dr. Ashley once said something like that to her?

While Clara went through the motions of her day, though, she considered a lot of things. She thought about Grandma and that house and her childhood, really *thought* about it, and not just the magical parts. She forced herself to think of some things, like the kids at school who were horrible to her and all the bad emotions she felt but had not understood at the time. She allowed herself to think of other things, embarrassing, shameful things, like all the times she cried or got sick in front of everyone. It was like twelve years had passed and only now was she finally confronting memories that she had tried to hide away, as if hiding was the way to make unhappy memories disappear. She sat on the couch in her apartment by the window and thought about these things for a long time, long enough that the sun began to set. And as she watched the pale, watery sunset, give way to dusk, she became more and more sure of the reality of her life, the past and its present.

She woke sometime later in the middle of the night and reached for her phone in the dark. She could hear Petra dreaming beneath the blankets. It was just past two in the morning, but Clara had woken suddenly, feeling awake and surprisingly clear-minded.

She had the Delta mobile app on her phone, which she used now to scroll through flight times from Long Beach to Hartsfield-Jackson Atlanta airport. Long Beach was a relatively new and small airport, and their flight options to the east coast were limited, especially since she was looking so last-minute. It was close to her apartment, and she liked it because it was so empty compared to LAX, which was a chaotic mess of an airport.

But it had the flight she was looking for. A non-stop trip from LAX to Hartsfield-Jackson at 8:40 AM the next morning. That was in about six hours. She checked her bank account, then booked the flight and got out of bed.

Unusually calm, she began to pack a duffle bag. She would only be gone for a little bit, as the return flight she picked out would bring her back to California on Monday by noon, just in time for work. A strange sort of resolve had settled into her bones, and she knew she had to go back to that house and find Lucinda one last time. Clara felt she was the key to all of this, her own past as well as something unresolved of her grandmother's past that she could not yet name. At the very least, she would go there to thank Lucinda for saving her life. And she would ask her what she needed in order to be at peace.

Wasn't that what people usually did when resolving ghosts, trauma, and memories? She understood now that Lucinda fit somewhere in those definitions, if not all three at once. This was the end-plan that Clara created in the hours between two-thirty and six in the morning.

She would have to drop Petra off at the kennel for week-end boarding, there was no way around it. She knew her picky dog liked the comfort of the sitter's house, but she'd have to make do for one weekend. She told Petra this as she kissed her little wet nose.

Just before seven, she picked up her things to go. She knew that Ryan was awake and up on the other side of her wall. The walls were thin, and she had heard him leave around six for his morning run. Right before she left, with her bag and Petra in her arms, she knocked once on his door. He came to open it immediately.

"Clara," he said, clearly caught off guard. Sweat glistened on his face and neck, which he quickly wiped at with the back of his hand.

"Hi," she said, feeling self-conscious but also too high on adrenaline to care much. "I...can't make it to dinner tonight. I'm sorry."

He looked her up and down, from her unbrushed hair to Petra squirming excitedly in her arms. "Are you going some-where?" The tilt of his eyebrows made Clara unable to tell if he sounded worried or amused.

"Yes," she said. "I'm going back to my grandma's house. There's something I need to take care of over there. But I'll be back. Soon." She added. "By Monday. And maybe then we can... reschedule." She didn't know why she said that last part.

But he smiled. "Okay. Sure, Clara. Text me when you get back. Actually, I'll text you." He leaned against the doorframe and gave her a silly smile. "I have a feeling you're one of those people who ghosts everyone that likes you until you inevitably run into them at the grocery store or something."

"Oh, yeah," Clara said, huffing out a breath like something

close to a laugh. "I think I've had enough ghosts for now, though."

"What?" He said.

"Ghosting. I mean." It wasn't actually what she meant, but after she figured this Lucinda business out, maybe next she could work on her social skills with Ryan. "I have to go now. But I'll see you later." She said that last part and meant it.

"Okay," he said. "I hope you go do whatever it is you need to do. And I'll be waiting for that dinner with or without your parents when you get back."

After dropping Petra off, she took an Uber to the airport. LAX was a nightmare outside of the airport even more so than inside, and she didn't want to have to deal with parking. Her mind was still buzzing from all she had done since two in the morning, and her head was throbbing with exhaustion. Once the city came into view, the morning light reflected of the shining buildings and hurt her tired eyes. Hopefully she could find some sleep on the plane.

It was a lonely, liberating thing for Clara to do this. She could hardly imagine being in that house without her family. It was too big for one person, like her soul could get lost in there.

But she reminded herself about Grandma, who had lived there alone for so many years at the end of her life. The thought brought her no comfort.

Only weeks before, less than a month ago, Clara and her parents had been on their way to Georgia for the first time in twelve years for her grandma's funeral. It seemed an eternity ago. At the airport this time, things went fast. She sped through check-in and quickly found herself at the departure gate, and then it seemed like she had only sat for a few moments before it was time to board. The morning had shifted from summery-bright and settled into a colorless June gloom, which she observed through her seat's little window on the plane.

A five-hour flight felt like the last thing Clara's overactive mind needed, but it seemed that she had done all her thinking from those hours between two and seven in the morning because now her thoughts were still. She put on a movie, something about old about two handsome vampires and their golden daughter, but as the plane rose into the air, she fell into a dreamless sleep for the first time in a long while.

Her eyes flew open the moment the plane touched ground, making a sound like thunder as the wheels hit the runway. People clapped. Clara sucked in a deep breath, already anticipating the muggy air.

As she stood waiting in the aisle, people slowly but surely getting off the plane, she switched her phone off from airplane mode and it instantly began to blow up with notifications, which was a rare occurrence for Clara. She rarely got texts or calls from anyone besides her parents or boss for work things.

Of course, her parents. She muttered a curse, feeling her heart begin to thump heavily. She purposely hadn't told them; they would have most definitely not allowed her to come back so soon, and likely not on her own. In the early hours of the morning, it had seemed like a good idea not to tell them.

She had eight unopened texts and six missed calls from her mom, four from her dad. The last, most recent text from her mom was

CLARA YOU NEED TO ANSWER THE PHONE OR WE ARE CALLING THE POLICE!!!!!!!

Shit, she thought, but she might have said it out loud. Her phone felt slippery between her nervous, sweaty hands.

The line departing the plane seemed to move fast now as she frantically tried to think what to do. She'd wait until she was off the plane and then call her mom first. As for how she would explain herself... she would figure it out when the time came in somewhere less than five minutes.

"Thank you, have a good day," flight attendants were saying as people exited the plane. Clara stumbled out of opening and scrolled through the messages and missed phone calls. They'd been calling over the past five hours when she was on the plane. What would she say? *Mom, I was sleeping.* True enough. Did she need to know it had been on a plane?

As Clara made it outside the arrival gate to the seating area, her phone lit up with another call. She reached to answer it but was caught by surprise. She rubbed at her eyes, not sure if she was seeing the letters on the screen correctly.

Cassie Graham?

Clara stared at the screen. She stared at her phone until the ringing stopped and the screen went to black. Then she unlocked her phone and called her sister back.

Cassie answered on the second ring. "Clara?" It was something of a question and an accusation. "What's going on? Mom and Dad seem to think you've gone missing."

"Oh," Clara cleared her throat. "Yeah. I missed some of their calls. I was just about to call back—"

"No," Cassie interrupted. "You'd better have some other explanation. I know they've been freaked out since what happened at the funeral, but they sound about ready to file a missing persons report." Clara heard her pause and huff out a frustrated breath over the phone. "Look," she said. "I don't know what's going on... but you should tell me."

Clara didn't know what to say, in fact she felt caught off guard, and in response to her silence, Cassie spoke again. "You can tell me, Clara. Are you... okay?"

Clara felt a stinging pressure behind her nose and eyes. "Yes, I'm okay," she said. "I'm back in Georgia."

"What?"

"I just got off the plane."

"Do Mom and Dad know? Actually, don't even answer

that. *Why*, Clara? What could possibly be so important that you have to go back so soon? And not tell anyone."

Somehow, talking over the phone felt easier, like it was easier for Clara to say the things that needed to be said like this than if Cassie was standing right in front of her in the flesh. "I had to go back. There's something I need to resolve back at the house."

Cassie didn't reply for a long moment, and Clara had to pull the phone away from her face to make sure she hadn't hung up. But after about ten seconds, Cassie said softly, "You mean, it's about *her*, isn't it?"

"Yes," Clara whispered. Did Cassie know about the girl? Or was she talking about Grandma. Was there a difference?

"I have to go back," Clara said. "I need to speak with her. There are things I need to understand."

"Okay," Cassie said, quietly. Then, "Okay," she said again a bit louder and surer. "But you need to keep your head, Clara. Okay? No falling out of windows or any bullshit stunt like you pulled last time."

"I promise." Clara said. Both sisters were smiling a small, sad smile on opposite ends of the phone, as if each was privately wondering what it would be like if they talked like this to each other more, what it might be like this whole time to have a sister as a confidant.

"What do you want me to tell Mom and Dad?" Cassie finally said.

Clara said the first thing that came to mind. "Tell them I came to visit you and Tristan in New York."

She made a noise like a snort. "They'll never believe that."

No, of course they wouldn't. "Then don't tell them anything." Clara said. "I'll figure something out. I'll call Mom right after this and I'll figure something out," she repeated, not quite sure which one of them she was trying to reassure.

"Clara?" Cassie said, her voice made strange through the phone's speakers.

"Yeah?"

"Do what you need to do over there and then be done with it, okay? Then go back home and don't let whatever it is keep haunting you. I want you there with me at my wedding, the normal Clara." After a pause, she said. "Normal for you, at least."

When they hung up, Clara walked through the airport with the ghost of a smile on her face. Hearing Cassie say those words, *I want you there with me at my wedding,* made Clara feel like things were going to be okay. It made her feel a bit braver.

She didn't know what was in store for her, waiting there at that lonely house, but she hoped it would be something of a second chance, a final dance with this past.

PART 3

Lady of the House

TWENTY THREE

The house loomed overhead like a black cloud heavy with rain.

Clara stepped out of the car, dragging her bag along behind her, and the Uber sped away. The driver hadn't seemed happy about Clara's request to go so far out of the city, but since it was a long drive, the fare had been quite expensive, and he'd agreed to take her.

Once the sound of the car's engine had melted into the distance, Clara felt the weight of being truly alone. How could this place truly be hers? How could it ever be. She was the only living soul on these four acres of land; her entire apartment complex back at home could fit in here. And yet, there wasn't silence, not even after the car was long gone. There's a certain sound that comes with being surrounded by a forest, something like a low hum, a thrum like a living heartbeat, as if the trees that made up Grandma's forest were one whole entity singing an unsung song of silence.

She walked up the driveway, dragging her bag behind her. The house seemed too still, towering above her with every step she took forward. She had never seen it look so solemn before, so sad, if a house could be sad.

At the side of the garage there was an old keypad, which Clara could still remember the code from twelve years ago when she would come back from school on the yellow school bus and run up the driveway. Back then, this garage had been her gate to heaven every day after school. She reminded herself of the feeling, telling herself that this empty house was nothing to be afraid of. It might be filled with memory, but now, today, she would be the only thing in it that was still real.

She flipped the cover up and punched in 0 2 2 5 with the tip of her index finger. For a moment, she wondered what the significance of those numbers was, but when the garage began to open, the thought slipped to the bottom of her mind as it was filled with other more pressing mysteries.

From the summer heat, the inside of the garage was warm and dark, almost as if she had opened a gate to Hell. But she hadn't come all the way here, put poor Petra in the kennel which she hated, lied to her parents, and then paid almost ninety dollars for the Uber ride just to open the garage and be afraid. She shook off the thought and stepped inside.

They had put the spare key inside an old shoe on the shoe rack by the door, which Clara fished out, feeling something like a dead bug before her fingers found the cool metal of the key. She imagined it would have been caked in dust, and perhaps something worse than a dead little bug in the shoe if they hadn't only been here weeks ago for the funeral.

The key turned smoothly and the door to the mudroom opened easily, inviting her in. But inside the house, it was darker than the garage, which had had one little dirty window on the side to let some light in. The mudroom was a little box with no windows, but she knew if she only walked a bit further into the pitch black, she would come upon a long hallway that led to the kitchen and living room, which had windows as tall as the ceiling. It was silly, she knew it, but she broke off into a clumsy run in the dark while she still had a little spark of bravery, scrambling with her bags to get out of the oppressive dark as fast as she could.

Her memory, refreshed by the last visit, served her well, and she came into the open kitchen area without running into anything or falling into the stairway that went down into the basement like another pit to Hell. She knew her imagination was running wild, but it was hard to shake off the theatrics, being alone in this big house. Though it had still been kept up well, Clara thought, it still seemed like a very sad, old crumbling mansion.

She didn't know how her grandma had done it, for twelve long years. They said she had been doing strange things in the last few years of her life, like wandering the neighborhood at odd hours in her nightgown, searching for a wisp of something long forgotten, or spending hours in her lovely, dark and deep woods. Making incoherent, feverish calls to her granddaughter only months before her death.

Maybe there was something haunted about this place. Even with the daylight coming in through the windows, the silence was enough to drive someone crazy.

She set her bag down on the floor and let go of the breath she hadn't realized she'd been holding in. What now?

She thought she should go through the house, into her old bedroom and Grandma's and see if there was anything she could find. But she didn't know what exactly she was looking for. A piece of paper, perhaps a book, that spelled everything out for her? She knew such thing didn't exist. It would be a miracle if life worked that way, if there was a manual that told you why things were the way they were and how to feel better about it all. If only such a book existed. Walking through the dark hallway, Clara told herself that she had gotten the hardest part out of the way. She had gotten herself all the way here, but now what? She still felt so far away from the truth she was looking for, and she didn't know where to begin to find it.

She didn't want to go upstairs quite yet, but she didn't exactly want to go out back yet either. When she had last seen her, Lucinda had been on the patio beneath her room, so close to the house. She could be anywhere now. Fear and uncertainty were beginning to paralyze Clara. She quickly forgot what she remembered about Lucinda, how they had been something like friends and that she had saved Clara's life. Now, clinging to a great and terrible fear, Clara could only remember the horns jutting out of her head, sharp teeth that looked wrong in a smile, and eyes glowing that unearthly yellow.

She hunched over, trying to catch her breath. Then, she sat down on the floor, right in the middle of the kitchen. She could feel panic crawling up into her throat, but there was no need to hide herself in the nearest bathroom. Nobody was here but her. She just needed to take a break and gather her wits and courage.

Her phone buzzed in her lap as if to remind her about the world outside this place. It was comforting to hear the notification and be reminded that she was not the only person left in this world. Because here, inside the house, it felt like she was the only living thing left on the planet.

It was a text from Ryan. She unlocked her phone to read the message.

> *Hey Clara, it's Ryan. Did you get to your grandma's house?*

Her phone buzzed again as another message came through.

> *Keep me updated on how it's going. When you get back, how about dinner next Friday?*

She was surprised at her own smile. A little while ago, a text like this would have reduced her to a jelly of anxiety. She would have pulled some fake excuse from her toolbox without a moment of hesitation. Now, she only smiled. Compared to what she was about to face at this house, Ryan's invitation seemed easy.

> *hi, yes I'm here. hopefully will be done soon. and yes, that sounds great?*

She sent the text back and then clicked her phone off. Then she stood back up. It couldn't be put off for any longer.

But the house, once so magical and big enough in a child's imagination to be a world of its own, now felt hostile, as if her presence was a violation. Not because of who she was, but perhaps the house itself wished to be laid to rest.

It was silly, she knew, but she was afraid to go any deeper into the house. Clara was used to living an invisible life, of always feeling most comfortable behind a closed door in the silence of her apartment, hardly daring to speak lest her voice be heard by another human, but this she feared would feel like thinning into a ghost.

And she knew that nothingness liked to devour.

Leaving her bags on the floor in the kitchen, Clara opened the door to the backyard.

She was a child again. A woman that was not her mother was gently dabbing at her bloody scrapes with a soapy towel that stung like liquid ice. There were tiny specks of gravel and road dust lodged into her skinned knees from where she'd fallen onto the road, pushed out of the way of the car by Lucinda's strong, spirit hands. It was like she had just flown for the first time in her life, except now her newly discovered wings had gone back to sleep forever. There were sirens around her, and she had been boxed in by strange, hovering adults and police cars and an ambulance. Couldn't they see that she only had a few scrapes and dried tear stains on her cheeks? Every day at school was worse than this, but the adults only seemed to notice her pain now that there was a little bit of blood. She was lost in the torrent of questions, noises, worried hands and faces of unfamiliar adults, and she wished that Lucinda was still here with her.

What was she to do? Call out the name? Clara shaped the word—her name, in her mouth, but she felt too scared to utter it out loud, because if her call went unanswered, she didn't know what she would do with herself. Because she didn't want to taste defeat so soon, she pursed her lips together and began her last walk into the backyard that was Grandma's Forest.

"Why did you do that?" A lady at the hospital who was not a doctor said to Clara. "Were you trying to die?" She sat in a chair next to Clara. When she had come in, she had asked Clara's parents to leave the room for a moment so they could talk together, and she had given Clara a small, pink teddy bear to hold. "I got this for you." Why, Clara thought. Who are you? But instead, she said, "I hate being there, I hate everything. I especially hate God because I prayed to him every day to not make me go to school, even if he wanted me to die for it. I'd rather die than go back to school. Please, don't make me go back." The lady had left, and the next time Clara saw her parents, they had gathered some of her things from school and home and packed them for her to take to the crazy place along with the pink teddy bear she had been given that day.

Clara reached the edge of the backyard, where the trees bent upward from the ground and towered over her like gnarled, reaching fingers. It was darker here, where the trees grew dense and close, so close and wild it seemed that only forest creatures were meant to wander through.

A pink teddy bear, one paperback book, a blanket from her bed at home, a soft notebook and a box of crayons. These were the objects that Clara had for two weeks, which she placed on the rounded shelf in her room there. It was like an empty box with all rounded edges. There was a chair

*that was round, and it was bolted to the ground. The bed
and shelf were also stuck to the ground. She couldn't wear
her own clothes from home because they had zippers and
buttons and string. Her parents brought a box of crayons
to write and draw with because pencils and pens were not
allowed here. Only soft, breakable things. She stared at
these things on her shelf for two weeks. She didn't touch
any of them, not even once.*

She had always been a bit terrified by the tall black gates at
the edge of the property, even though they kept the woods
out. Six feet tall by state rule, yet adult deer could still clear
it in one great leap, because things so trivial as fences would
never be enough to keep the wild things out. She wrapped
her fingers around the rusty latch and slid it back until the
gate sprung open.

*Two weeks of endless days passed, but Clara didn't find
being here to be much worse than having to be at school.
She didn't talk to anyone, and no one talked to her. A lot of
the kids there had the same sort of look as her. Sallow and
sad faces, they moved slowly and ate nothing. Many of the
other kids here cried much more than Clara, and some of
them screamed and kicked too. They did family therapy,
which was the one time Clara got to see her parents in that
two-week period. They looked at her like they didn't recognize her. Her mom cried a lot, her dad was silent. Clara
thought that they were both angry with her for running
away from school and getting herself in all this trouble.
"Your daughter is depressed," the man said, who was not a
doctor but a psychiatrist. "Depressed?" Megumi Graham
had said. "She's just a child!"*

She stepped through the gates and into the mouth of that

dark wood, and though it felt like stepping out into the open world with nothing to protect her, it also felt like there was nothing to hold her back. She began to walk forward, and her footfall made only the faintest sound against the forest's soft undergrowth. There was a fullness here of life and death, little weeds and mosses blooming on top of rotting, water-damaged tree stumps. Clara walked and kept walking until she knew where she was going.

Nobody listens to children, especially not adults. But children can see horrible things, and they know horrible things too. Things that would terrify adults. The eyes of children are more attuned to what is invisible, and in this way, knowledge can enter the body in a way that defies time and experience. Clara could see Lucinda as she was and all that she represented: beautiful and terrible, something unspeakable and altogether shameful, a secret as guilty as the Devil. She was something very bad, very strong, and very, very sad. And after that day on the street, she disappeared from Clara's sight and strayed out of remembrance.

But memory is a living thing, and it demands to be seen and accepted. Because when it is neglected, it will morph and twist into something overgrown and monstrous. It is never something that can be consciously forgotten or snuffed out of existence. In fact, the deeper you try to hide it, the harder it will push back.

She came to a clearing in the woods where the trees grew less dense, and the air felt a bit less stifling. Her feet slowed and she came to stop in front of a little mound against the knotted trunk of a tree.

What she found sent a shiver down her neck despite the muggy summer air.

Once, back when she was still in college, she had visited some cluttered little antique shop packed so tightly with lost trinkets and useless baubles that there wasn't even room for dust to gather. It looked now as if one of those sorts of shops had been set up here in the middle of the woods.

Looking closer, she realized the little mound in front of the tree was actually a filthy blanket, so caked with mud and dirt and mold that it appeared frozen solid. And then around the base of the tree there was an odd collection of items that had no place in the middle of a forest. Some things she recognized, like the cornflower blue mugs from her grandma's kitchen that were painted with yellow and purple pansies. Other things were strewn across the ground nearby, and many of them were dirty, old toys that looked as if they'd spent over a decade out here. It looked like a shrine for a dead child.

Clara thought about Grandma, and the things that had been whispered about her in the last years of her life.

She wanted to turn back and run as fast as she could with her eyes squeezed shut.

A week after Clara had returned from her stay in the children's psychiatric hospital, the Grahams packed their things and returned to California. School had ended during her brief stay. Mom said Dad got a new job so they were going back home, and they would be living in a new house too. Home? What about here with Grandma? And how could it be home if it was a new house? Why had they moved here in the first place if only to move back a year later?

The woods were silent, but she felt Lucinda's presence by the way the hair on her bare arms stood up. She couldn't bring herself to turn around and face the past, now that it was here behind her, just the two of them, with no distance to blur the memories.

She and Grandma barely spoke, and they barely said good-bye. They just looked at each other with sad watery eyes and Grandma said, "Please come back. You'll always have a home here."

She remembered seeing those words written in her grandma's shaky cursive letters on the slip of paper she'd found under the bed when she and her dad were going through the house.

"Clara."

It was the sound of her name, called by a voice that sounded both young and old, but also incredibly real.

At last, she opened her eyes.

After that day on the road, Clara never saw Lucinda again. Not until many years later when she was an adult. But by then her memories of the magic and horror had dwindled and faded to nothing more than a wisp of imagined childhood fairytale. Growing up is never the problem. Forgetting is.

She was standing there, a dark outline of shadow in the forest, looking very much like herself. Horns, teeth, and yellow eyes. Instead of being afraid, Clara looked at her with a child's knowing eye.

"You don't need to forget," Lucinda said. "You don't need to be afraid."

The two girls stood face to face and there was no past or present, only the vast, open sea of memory. Clara began to cry, first slowly, and then all at once like a dam letting go.

"Goodbye," she said, and as the words left her mouth, she glimpsed Lucinda, her beautiful monster, one last time.

Clara left. She made her way out of the woods, through the backyard, and into the house. She grabbed her bags from the kitchen floor and locked up the house, putting the spare key back into the old shoe in the garage. This far away from the city, an Uber wouldn't be able to pick her up for a long while, but she started walking anyway, dragging her bags behind her. And as she turned back to look at Grandma's house one last time, she saw it as a fragment of a dream stuck in time, shrouded by those dark woods that reached up and over the house like they would one day grow over the entire property. But now that the past had moved on, it was just empty woods, and nothing more. Clara knew that she wasn't truly gone, and it was enough for her to walk away from that house and still have those terrible, wonderful things within her heart.

ACKNOWLEDGMENTS & AUTHOR'S NOTE

This book is the product of unrelenting love, support and community from my family, friends, and our 2022-2023 Novel Writing Workshop at The University of Utah: Sophia Burkemo, Henry Harrison, Matthew Mitchell, Brekke Pattison, Audrey Pozernick, Nayla Rodriguez, Gillian Ruppel, Lauren Wigod, and our outstanding professor and mentor Dr. Michael Gills. It would have been a very lonely process without you all. Thank you for helping me and this story grow, and for taking Clara's world into your hearts.

Fiction is a wonderful, magical thing, and I hope this story has let you in on experiences you've never had before. As both a reader and writer, I think the true power of fiction lies in its ability to build empathy in readers and find a deeper connection to humanity. The world we live in today is in desperate need of kindness and unity, so I urge you to keep reading diverse literature to expand your understanding of different people, places, and situations. Find solace in shared experiences. Embrace what is foreign. Never stop learning. And because literature helps us understand not just ourselves but also each other, I believe it is the key to fighting for a better world.

ABOUT THE AUTHOR

Katie Sanyal is a debut novelist from Utah with roots in Georgia. She is an English major currently studying at the University of Utah. When she is not writing, she is reading, and when she is not reading, she can be found enjoying Salt Lake City with her friends and family.